RETURNING
LOST LOVES

RETURNING
LOST LOVES

a novel

Yehoshua Kenaz

Translated from the Hebrew by Dalya Bilu

STEERFORTH PRESS
SOUTH ROYALTON, VERMONT

For information about permission to reproduce
selections from this book, write to:
Steerfoth Press, L.C.
P.O. Box 70, South Royalton, Vermont 05068

First published in Hebrew 1997 by Am Oved, Tel Aviv.

The poem on page 50 was translated by Chana and Ariel Bloch.

LIBRARY OF CONGRESS CATALOGING-IN-PUBLICATION DATA
Kenaz, Yehoshua.
  [Maḥazir ahavot ḳodmot. English]
  Returning lost loves : a novel / by Yehoshua Kenaz ; translated
from the Hebrew by Dalya Bilu.— 1st ed.
     p. cm.
  ISBN 1-58642-013-5 (alk. paper)
  I. Title.
  PJ5054.K36 M313 2001
  892.4'36—dc21

                              00-012132

FIRST EDITION

ONE

A moment would come when one of them would ask: When will I see you again? And this would be a sign that something was ending and something else was beginning, and the grace of the first days, if indeed they had both been in a state of grace then, would disappear. This was more or less what the lecturer she'd been with for a time in her student days had explained to her. The writer he was quoting (she had forgotten his name) argued that the first of the two who asked: When will we meet again? had "lost the love." So, Gabi had wondered then, was the whole thing just a power game? She wasn't convinced. After a while she split up with the lecturer, and at the same time she also dropped out of her course at the university, which wasn't giving her what she had hoped for.

In the years that had passed since then, there was also a short marriage that didn't work out, but which hadn't, at least in her opinion, done her any harm. She looked younger than her age; she was still slender; her face was unlined, her complexion fair and matte; her straight dark hair fell to her shoulders (in the office she wore it gathered up into a dancer's bun on her neck); her dark eyes were long and alert and her snub nose gave her an expression of being shrewder and more sophisticated than she really was.

While approaching the building entrance she glances back over her shoulder, quickly inserts the key in the lock, enters the stairwell, and climbs the stairs to the apartment. Despite the plastic shopping bags holding the groceries she bought on the way, despite her high heels, and despite the fact that she hasn't switched on the stairwell light, she climbs quickly from floor to floor, enters the apartment, and immediately locks the door behind her.

She got her job as a clerk in the firm as a result of a chance meeting with an acquaintance who was about to leave Tel Aviv for a settlement in the Galilee. For a few weeks they worked side by side and she taught Gabi the ropes, and among the other good advice this friend gave her, there was one warning that Gabi particularly took to heart: to keep away at all costs from a shit called Hezi, who was away at the time doing his army reserves duty. It didn't take more than a few days, and even before she set eyes on him Gabi was already in love with him. She waited impatiently for him to come back to work, and when he returned and passed her in the corridor, she had no doubt that he was the man, even though she hadn't yet heard anyone address him by his name. And she knew she had to have him at any cost.

But he showed no signs at all of being interested. Although he worked on a different floor of the building, he would drop in several times a day at the secretary's office where she worked and joke with the other girls, but he didn't even ask who the new girl was, didn't introduce himself to her, didn't say a friendly or encouraging word, didn't pay her any attention at all. And by then she couldn't think of anything else. From snatches of conversation between the girls she shared the room with, who like her friend didn't speak of him with any affection, she learned that he was a married man with a family, and that his father-in-law, a person with influence in economic circles, had helped him obtain his job in another department of the firm. Gabi wasn't a gullible young girl anymore, the experience and lessons of life had taught her caution and responsibility, but Hezi's reputation as a shit and his striking appearance, the face of an arrogant child with a head of snow-white hair, cast a spell on her that she couldn't resist.

They first made love in a little hotel on one of the streets going down to the sea, a few days after he condescended to smile at her for the first time as he walked past the door of her room. Gabi went down to the little diner next to the office building, where she usually had lunch. He was sitting there. He looked at her and she smiled at him. He came up to her table and said quietly: "I want to get to know you." When she said "Okay" he took a notebook out of his jacket pocket, tore out a page, wrote something down on it, folded it, put it on the table, and walked out of the diner. The note contained the name of the hotel and the time they were to meet. The first time he heard her hysterical cries of pleasure, his body froze and he raised his head and examined her face with suspicion and concern.

He laid down rules governing how they were to behave when arriving, while there, and on departing, so that the apartment he rented for their meetings would be protected, secure, impenetrable as far as possible by the outside world — like a nuclear war shelter, he said. No one, apart from themselves, was to know about it. They were never to arrive at the building together and never to leave together. He usually arrived in a cab, not in his own car. In addition to the apartment's old telephone line, which he left unconnected, he had a line with an unlisted number installed, to be used only by them in the few hours they spent there. And it too was not to be answered at once when it rang; she had to wait for the signal they agreed upon: three rings, a pause, and another ring. Calls on the intercom and knocks at the door were to be ignored. And of course, no contact with the neighbors, not a single word. The name of the previous tenants, Neuman, was left on the intercom outside the building entrance and on the mailbox. And at work they ignored one another, as if they had never met.

She accepted his conditions without asking his reasons. This game — and perhaps it was only a kind of test she was being subjected to — didn't put her off. On the contrary. After all, it was only a few hours a week, usually during the day, and she went on living her life as before. And if her heart warned her that she might be in danger from this peculiar relationship — this was precisely what drew her to it.

In the kitchen Gabi unpacks the groceries and starts making a light meal for the two of them. The dog in the apartment on the other side of the wall howls like a wolf, long, savage, painful howls, like moans of longing or complaint at some terrible injustice. This is how he howls when his master has gone out, as she has learned from experience; for she has heard his other barks too: the cries of joy and gratitude when his master comes home, the proud announcements that he is about to be taken out for a walk, the angry growls warning of an undesirable presence outside the door, and also the nagging, self-righteous scolding on the other side of the bedroom wall, when she is in bed with her lover. And although she has never had any special affection for animals in general or dogs in particular (if she had wanted a pet, she would definitely have chosen a cat), she feels that a strange bond has come into being between herself and this dog on the other side of the wall. To such an extent that when she saw him for the first time, leaving the apartment with his master and walking past her, big, shaggy, and slow, she wasn't afraid of him when he barked at her and when the fur of his neck brushed against her thigh, she was so sure of the secret intimacy growing between them. His master is a rather repulsive man of about fifty, short and very thin, his face hidden by a wispy gray beard and glasses whose lenses cast a gray-brown shadow over his shifty eyes. The name on his mailbox is Aviram, and there's no knowing if it's his first name or his surname.

After finishing her work in the kitchen, she goes into the living room, switches on the radio, which is always tuned to the "Voice of Music," and sits down to read the paper. About half an hour later Hezi opens the door, she doesn't turn her head to look at him but goes on studying the newspaper, and he comes up to her from behind, puts his arms around her shoulders and chest, and buries his head in her neck. On the radio there's a pause in the music and the announcer recites a poem, slowly and in a reserved voice. Gabi feels his warm breath melting her neck. Again she is flooded with the joy of the meeting, always new and surprising, conscious once more of the closeness of his body, hungry for her, about to pounce ungently on its prey.

The day they moved into the apartment she shouted again at the top of her voice when she climaxed, and not only did the dog in the next apartment burst into loud, threatening barking, but one of the neighbors rang their bell and knocked on their door, calling: "Hello! What's happening?" until Gabi was forced to call out in reply: "Everything's all right, everything's all right!"

"From outside it sounds as if somebody's being tortured to death in here," Hezi said then, got out of bed, went to the bathroom, came back and immediately got dressed, refusing to eat anything. Gabi didn't appear embarrassed in the least. Half-serious, half-humorous, she promised that from now on she would shout softly. But she didn't keep her promise and he never mentioned it again. Perhaps he resigned himself to this breach in the nuclear shelter he had erected and decided to take a calculated risk. In any event, he no longer allowed his lovemaking to be disturbed by the fear of attracting the attention of the neighbors with her shouts.

Now they sit in the kitchen, eating the light meal that Gabi has prepared, a niçoise salad. As usual, he eats in silence. In general, he doesn't talk much. And although she doesn't break the silence, she can't help glancing at him from time to time, to examine his face, whose riddle becomes harder for her to solve the longer she knows him. And when her look arouses him from silence, he smiles at her questioningly and murmurs a compliment about the food. And she doesn't want to tell him what a good cook she is, how she can prepare far richer and more complex dishes than this, whole meals, in case he thinks she's trying to expand their meetings to include other hours too, for example, in the evening. She knows that anything like this will arouse his resistance, be interpreted as an intrusion on his freedom, because any such invitation to extend their relationship has to come from him and not from her. And so she confines herself to a smile of thanks and goes on looking at his childish face, which in the eyes of someone not in love would no doubt seem a very ordinary face: only the mane of white hair surrounds it with a kind of halo of spirituality. But even though he talks about himself so little, she already knows enough about him to be certain that there is nothing spiritual about him at all. He himself told her, in a rare moment of frankness, that the only things that interest him are money and sex, and if he had to choose between them, he would definitely choose money, which could procure sex — but not the other way around.

To Mr. Barzilai Nachman,

Even though we haven't spoken to each other for years due to a certain subject because of which I quite rightly stopped talking to you now I haven't got any choice in the matter. I could have sent this letter to your lady too like I did the other times on the subject of money for special expenses on the building but this time the subject isn't suitable for a woman. As follows, I'm writing this letter to you not personally but only as the head of the House Committee. Ever since Neuman left and other people moved into your apartment the situation here has become intolerable. Nobody lives there by day or night and only in the afternoon there's a woman there who receives men for intimate relations and begins screaming Oy oy oy so that the whole building can hear. At first we didn't know what was happening we thought there was some catastrophe and we went to knock on the door to offer help but we saw that it was something else and it's been going on like that to this day a few times a week. It wouldn't be so bad at night when everyone's sleeping but in the middle of the day it's not normal. Lucky there are no more children in the building to hear such things and ask what's going on but it's a shame and disgrace for the women who live in the building too. You must remember what happened in apartment three after Moyal died 7/18/1981 and his wife went to the old-aged home and a person moved in who brought girls and turned the place into you-know-what. People were waiting in line in the stairwell. You yourself were on the committee then. We went to the police and put an end to it. What's to be done now with this girl? We would have gone to the police a long time ago but I know what your temper's like and I thought I should first give you an account of what's happening in your apartment.

And now in the name of the committee I demand with all due respect you put a stop to it. Not only is it unpleasant and shameful for everybody but the value of the property is going down too because nobody will want to buy an apartment in a place like this and we wasted our money on the new entrance door and the intercom so everything should be dignified. If nothing comes of this letter we'll have to go to the police. Please give us the name of the person you rented the apartment to which the committee is entitled to as you yourself know. And in addition they don't pay their dues to the committee either, they owe two months, notifications in their mailbox don't do any good or under the door either, they don't open the door or pick up the phone even in the afternoon when you can hear her in there.

Respectfully yours,
Shwartz Ariyeh
on behalf of the House Committee

"Tell me, what's eating you?" Ilan suddenly asks, getting up from his desk, standing next to him, and examining him with concern.

After the two clients had left, there was an unexpected lull in the office. Ronit went to the diner down the street, the telephones were silent, even the roar of the buses in Ibn Gvirol Street seemed to subside for a moment, and only the Russian's accordion, next to the bank entrance, went on creaking out its regular repertoire of light classical music. From the big window part of Malkhei Yisrael Square is visible, bathed in spring sunshine.

Aviram raises his head from the computer and looks at him in surprise.

"Nothing's eating me, what's the problem?"

"Lately I've had the feeling that you're angry with me," says

Ilan. "You hardly talk. Are you depressed or something?"

Aviram doesn't know what to say to him. He rubs his beard with the back of his hand and prays for Ronit to come back quickly and for this conversation to end.

"Forgive me for saying so," Ilan adds, "but it doesn't exactly make the clients feel good either to sit opposite such a sour face. They'll think we're about to go bankrupt."

"That's just the way I look," says Aviram.

"No, no, it's only lately, something that makes me feel as if you're mad at me, as if I did you some harm."

"Not at all. Sometimes people have personal problems, you know. The trouble with me is that you can immediately see it on my face."

"Is it something to do with your parents?"

"No, no."

Ronit finally returns, bringing three toasted cheese bagels, and goes into the kitchen to make coffee.

For a few years now the two of them have been working together in the same room, partners in the Northern Star Rental and Sales Realtors, without establishing any personal relationship. The only time the framework of formal relations between business partners was breached was when Ilan threw a bar mitzvah party for his son in a reception hall in Holon and invited Aviram. Not knowing anybody there, Aviram barricaded himself in a corner and fled for his life as soon as the guests got into line for food.

Ronit brings in the coffee cups on a little tray. She puts the cup containing half a saccharine tablet on Ilan's desk, the cup with two spoons of sugar on her desk, and the cup with neither on Aviram's desk. In that order. And while they restore themselves with the coffee and the toasted bagels he wonders, not for the first time: Even in something as silly as the order in which they are served, Ilan always comes first. It seems self-evident, but why, in fact, should it be? They're equal partners, with exactly the same status, and Aviram is older than Ilan. And why does she serve herself second, and him last? Why is it so self-evident? He's her boss, after all, just like Ilan. But why pre-tend — Ilan's sleeping with Ronit, and this, too, is a classic fea-ture of being the boss. They don't even try to hide their intimate relationship from Aviram, with all kinds of whispers and stolen caresses and inexplicable bursts of laughter. They feel no embarrassment in the presence of the wretched little clerk.

It is not the order in which they get their coffee, however, or the erotic amusements of Ilan and Ronit that are preoccupying Aviram, but a deeper and more fundamental order of things, which in his opinion is also reflected in these trifles. In his eyes he is a rejected person, crushed by life and cast beaten and help-less by the wayside.

Would he have dared to speak to Ilan, who is several years his junior, in the way that Ilan had just spoken to him? But anyone casting a glance at the two of them would have no doubt as to which of them was the boss and which the lowly clerk. Ilan feels like a boss. Look at his executive airs and the self-important expression on his face when he speaks to clients or answers the phone and you'll see that he relates to their brokerage agency as if it's an international concern, especially since it was decided, on Ilan's initiative, to expand the activities of the office to include "real-estate management" — which in the eyes of Aviram's ambitious partner was more promising, profitable, and dignified than plain old apartment brokerage.

First thing in the morning, when he comes into the office, Ilan sits down to study the financial newspaper, to bring himself up to date on what's happening in the business world, which he sees as his natural arena. Look at what he's wearing: always a necktie, white shirt, and dark trousers. In winter, a dark blue jacket with metal buttons; in summer, a well-pressed short-sleeved white shirt and, of course, a necktie. And a smell of aftershave, patted onto his always shining face, envelops him like a cloud of incense. And Aviram always in the same shabby gray slacks and checked or striped shirt, and in winter a dark blue cardigan with a zipper or little leather buttons. And about this too, Aviram knows, he can expect to hear from Ilan.

Every dog knows who his master is and obeys him. Not only Ronit, who sees herself as Ilan's secretary, with everything implied by this position, and awaits his instructions, but also the clients coming into the office know at once who's boss and address themselves immediately to him. Ilan enjoys the contact with the customers, which affords him the opportunity to demonstrate his importance and speak in a voice full of authority, a quiet voice, almost suffocated by the weight of the responsibility he bears. And thus, of their own accord, things arranged themselves to their mutual satisfaction. As a rule Ilan is the one who goes out with the clients in his car to show them the properties for rent or for sale, or meets the home owners wishing to sell or rent their property. And Aviram, who in any case doesn't own a car or know how to drive, and who hasn't got the patience for conversing with his fellow men, usually stays in the office to do the bookkeeping and other chores that are beyond the capacities of Ronit, who is employed at the office part-time. He lives on one of the streets close to the square, which allows him to go home every day at lunchtime, to take the dog for a walk, to buy a newspaper, to have something to eat, to rest a bit, and to return to the office after an hour or an hour and a half. He often spends the afternoon alone in the office, while Ilan goes out for meetings and all kinds of activities.

There was a moment in his past when he gave in and surrendered to the crushing force of life, and after that he no longer had any control over what happened to him. When that moment was, he is unable to remember. But he is certain that it existed. The image of himself lying wounded and helpless by the roadside accompanies him always, in two versions: in one he is a pedestrian walking on an expressway full of cars driving at a dizzying speed; in the other he himself is driving one of the cars, although he has never learned to drive in his life. And both of them include the moment when he decides to go on walking and not to take any notice of what's happening around him, or alternatively when he takes his hands off the wheel and covers his face in order not to see anything. But when did this accident happen in his real life? When did he decide to give in? This he doesn't know. He sometimes tries to discover this moment, as if the discovery would solve some mystery for him, and at the same time he knows that it couldn't have any practical value. And perhaps there was no such moment and there was no decision and no accident but a gradual process of wearing down until the last fiber tore.

This time on his return to the office after his lunch break he finds Ilan there. He dreads a continuation of the morning's conversation and he tries to smile at him and look relaxed, hoping to escape his doom.

But no. "I don't think there are many partners who've been working together for years like us, without any tension or conflict or suspicion and so on," Ilan says and sits down on Aviram's desk. "I, at any rate, like working with you. Even though we're so different, we're of one mind in everything concerning the business. That's why we can be honest and even criticize each other. Because I've got a lot of respect for you and whatever I say is always well meant. I wanted you to know that and not to take things personally."

"It's okay," Aviram says. "I've got no complaints."

"I want to say something about your appearance. You said this morning 'that's the way I look.' That's not true. You can look good, you're not an ugly person, but you do everything you can not to look good. What about that beard, for example? You have a nice face but nobody can see it. What's that beard supposed to mean? And your clothes."

"I knew you'd get to this."

"Avi, believe me that I'm telling you this as a friend. You can afford to buy normal clothes, and change them occasionally, and wear proper shoes instead of Adidas or sandals with socks like you do."

"You know very well that even if I shaved off my beard and wore different clothes, I won't change and nothing will change," says Aviram. "You'll just have to accept me as I am."

"Of course! What a question! Of course I accept you whatever you look like, I like you just as you are. But you'll feel different, believe me."

Ilan looks at his watch. "Ah! I'm late for an appointment." He gets off Aviram's desk, says, "Think positively about what we spoke about, okay?" gives him a paternal smile, squeezes his shoulder, picks up his big leather briefcase, and winks at him before closing the door.

Dear Mr. Shwartz,

In reply to your confused letter, I must ask you not to trouble me any further with your nonsense. The man renting my apartment is a respectable person from a large city in the north of the country, a senior member of an important commercial concern in Tel Aviv, who requires a place to rest during the day. He may have brought his wife with him to Tel Aviv on a few occasions, and when she was in the apartment she said "Oy oy oy." It's a shame and disgrace for a man of your age to think of such things. Is this what concerns you? When I lived in the building I never knew that you had the fantasies of an old lecher. It's not dignified, Mr. Shwartz, I'm ashamed for your wife.

In general people should examine themselves first, to see if everything is as it should be in their own homes, before going to listen at other people's doors. First ask themselves, for example, why their daughter got divorced twice, and then go and complain about someone who they claim they heard saying: "Oy oy oy."

Of course I can't give you the name of the tenant, or any other details about him aside from those I gave you above. With all due respect to the rules of the House Committee, there are more important rules, to respect other people and to respect their wish for privacy. He is perfectly entitled to protect himself from nuisances like you. A man in his position has the right to remain anonymous in the few hours of rest allowed him by his work, without being bothered by the media and interviewers and all kinds of hoi polloi wanting favors. If you wish to go to the police, I can't stop you making a laughingstock of yourself and the rest of your committee.

And as long as we're on the subject of laughter, I read your letter two or three times and I couldn't stop laughing. After fifty years in the country you write Hebrew worse than a new immigrant. As a teacher for many decades I had the opportunity to read all kinds of strange compositions, but such a ridiculous pile of nonsense I have never seen before. We laughed, my wife and I, unrestrainedly, as if we were reading a parody, and my wife even read the letter aloud and it sounded even funnier. We decided not to throw it away until we show it to the children when they come to visit us on Saturday. To give them some pleasure too.

Nevertheless, Mr. Shwartz, we have had enough of this joke, and if you intend to amuse us with another act in this comedy, we would be grateful if you spared us.

Respectfully yours,
Nachman Barzilai

On Saturday morning Gabi wakes up earlier than usual but goes on lying in bed with her eyes closed. The phone rings. Last night before she went to sleep she forgot to bring it closer to her bed. By the time she reaches it, it stops, after three rings. She stands next to the phone waiting for the next ring of the agreed signal, as if she's in the other apartment. And then she comes to her senses and goes back to sit on the edge of the bed, wondering how the clandestine rules of the nuclear shelter could have invaded the old, familiar world of her home so quickly. For the first time since the beginning of her affair with Hezi she feels a kind of shrinking from the unknown toward which she is advancing.

She goes to wash, hoping that it will refresh her and clear her
mind. She pours the bubble bath with her favorite scent into the
tub, and while the tub fills with water the phone rings again. She
runs naked into the room and hears Ada's voice on the other end
of the line. "Did you ring before?" she asks. "Yes," Ada replies,
"but suddenly I had second thoughts, I was afraid you were still
sleeping, and I hung up. But when I saw the time . . ."

"Listen, I'm running water for a bath. I'll call you back when
I get out."

Immersed up to her neck in the warm water, breathing in the
fragrant steam, the radio playing music on the stool next to her,
Gabi wonders whether to tell Ada. It would be a betrayal of his
trust. But she can rely on Ada, she's loyal and she knows how
to keep a secret. Still, it would be a betrayal of the pact between
them. And he, what does he do on the days and in the hours
that they're not together? Does he tell people or doesn't he?
And what does he tell them? But all this secrecy is important to
him, very important, he needs it to protect him. Protect him
from what, from who?

When she gets out of the bath, she still doesn't know which
of her two inner voices has the upper hand. She dries her hair,
puts on a white bathrobe, makes herself a cup of coffee, and sits
down by the phone.

"Why did you leave so early yesterday?" Ada asks. "It was
actually a lot of fun. That guy, Oded, was obviously interested
in you, and you barely took the trouble to answer him."

"He looked so uninteresting," says Gabi, "so normal, I could
hardly keep awake."

"What's the matter with you, Gabi?"

"Why do you ask?"

"Because lately you haven't got any patience for anyone or
anything, your head's always somewhere else."

Ada's perceptiveness, the intuition she doesn't always know
how to make use of in her own life, always give rise to Gabi's
affectionate admiration.

"I have to talk to you," Gabi says, "today."

"Either I don't hear from you for weeks, or else it's terribly urgent."

"When are you free today?"

"This afternoon, at five, six?"

It isn't easy to decide on a café that's open on Saturday and has air-conditioning — there's a hamsin blowing and the heat is unbearable — and where there's no chance of bumping into people they know. In the end they settle on a café whose dim basement is the meeting place, according to legend, of secret lovers and scheming politicians.

Ada, an ex-kibbutznik with a broad body and unruly fair hair, and Gabi, tall, slender, and dark-haired, met and became friends when they were students at the university, and since then their friendship has survived their respective marriages and Gabi's speedy divorce. They have never lost touch. There have been periods when they met frequently and spoke on the telephone almost daily, and others when weeks or even months passed without them hearing from one another.

The dark hall of the basement café is almost empty at this hour of day. Apart from the two of them, one of the tables is occupied by an elderly couple who look neither like scheming politicians nor like secret lovers. Gabi tells Ada about what has happened in her life.

"Where's it supposed to lead?" asks Ada.

"Nowhere," says Gabi. "As long as it makes us happy, what does it matter?"

"And you think it can go on like this?"

"Why not?"

"You know that one of you will get tired of it first."

"And you're sure that it will be him."

"Right."

"Well I'm not so sure. But let's say you're right. So it'll be over. It was good while it lasted. What did I lose? In any case I'm living my life as usual. The whole thing doesn't take up more than a few hours a week."

"You're not in love with this man?"

"I hardly know him. Everything that happens between us happens in bed."

"And is he so good in bed?"

"He's all right."

"Just all right, or more than that?"

"No more than that."

"So what's the big deal? If you're not in love with him and in bed he's nothing to write home about, what do you need it for? All that hole-in-the-corner secrecy, being dependent on him, waiting for him to show up when he can or when he feels like it, everything by his rules. And where does he get the money to keep an apartment like that, just for your meetings?"

"I don't know. To this day I've never asked myself that question."

"So then, you enjoy playing the role of some kind of mistress or prostitute?"

"Perhaps I do. The thing that attracts me in all this," says Gabi, "is precisely that it's not easy or simple, that we meet like two spies in enemy territory, in that apartment, with all that exaggerated secrecy and those insane precautions. It's all based on some fear of his, and I don't know what this fear is, but he passes it on to me, and I feel as if I'm fighting a war."

"Against who?"

"Against him."

"What for?"

"For him to be prepared to risk everything he has for my sake, everything he's afraid of losing now."

"And if you succeed, do you want to live with him?"

"No."

"What are you trying to prove to yourself?"

"That I can do it."

"If you ask me, you're simply deceiving yourself. You're madly in love with him already."

Gabi looks at the old couple sitting silently in the corner, taking little sips from their tall glasses of iced coffee with ice cream. The air conditioner is on too high for the empty hall and she rubs her bare shoulders with her hands.

Ada says: "And if I was in your place I'd get out while it's still possible."

"It's already impossible," Gabi says.

"It sounds really perverted," Ada replies, shaking her head. "Can't you find yourself someone normal who you can meet outside bed too, live with, find interests in common with, develop a deeper and richer relationship with? Why are you so contemptuous of these things?"

Gabi doesn't reply.

Ada was one of the most brilliant students in the department. She finished her BA with honors and great things were predicted for her. She was curious and full of life, erudite, a lover of books, and an original thinker. She was herself, she always said what she thought, she was incapable of lying and pretense. In Gabi's eyes she was a rare example of authenticity. There were already strands of gray in her fair hair; her skin, always dry and sensitive, had aged prematurely, and her body, naturally broad, had grown fat around the hips and waist. She had married a man she didn't love and devoted all her time to her charmless children. The spark had dulled, the originality, the intellectual curiosity, the candor, the authenticity had worn away. And Ada too had adjusted to a life of pretense and self-delusion, even if she wasn't aware of it. And now she's preaching women's-magazine clichés about developing common interests, about deep, rich relationships, and on Friday nights she invites over some traumatized divorced man to fix him up with "our poor Gabi." Ada's sensitivity and empathy have turned into resentment and envy. Isn't it obvious that in her own wretched, not to say tragic, existence, Ada is simply jealous of the great adventure that has come into Gabi's life?

But Ada's sensitivity and empathy have presumably not yet been entirely eroded, for she smiles at Gabi with an irresistible sadness, a resigned, accepting sadness, and says in a whisper, as if afraid to pronounce the words:

"I know that you hate me now."

Gabi shivers, because of the chill of the air conditioner or because she feels ashamed. She stands up, bends down to kiss Ada's cheek, and says: "How could I, Ada, how could I?"

Ruthie and Ezra's Eyal got into trouble in the army. This was the last thing that the family, the neighbors and friends, and everyone who knew him in school and from the neighborhood could have expected to happen. He was a quiet, well-behaved youth, he graduated from high school without any problems to speak of, without being conspicuous for good or for ill; he liked watching sports on television and listening to pop songs popular with his peers, he got along well with his parents and was nice to his sister and brother, eight and ten years younger than him respectively. Before he was drafted he even took a course to improve his physical fitness, in order to get accepted into a select combat unit and cope with its stringent demands. But it turned out that somewhere or other there was an invisible crack, which in certain unclear circumstances widened into a break, not to say total collapse. Because now he's landed in a military jail, and what's worse: he's escaped, which is tantamount to desertion.

In fact, from the beginning of boot camp it was already evident that there was something wrong. His rare calls home were impatient and sparing of words. Today Ezra wonders: Were they distress signals that we failed to interpret? And Ruthie replies: No, Ezra, he called out of a sense of duty, so that we wouldn't worry about him and we'd let him cope with the challenges by himself. Ruthie is a kindergarten teacher by profession, and thanks to her psychological training her perceptions are sharper than those of Ezra — a renovations contractor, always dreading the worst.

When the boy came home on leave for the weekend, his first leave since his conscription, he answered in monosyllables the questions showered on him by his parents, especially by his emotional father. He threw his kitbag and weapon into a corner of his room, took off his uniform, got into bed, and slept for almost two days. He got up only to go to the toilet or when summoned to meals, and then he didn't wash his face, and he sat like a stranger with his parents and siblings at the Sabbath table. Ruthie set his favorite dishes, which she had gone to a lot of trouble to prepare, before him, and he tasted a little of each and hardly ate anything, maintained a gloomy silence, and didn't look at them. As soon as the meal was over he stood up, shut himself in his room again, and went back to bed. Ezra's heart broke inside him.

Ruthie reassured him by saying that it was only a passing crisis of adjustment and they had to leave the boy alone to overcome his difficulties. But Ezra could not rest. On Sunday morning, after Eyal left for his base, he phoned a few of the parents of classmates who, he knew, had been inducted on the same day as his son. A number of the boys had also come home on leave, but their parents didn't know if they were in boot camp with Eyal, they hadn't heard them say anything about him, and there was nothing worrying about their sons' behavior, on the contrary, they had been happy and lively and, most important, their morale was high. Afterward Ezra tried to locate parents whose sons had been with Eyal in the fitness improvement course. This was much more difficult, since the participants in the course were not necessarily from their neighborhood. Nevertheless, with a lot of effort, he succeeded in getting hold of the phone numbers of two families whose sons had been in the course. But they didn't know who Eyal was and were unable to help his father.

Ruthie said: "Leave it be, Ezra, stop thinking about it all the time. You're killing yourself, you can't work or think about anything else. It will all work out, he'll grow up, like everyone else, and everything will be all right." And Ezra replied: "It's killing me, Ruthie, to think that my son is unhappy, that maybe someone's giving him a bad time, that he's suffering and I can't do anything to help him."

He smoked one cigarette after another. His throat was hoarse and he couldn't stop coughing and racking his brains with the question: How could he get to someone high up in the army, in security or politics, who would be able to find out for him what had happened to his son, to rescue him from his troubles? Who could help him make contact with someone like that? He thought about his friends in his company in the reserves, about their officers, about people whose homes he had renovated, about forgotten acquaintances who might have gone up in the world, but he couldn't come up with anything. From the immediate members of the family he hid his distress, out of shame. When his oldest brother, Menashe, the closest to him of all his siblings, asked him how Eyal was getting on, Ezra answered in generalities about the period of adjustment to a new framework and expressed his confidence in the successful future awaiting his son in the army.

Ezra was always sure that he was the salt of the earth, that even though he was ostensibly an anonymous citizen, the man in the street, everybody knew that he and those like him were the secret strength of the state, the backbone of the country. And now he's a man without a people, he doesn't belong to anything, and the state is busy with its own affairs, which have nothing to do with Eyal's problems.

Ezra's agony lasted for about a week, until the phone rang at home. It was someone speaking on behalf of the army. A sergeant called Hagai informed them that Eyal had been given a prison sentence and on his way from the court to the army jail to serve his sentence he had given his guards the slip and escaped. Now he was officially a deserter, nobody knew where he was, presumably he would soon be caught. In any case, if they came into possession of any information about his whereabouts, they were to contact the following phone number immediately and hand him over to the military police, or else they too would be breaking the law and liable to punishment. After Hagai completed his announcement and said good-bye politely, the shocked and agitated parents realized that they had forgotten to ask him what Eyal had been sent to jail for, what crime he had committed. Nor did they know where they could contact this Hagai, where he was from — the boot camp, the town adjutant's office, or maybe the military police? But Ezra lit another cigarette and said: "Ruthie, believe me, I feel a lot better now. At least I know what happened, and I've got a phone number for the army. The question is what's happening to him now, where he's hiding and how we're going to find him."

Looking back, it appears that the first sign of Ilan's scheme was his suggestion that they should hire Ronit. There was no need to do so, the two partners could cope with the work very well on their own. Ilan justified his proposal with their plans for expansion, and he showed Aviram his calculations proving that in the long run hiring Ronit on a part-time basis would not adversely affect their income. Ilan's keenness to hire her had aroused Aviram's suspicions even then that his partner was having a love affair with the girl, and he didn't hesitate to mention his suspicions either, with a smile and in a spirit of good humor. Ilan denied it vehemently. "On the contrary," he said, "maybe you'll fancy her yourself and have an affair with her. Wait till you see how cute she is." Aviram said: "Sure, as soon as she sees me she'll fall in love with me." And Ilan said: "I don't understand you," and he pretended to be hurt to the quick by his partner's suspicions, by the aspersions cast on the purity of his intentions. But when she started working in the office, he wasn't ashamed to flirt and giggle with her in Aviram's presence. And now he was proposing to give her a full-time job. Aviram decided to object.

It's quite simple, he says to himself — Ilan is trying to get rid of him. After a logical examination of the various possibilities, there's no escaping this conclusion. Nothing else can explain Ilan's recent behavior. The new policy is to shower Aviram with affection and friendship, to consult him on every matter, never mind how trivial, especially on questions that according to the traditional division of labor between them were left to Ilan's discretion. And inside this deceitful wrapping of amiability, Aviram is supposed to feel more and more that a noose is tightening around his neck; that he is superfluous, and even worse, a handicap to the development and expansion of the business, like a grain of dirt stuck in the delicate workings of a machine and spoiling its performance.

Ilan is fed up with the petty business of apartment brokerage and has set his sights on the wider, more promising field of "real-estate deals," which involves a lot of trips and appointments outside the office. And so Ronit stepped into the gap and offered to take clients to view apartments for rent. In the end she was also entrusted with the keys to the empty apartments, which were always kept in a locked iron box. When he is left alone in the office, Aviram finds himself answering the phone, doing various secretarial tasks, and performing more and more of the job Ronit was hired to do. Now Ilan is proposing that they employ Ronit on a full-time basis. The object is clear: to make Aviram feel that he is superfluous in the office, that he has no place in the new era toward which Northern Star is advancing, up to the point where he demands the dissolution of the partnership. And according to the terms of their contract, this would suit Ilan to a tee — for Aviram to initiate the breakup of the partnership and retire of his own free will.

And perhaps all this is nothing but the distorted interpretation of a person losing touch with reality? For hours Aviram sits alone in the office, trying to concentrate on his work and distract himself from this question. Sometimes Ronit returns to the office and conducts loud, lengthy telephone conversations with her mother or her girlfriends, as if she were alone in the room, as if there's nobody there trying to work. She is in her early twenties, still reliving the experiences of her military service, to judge by her conversations with her girlfriends and perhaps also by the way she relates to Ilan, as if he were her commanding officer, with everything that implies. Her short hair emphasizes a certain coarseness in her features, but her tanned body is shapely and bursting with youthful vitality. In the summer heat she usually comes to work in tight-fitting jeans that show off her figure and short tank tops in which her breasts quiver erect and free, with a wide gap between the tank top and the jeans, exposing a slender waist and an expanse of golden stomach with the navel as its crowning glory. And sometimes she wears the shortest of skirts, ending at the top of her thighs and revealing the glory of her legs in all their length.

At this midday hour she has already finished her half-day's work and is free to go home. But after completing her telephone calls she approaches Aviram's desk and leans over him until he can feel the warmth of her body. In the framework of the new policy she too demonstrates friendship and interest toward him. Obviously, she knows about his objections to hiring her full-time, Ilan tells her everything. And consequently she sees Aviram as her enemy. It would be better if she took no notice of him at all. Suddenly he feels sorry. Sorry for her. Sorry for himself.

"What are you doing?" she asks, coming around to his side of the desk to see the screen of his computer, trying to show off her knowledge. "Ah, you're bringing the lists up to date," she says, standing next to him with her bare midriff brushing lightly against his arm, above the elbow, radiating a dreamy warmth. And before he recovers from the surprise, she returns to her desk, to the telephone, and carries on with her conversations. He has the impression that she is deliberately drawing out her telephone calls until he leaves and she remains alone in the office. Maybe she's waiting for Ilan.

On his way home for lunch he goes on thinking about the touch of her bare body on his arm, and the dreamy sensation still accompanies him. And even though he is not a man to be led astray by illusions and false promises and to part from his identity as a person excluded from love, excluded from friendship, excluded from every human relationship, superfluous in the world — nevertheless something arouses him to believe in his ability to attain his wish.

In the backyard of his apartment house people have gathered and there are sounds of an argument. He slips into the entrance and quickly climbs the stairs. The joyful barking of the dog greets him from inside the apartment and his heart is flooded with love. As soon as he opens the door the dog jumps on him, barking all the while. Once inside, Aviram kneels down next to him and embraces him and presses his face to his. The dog licks his bearded cheek, and Aviram closes his eyes, stroking the dog's neck and saying: "Nice boy, good boy, my sweet, my soul." Then he stands \up and wipes his beard with a paper towel where the dog wet it with his tongue. In the bedroom he presses his ear to the wall, and there is no sound from the apartment next door. After a while he goes out with the dog.

The argument outside is still going on. Mr. Shwartz, the head of the residents committee, his face red with rage, sees him and calls him to come over. At the center of the dispute are a strange man and woman. The man, tall and thin, is wearing a red baseball cap featuring the logo of the Olympics and that of its soft-drink sponsor; his eyes are embarrassed and worried. His wife, a heavyset redhead — dressed, in spite of the heat, in tight yellow pants and a loose green and brown shirt covering her body down to the knees — is shouting and cursing. Inside the pit being dug at the foot of the back wall of the building, a basement wall half underground, stand three Arab boys who have stopped working, leaning on their spades and picks, their eyes raised questioningly to the Jewish contractor, a short, broad-shouldered man who is standing on the edge of the pit with his arms crossed, smoking a cigarette, as if all this has nothing to do with him. A few of the neighbors, most of them from adjacent buildings, have gathered at the sound of the yelling, and others are watching from their rear balconies.

Mrs. Shwartz tries to calm her husband, and she explains to the people standing next to her: "No good him to lose temper. Sick blood pressure. He better to leave them alone, let them to go to hell with their storeroom." But he ignores her advice.

"Just like that they come and dig under the wall of the building?" Mr. Shwartz grips Aviram by the arm to prevent him from getting away: "Who are they? Nobody knows them. Without asking the House Committee? What do they think — this building belongs to them, this land belongs to them? Who do they think they are? Who gave them permission to dig here? Have they got a license? I phoned the municipality and the police and they're on their way."

"It's our storeroom, we bought it," the husband mutters to pacify him. "Show him the papers."

The redhead takes some papers out of the plastic bag in her hand and shows them to Aviram. "It's ours, we can do what we like here."

"Get inside the storeroom, if it's yours, and stay there as long as you like. But what business have you got digging outside here? The yard is the common property of the whole building; it isn't yours!" Mr. Shwartz cries in a voice hoarse with rage.

"What's the matter?" yells the woman. "Why are you talking to us like that? Aren't we Jews? What harm are we doing you? Do you know who you're dealing with? You think you can get away with making trouble for us? You go home and leave us alone!"

"It's only to put tar on the wall," the man with the Olympic cap tries to calm things down again, "so it won't be wet inside in the winter. Afterward we'll fill in the pit again and you won't see anything."

"So why should you care?" Aviram asks Mr. Shwartz.

"Look here," says the old man, and he points to the edifice of cinder blocks that has been erected over the steps leading down to the basement. "Can't you see, they want to build an apartment here and they're putting the entrance there, where they're digging, in order to take over the whole wall. It's against the law to make changes outside, it's against the law to build on the yard of the building. They're stealing our land."

"No, no," says the man. "Only to put tar on the wall."

"And what are you building there instead of the steps?" asks Mr. Shwartz.

"What do you care?" yells the woman.

"Blood pressure," warns Mrs. Shwartz. "If he lose temper, go straight to hospital in ambulance!"

"Go, old man, go, go!" says the woman who owns the storeroom. "Go die!"

25

"You hear her cursing?" says Mr. Shwartz, keeping a firm grip on Aviram's arm. "These people are gangsters. In the end they'll take the whole building from us." He looks anxiously at his watch. "And they're still not here from the municipality. They said they'd come soon to see what these people are doing here. It's against the law. You're witnesses," he announces to the people gathered around. "You're witnesses to what they're doing. Afterward in the court case they'll say that it was like that all the time and they didn't change anything."

"You should film it with a video," one of the onlookers suggests, "that's the best proof."

"These people are worse than the Arabs!" screams the redheaded woman. "Go and die with the rest of your families!"

A policeman comes into the yard. Mr. Shwartz calls out to him: "At last!" and explains in detail what's happening. The redheaded woman yells: "I'm afraid of the police? I'm afraid of the municipality? You can all kiss my ass! I've got a lawyer! I can do what I like in my own home! If I like I'll dig a pit from here to America! What will you do to me?"

"Make peace between you," the policeman suggests. "And I'm warning you, don't get violent and don't break the law."

"But what they're doing is against the law!" cries Mr. Shwartz. "It's against the building laws! They can't build here. And the land belongs to all of us, it's common property!"

"Take them to court," the policeman suggests. "I can't interfere here, we don't interfere in disputes between neighbors. Work it out between you."

"We're not gangsters," says the husband, "we don't mean any harm to anyone."

Aviram extricates his arm from the grip of Mr. Shwartz, who is trembling with agitation, and goes for a walk with the dog. On the pavement he can hear the woman shouting at the contractor: "What are they standing around for? Tell them to carry on working, everything's all right! You heard what the policeman said. There's no problem. They can kiss my ass."

The dog wants to go to the boulevard, along their regular

route, but Aviram doesn't want to go so far. He fails to persuade the dog and gives in. The midday sun beats down on his head, the sweat pours from his beard to his neck, his shirt is wet, but it's easier for him to bear, something has awoken in him, like the vestige of a strength that has gone to sleep and been forgotten long ago. The dog stops to sniff a tempting wet stain on the pavement, and Aviram raises his head and sees her coming from the end of the street, wearing white, as usual, holding the plastic bags containing her groceries, walking slender and erect with her haughty step, the walk of a dancer. The dog has abandoned the damp stain and is advancing along his route. When he sees that Aviram isn't coming, he stops and barks at him as a reminder that they still have a ways to go. But Aviram bends down and says: "We're going home." The dog ignores this announcement, goes on barking and advances up the road, stopping again and again and turning his head to see if Aviram is following behind. But Aviram is rooted to the spot, he can't take his eyes off her. She comes closer and he looks straight at her dark glasses. Up to now he has caught only a glimpse of her in the stairwell, this is the first time he has had the chance to get a good look at her. The dog doesn't stop barking, calling him to come. As she walks past them he nods, but she ignores him, her face as blank as if he isn't standing there right in front of her.

He hurries up to the dog, attaches the leash in his hand to the dog's collar, and pulls. The dog refuses to move, his paws scrabble on the pavement with the jerking of the leash, and he barks with loud, baffled complaint: Why change the old familiar route? What's wrong with the safe, regular path? What good will come of it? In the end he gives in, accepts the inevitable, and his legs run at the pace dictated by Aviram, who doesn't even look back to see if the collar is tightening around his neck but quickens his steps in order to keep up with the woman in white walking in front of him.

In the backyard of the building the work is continuing energetically, the roar of the drill and the blows of the hammers sound as if they are bringing down the walls, if not destroying the actual foundations. And she approaches the entrance at a run, immediately opens the door, and hurries up the stairs without switching on the stairwell light. Precious seconds are wasted until he takes the key out of his wallet, opens the front door, and follows her up the stairs. She is one floor ahead of him, and on the landings he manages to catch a momentary glimpse of her before she disappears from view again. By the time he reaches their common landing, she has already locked the door behind her.

He goes inside, takes off his shirt and trousers, and puts on a pair of gym shorts. His body is bathed in sweat and he puts on the air conditioner. The dog stands in the corner of the room and looks at him in bewildered apprehension and Aviram leads him to his bowl of water and urges him to drink before going into the kitchen to make himself something to eat.

When he hears the dog barking in the bedroom Aviram gets up from the kitchen table and goes into the bedroom. Through the hum of the air conditioner and the wall-shaking hammer blows and the furious barking, the sound of her moans rises from behind the wall, moans of pleasure so much like cries of pain. In vain he tries to calm the dog, then he sits down on the bed, closes his eyes, and tries to imagine how the tall, slender figure with the proud walk looks naked, white, on fire with passion and lust in the moments of climax.

Something wakes me from my sleep and I can't remember what it was. A dream? I don't remember any dream, and when you wake from a dream you remember it, you remember at least having had a dream. I know it was something sudden, some powerful shock that came from inside me, like an inner collapse. Another stroke? I feel what little remains alive in my body after that other stroke, move what I can, and nothing has changed. The way I feel in general hasn't changed either. The only sound to be heard in the house now is the sound of her breathing, the weak, rhythmic snores of someone who breathes through her mouth. At night she leaves the sliding door of the porch, where she sleeps, open, so that she can hear if anything happens to me, if I need her. And as always, when I wake up at night, I am confronted by her particular smell, the smell she brought with her into the house.

What is this smell? To this day it's a mystery to me. Perhaps it's some medicine, some special soap she uses, a cologne she brought with her from her country, perhaps they like this smell over there? Perhaps it's the smell of her body, the smell of their race? A sharp, unpleasant smell, like the smell of the food she cooks, apparently with some spice of theirs, and it takes over the house. In the first weeks I couldn't get used to it, there was something bitter and sweet about it that reminded me for some reason of the smell of a corpse. Whenever I woke up at night I couldn't go back to sleep because of that smell, and I hated her and cursed her. I reminded myself in detail of her ugliness, her round face with its broad, flat nose, her little eyes, her big back-side and short, fat legs. When she first appeared and I saw how ugly she was I was angry: why her of all people? I decided to make her life a misery until she left.

At first they wanted to bring a man. I heard them talking on the phone to the agency that brings them to the country. I yelled and gesticulated with my hands to signal my objections. (Thus I was forced to reveal that I understood what they were saying — up to then they thought that if I couldn't speak I couldn't hear or understand either.) They explained to me that I would feel better if a man took care of me and not a girl, what with the bathing and help in the toilet and so on. A lot of nonsense along those lines. I stood my ground, and I don't regret it.

My daughter had a different plan altogether, to send me to a nursing home, but my son objected, because to get me in they would have had to sell the house, and he had plans of his own. I didn't imagine that he was thinking of what was best for me. He isn't a particularly intelligent lad, in this he resembles his mother, but unlike her, he's always thinking about money, he always needs money urgently, I have no idea why, and it doesn't interest me either. His mother too wanted me to stay at home, so that she could show everybody how she was sacrificing herself for me. For some time she pretended that she was taking care of me together with the girl, but in fact because of her heart condition she couldn't help much, and she only "supervised" her. After a while she died, and again my daughter tried to persuade everybody that a nursing home would be best for me. She's no fool, and she's a bit of a bitch too. Maybe she knows something about her brother's plans as well, and she doesn't think they're in her interest.

To this day the apartment is exactly the way it was when my wife was alive. The girl didn't change a thing. The children gave her the closed-in porch, provided her with a bed, closet, and chair, and she arranged her things in there. And her peculiar smell invaded the house.

The light goes on in the porch and she crosses the living room. Her steps are soundless. In the light coming from the porch I can see her passing the open door of my room, in her pale pajamas, a squat shadow to which even the dimness of the night fails to lend an air of mystery or feminine grace. She goes into the kitchen and switches on the light, opens the tap and pours herself a glass of water. Perhaps I'd like a glass of water too? I yell at her. Time passes until she emerges from the kitchen, comes into my room, and switches on the light. Her pajamas are a white T-shirt, with a picture of Mickey Mouse and Donald Duck in red and blue, over loose white pants. I signal with my hand that I want to drink, and she says in her English: "Okay, now sleep, good night," switches off the light, returns to her porch, and once more the house is quiet and dark. After a while the sound of her rhythmic breathing resumes.

On fine winter days and on summer mornings she dresses me for a walk outside. In summer she puts an old cap on my head to protect me from the sun; in winter, so my head won't get cold, a red woolen hat with a pompom, apparently a child's hat, which she got hold of somewhere or other. Because for her I'm like a baby in a baby carriage. I realized this when I saw myself for the first time in the hall mirror before we went out, with that hat on my head. At first I felt angry and insulted, the reaction of a self-respect dating from another life, like a limb considered dead suddenly emitting a wave of pain. But when I looked in the mirror again, I began to like it and I realized that it was right.

And so she takes me for a walk in the wheelchair around the neighborhood and then in the public park, where she meets friends of hers who work nearby. They too bring their old people in wheelchairs. When they sit there together in a group, they are no longer so discreet and shy and quiet as they seem. They gabble away in their strange language, producing sounds from their throats that you don't hear among our people. They all talk together, laugh at the tops of their voices. My minder is more restrained. The other old people in wheelchairs don't seem bothered by the noise. One of them I remember from the neighborhood we once lived in. His family had a grocery store, and he was also a handyman. He had a thing for collecting old junk that people threw out for the garbagemen to take: an old chair, a tattered blanket, a broken washing machine, and even a broken toilet bowl. He would take them all home and try to repair them. His wife complained to customers in the shop that their house was full of junk, jammed up, it was impossible to move, and their children had left home because of this. For a long time now he hasn't known what's going on. He stares at his knees all the time; every few minutes he makes an effort, fills his lungs with air and heaves a long sigh, and goes back to staring at his knees. The two others, one a fat little Romanian, the other a pious Sephardic Jew called Tzarfati, talk and I try not to hear their nonsense. They know that I don't speak, they think I can't hear what they're saying and they don't bother me. I don't look any better than they do, I know, and nevertheless sometimes I have a silly urge to suddenly take off my hat and show them my full head of hair, with hardly any white, only gray! My son's hair is already completely white. He inherited that too from his mother. And when I feel this urge, I'm ashamed of myself.

———

"You hear what's going on here?" demands Mr. Shwartz. He stands in the doorway and prevents Aviram from shutting the door. Only the dog's barking stops the old man from crossing the threshold and walking into the apartment. "I called the police and they told me that until half past ten at night it's permitted to make that noise. You understand, they'll work day and night to finish everything before they get the order to stop building. They know what they're doing. And the municipality's not in a hurry; by the time they came to see, those people had already put up the terrace in the opening they made there, and the room over the steps to the storeroom, and now they'll finish putting in the toilet and the shower inside it. What will there be left to stop, I ask you? Everything will be finished."

"So what can you do about it?" says Aviram, and he tries to gradually close the door, but Mr. Shwartz holds the handle and stops him with a strength surprising for someone in his physical condition. "And what's so terrible about there being an apartment there anyway?"

"What do you mean?" says the astounded Mr. Shwartz. "You heard that woman, the way she talked? You want people like that here? You want to turn this place into a slum like Hatikva? For them to sit outside all night, on their terrace, and talk in shouts, with the radio playing Arab music full blast? For them to barbecue their meat under our windows?"

"I can't help you," says Aviram. "What can I do?"

"I want you to come down with me now and see what they're doing there. So we'll have witnesses when the municipality takes them to court."

"I can't now," says Aviram, "I'm very busy."

"What?" the old man yells. "It's all up to Shwartz? It's all up to one sick old man and nobody can help?" He raises one of his trouser legs, revealing a skinny white shin knotted with blue veins, and pulls it over his knee to show Aviram the edge of the bag of urine hanging on his thigh.

The yard is illuminated in the light of a powerful lamp connected to an electric cable emerging from the basement, a small cement-mixer chugs without stopping, and the sound of the blows coming from the new toilet facilities is deafening — they must be demolishing the old stairs that led down to the basement. The back wall is exposed in all its length and an opening has been made in it for a door. At the foot of the square pit they are laying the porch floor and erecting a low wall, about half a meter above ground level. The builders are rushing around in a frenzied attempt to complete their work by half past ten, and in the surrounding buildings people are standing at their windows and on their balconies, shouting: "Quiet! Quiet! Enough already! From morning to night without a break!" And the red-headed woman — actually, Aviram notices, more ginger-haired than red, yes, she's a gingie all right — is yelling back at them: "What do you care? Go to sleep and don't get up again!" The contractor is standing and smoking a cigarette, looking at his watch and urging his workers to hurry. And off to the side, on a slab of stone, her husband is sitting in his red baseball cap, as if all the commotion has nothing to do with him. When he sees Aviram, whom Mr. Shwartz has left by himself for a minute in order to go and argue with the contractor, he comes up to him and claps his hands together and complains, in a voice that is almost tearful: "Look at the trouble they're making for us. They're all against us. The neighbors, the police, the municipality. What harm have we done them?"

"I see that you're making a door and a porch there," says Aviram.

"Sure," says the man, "how else will we get in?"

"But you said you were only tarring the wall against dampness and afterward you would return everything to the way it was before."

"No!" the man argues. "We'll tar the wall and everything will be okay. What's the matter? Why don't you want us here? What are we, Arabs?"

"You're thieves!" Mr. Shwartz, who has come back to stand next to Aviram, yells at him. "You stole a piece of land that isn't yours and you're building on it against the law! It's going to be pulled down!"

The ginger woman, who up to now has been busy exchanging shouts with the people from the adjacent buildings, turns her attention to Mr. Shwartz. "Nobody's going to pull anything down!" She pushes her face into his until it's almost touching: "You hear, you old maniac? Nobody's going to touch our house! Not the municipality and not the police and not the court, they'll all side with us. You know who you're dealing with here?" she addresses this rhetorical question to Aviram. "If you don't stop making trouble for us, I know people who for fifty dollars will throw acid in your face so you won't be able to go outside anymore. Do you understand me?"

"You hear?" demands Mr. Shwartz. "These are the kind of neighbors you're going to get here. Remember to tell them in court what she just said. Going to tell the police won't help you. They're not interested. Until somebody gets murdered they don't do anything."

Aviram calls the dog, which has gone off to look for something in the hedge, and prepares to set out with him for his nightly walk. But the husband stops him: "Just a minute, sir, I want to say one more word to you. I see that you're an educated person with a kind heart. Our daughter's in the army, soon she's getting out, and she wants to go to the university. She's a good girl, she's got brains. Why shouldn't she live in a quiet place, without drugs, without gangsters, with people who go to the university? What's wrong, hasn't she got the right to a good life?"

"Don't let him tell you stories!" says Mr. Shwartz. "They're doing it in all kinds of places around here, buying storerooms and basements and building apartments to make money! In one place they made an apartment out of a laundry room on the roof of some building where the people don't pay any attention to what's going on right on top of their heads. It's all business."

"No, that's not true," protests the man in the Olympic cap, "it's only for our daughter, so she can have a life like that of your children."

34

"Yes," yells his wife, "we'll build apartments in all the buildings around here, in every hole, on the roof and under the
ground, and we'll bring Arabs to live there! Arabs, every one of
them two meters tall! So that no young girl will be safe here! So
you'll all run away!"

Aviram leaves the yard with his dog and says to himself: Maybe
the time has come to leave this place and buy an apartment somewhere else. But not yet. Something rivets him to this house. In the
apartment next to his, on the other side of his bedroom wall, the
young woman shouts her shouts of lust. And he listens as if it's a
message intended for his ears: Try to win me. He has always felt
excluded from love. The only women that ever showed any interest in him were ugly, and he was repelled by them at the outset.
And if they weren't ugly, they were prostitutes whose services he
paid for — and when it was over he hated them and himself.
Only in the white cat behind the wall will he be able to find the
real thing, whose absence tortures his soul.

TWO

"Do you live here?" A young man in jeans and a white sleeveless T-shirt is standing in front of the entrance and barring her way.

"No," Gabi says quickly.

He ignores her answer. "I'm looking for the people who live in number 17. I've been coming around for a few days now and nobody answers the door. It's written here Neuman," he points to the mailbox, "but the neighbors told me that the Neumans left a long time ago and other people live there now. I have to deliver a letter to them by hand, I'm from a delivery service."

"And there's no name on the letter?"

"No, only apartment 17, and the address."

"Who sends a letter like that? Show me the envelope," says Gabi.

"I can't. It's private."

"If you like I can take it and put it under their door," says Gabi.

"No, that's forbidden. I need them to sign that they got the letter," says the youth, and he looks at her with interest. "You don't know them?"

"No, I told you, I don't live here, I've come to visit someone."

"And those shopping bags?"

"They're for a sick woman who can't leave the house and I help her out. Are you investigating me?"

He bursts out laughing. "I'm just trying to start a conversation."

"Look, she even gave me her key to open the door," she shows him the key, "because she can't get out of bed to let me in."

He stands opposite her, his back to the entrance, and smiles.

"You're in my way," says Gabi.

"Can I help you carry your bags?"

"No thank you, they're not heavy."

She waits and he moves aside.

When she goes upstairs she sees that he is still standing behind the glass door and looking at her. And on the second floor the door of one of the apartments opens and the old man from the residents committee appears on the landing and glares at her angrily. "What about the house dues, miss? Soon that's three months owing. What are you going to do about it?"

"I'll pay," she replies and hurries up the stairs.

Inside the apartment, as she unpacks her groceries, she suddenly remembers the question Ada asked her in the café on that sweltering spring day: Where does he get the money to pay for an apartment like that? Up to now she hasn't given it a thought, not even after the conversation with Ada. Now she feels the beginning of a certain uneasiness, a kind of vague anxiety. There are too many things she doesn't understand. Up to now these shadowy areas have seemed like an added attraction to the whole adventure, but now they begin to unsettle her. Is this a sign that the fire is beginning to die down? In any case, her anticipation of the joy of the meeting is beginning to feel more like the dependency of an addiction, the need to satisfy a craving, which in her opinion only he can satisfy.

When he comes in, his face looks harassed and tired. He gives her a quick hug, evades her embraces, doesn't even look at the bed — he's not in the mood, is what he says. He sits down opposite her and looks at her in silence, examining her face just like she sometimes tries to solve the riddle of his. Two strangers, she says to herself, this is what it's like all the time, and that's what he really wants. All this secrecy and all these extraordinary precautions, and his refusal to know anything about her and her life outside the nuclear shelter, his reluctance to talk about himself, the long silences, and now, this searching look — it's all so that they'll remain strangers. He frightens her, she's afraid to lose him, her heart goes out to him.

They sit down to eat in the kitchen and she tells him about the young man from the delivery service who was looking for the tenants in number 17. He stops eating, his tired face tenses: "Did you talk to him?"

³⁸

"I told him that I don't live here."

He raises his voice: "Why do you talk? I told you not to talk to anyone!"

"If I hadn't answered, it would have seemed suspicious."

"I told you not to talk!"

"I want to understand what's going on here," says Gabi. "What's the story here? Is somebody after us? Are we being hunted?"

"Now you remember to ask? It's none of your business."

"You really think it's none of my business? I'm not involved?"

"No! You're not involved!"

He starts eating again and seems to calm down a little.

"Are you afraid that your wife will find out about us?"

"We don't talk about those subjects."

"What subjects do we talk about?"

"There's no need to talk much about anything."

"So for you I'm just a body?"

"Yes. And I'm just a body for you too."

"How long can we go on like this?"

"It'll last as long as it lasts. You're talking now as if all this is new to you. But all these things were there from the beginning, you knew about them. They were the conditions and you accepted them. Nobody forced you. Nobody's forcing you now either. You can decide at any minute that it's not for you and leave."

She is silent and then she tries to change the subject. "The old man from the house committee yelled at me on the stairs that we owe him money."

"I'll leave the money for him in his mailbox." He reflects for a minute. "I won't be coming here for a while."

"Are you punishing me?"

"No. And you do what I tell you, even if you don't under-stand why."

"Perhaps you just don't love me anymore. The decent thing to do would be for you to tell me so and for us to stop seeing each other."

"You're talking like a child. If I stop loving you, you won't see me here. And if I pretend, you'll sense it at once."

"You mean that your body will tell me."

"Exactly. Or to be more precise: it'll keep quiet."

And after their meal he suddenly is in the mood, and he pulls her to the bed.

The ginger woman who owns the basement waits in front of the glass door to accost the people coming out of the building. She follows Gabi as she goes to throw the garbage bag into the can. She calls after her, and Gabi, having learned her lesson, doesn't reply.

"You think you're too good to talk to me?" yells the woman. "What is it with you people, are we Arabs? Who do you think you are? Go die! Who needs you? Our apartment is already finished, there's nothing you can do about it. Our daughter will live there like a queen! We'll just move the garbage cans to the other corner of the yard so the porch doesn't stink, and we'll make a nice garden around. Come, come, come inside, I'm inviting you, come and have a cup of coffee, come and see how beautiful it is inside, so your evil eyes will pop right out of your head!"

The construction work has indeed been completed, and the sunken porch at the new entrance to the basement gleams white, there are lamps planted at the sides of the path to illuminate it at night.

When Gabi turns onto the path leading to the street, the woman stands in front of her and bars her way. "Wait a minute, I want to show you something." She takes a bundle of papers out of a plastic bag and waves it in front of her eyes. "I'm a sick woman, you know that? Cancer in the head. Look, look, it's all written here, from the HMO. You know what it means, cancer in the head? All the time treatments and soon I have to have an operation on the head. Why are they making trouble for me here? Haven't these people got a heart?"

Gabi steps off the path, squeezes past her along the hedge, and quickens her pace. The woman follows.

"From the way you look, you don't know what it means to have children," she shouts, "you probably haven't got a husband, you probably live alone, like everybody else in this building. Maybe you're a lesbian! You'll never know what it feels like to hold your baby in your arms."

On Sundays the girl goes to Jaffa to pray in their church. It's her day off. Apparently that's where they meet, all those boys and girls who work in Tel Aviv. At first my daughter came to take her place on Sundays, but after a few times she got fed up with spending such a long time with me, and I got fed up with it too. The girl brought Pedro. He's from there too, with their special smell, which with him is mixed with the smell of cigarettes. Apparently he's not so religious, or else he wants to earn a bit more money. He sits here on the sofa in the living room, smoking all the time, drinking beer from cans and watching sports on the television. I look at him from the side and see how he jiggles his knees all the time out of nervousness. It's not a nice thing to see.

He's short too, fatter than she is, with the same short legs and big backside. You can hardly tell the difference with them between male and female. You can't even see if he shaves his round face. But he's very strong. When he moves me from the bed to the chair or takes me to the toilet he lifts me into the air and throws me down hard. Maybe it makes him angry that he has to do a job like this. And in his little eyes there's always a savage look, scary to see.

It's not that I can't talk, I just don't want to. I don't want to so much that it's almost on the borderline of not being able to. But sometimes, to prove to myself that I can still speak, I say words. When the girl's not next to me I say: "Linda." It's easy to say, I don't even have to move my lips: "Lin-da, Lin-da." Once Pedro was watching football and I said out loud, "Linda." He turned his head to me and smiled. I'd never seen him smile. He said: "You love Linda?" I nodded my head: yes. "You love Linda?" I nodded: yes. It gave him as much pleasure as the clever trick of a baby. "You know what is Linda?" he asked, and answered: "Linda is beautiful!" And again he laughed.

I often ask myself if she has any sexual urges at all. It doesn't look like it. Can it be that she hasn't got any? The fact that she isn't beautiful doesn't mean that she doesn't have thoughts or dreams on the subject. As long as your mind's still working you don't stop thinking about it, even after your body's finished. When she takes me to the park and sits there with her girl-friends, I examine every one of them and try to guess about them. They all wear jeans and high, white, men's running shoes, and in summer, white T-shirts. There are two or three of them who show signs of having sexual urges: in their movements, their expressions, the way they touch themselves. One of them wears lipstick too. But with Linda there's no sign.

The boy sits opposite the television, in one hand he holds a cigarette or a can of beer, and the other hand lies between his legs all the time, feeling, stroking, and sometimes he pushes it into his trousers, deep inside, and rubs himself there savagely.

On Sundays I feel her absence. It was hard for me to get used to her appearance and to her smell filling the house, but she's become a part of my life. In the summer, when she's wearing short pants and a tank top, without a bra, washing the floor, bending over the pail to wring the floor rag, I try to guess what she looks like naked. A few times I pushed myself over to her porch in my wheelchair when she was getting dressed, and she immediately closed the curtain and wagged her finger at me as if she were scolding a naughty child. Apparently she went and told my daughter, who found it necessary to come and lecture me and threaten me that Linda would leave if I went on behaving like that. But I pretended that I didn't understand what she was saying.

I didn't see my son for a long time. We were never on good terms, we hardly spoke a word to each other. He was always a mama's boy, and whenever there were arguments, she always took his side. And his face reminds me too much of her. On Saturday he suddenly showed up to talk to Linda.

He offered her a job for Sundays cleaning some place connected with his work. I shouted and gesticulated: No! No! And he left immediately without saying good-bye. She came up to me, put her hand on mine, a fat hand like a pillow, with short fingers, and asked me in her English to agree. She explained how important the money she would get for the work was to her, work that wouldn't take more than an hour, an hour and a half on Sunday afternoon. The money she gets from me she sends home to her family, without it they'd have nothing to live on, and with this little extra she'll be able to buy herself something to wear or whatever she needs. I knew that nothing good would come of anything he offered her. I would be happy to give her the money she needs to buy things. But her hand held mine and its touch was so soft and pleasant that I couldn't help nodding my consent.

When I wake up I don't know what day it is, and I feel uneasy. In fact, what does it matter, but still, I have to know. It's a habit left over from the days when I was busy. When the boy comes to take her place, I know that it's Sunday. The next day I still remember sometimes that it's Monday, but after that the calculation starts getting muddled, and I feel that I'm a little less alive and a little more dead. When she doesn't take me to the park, I sit out a lot on the little kitchen porch. I hear her cleaning the apartment, washing the floor, all day long in her short pants, which draw attention to her short, fat legs. Then she comes into the kitchen to cook my food and hers, with that smell. And with that strangled voice of theirs, she sometimes sings cheerful, strange songs, or perhaps they're just ordinary songs. Sometimes I can hear familiar words in them, English words, but she sings them strangely. Her singing doesn't bother me, but I ask myself: What kind of a life does she lead? What has she got to sing about?

You can't tell their age, but she must be young — twenty, twenty-five, something like that, and all the time, day and night, with a crooked old man in a wheelchair who can't do anything for himself and has to be taken care of like a baby. She has only Sundays left to live her life, and then she goes to pray and meet the others, who live the same way. And even on her one free day she takes time in the afternoon to do cleaning work in my son's office. Is this how her whole life will go by? When will she go back there? By then she'll be too old to find a husband and have children. And she sings cheerful songs. Doesn't she care? Young people believe in life. Has she already given up her life?

From the little kitchen porch I can see part of the playground. From up here I can see little children flying on the swings, climbing the ladders and sliding into the sandbox, running after each other, and sometimes I can hear shouts of joy or pain from a child who fell down and hurt himself, and I want to be there, so that they'll see me next to them. When she goes to do the shopping at the supermarket she usually takes me with her and leaves me outside the entrance. Because inside she has to push the shopping cart. Sometimes people who know me from before walk past and try to talk to me. When they see that I don't answer, they think that I've lost the power of speech and they leave me alone. I used to work with the bank next to the super-market. I know the manager and the clerks. Today all these things are foreign and annoying. I think only of the playground. When she comes back to me, I show her the way there, and if she has time, she takes me. What is it that draws me so strongly to show myself there? Maybe it's some evil impulse, like people who're not normal and want to pull down their trousers in the street and stand there with the whole business outside, in front of all the women passing by, and see how they react. That's more or less the kind of pleasure I take in appearing in front of them disguised as a baby, with a little mother pushing me in a stroller.

When they see me, some of them stop playing, a few of the little girls run to their mothers or their nannies, cling to them and whisper. At first the children look at me from a distance, with sidelong glances, as if by accident, then they gradually come closer, and one braver than the rest stands right in front of me and stares me in the eye with a defiant expression as if to say: I'm not afraid. Until his mother comes to take him away and gives the foreign girl a rebuking look for bringing this scandal to the playground. The girl is embarrassed, she doesn't want to frighten the mothers. She wants us to go away, but I object. She knows that I'll shout if she takes me out of the playground and this scares her. And gleeful laughter rumbles in my chest. In her English she says to me: This place for children, you not a child. And in my heart I say to her: I'm your child.

On the face of things, the right thing to do was to take advantage of the period when she was forbidden to meet him in order to take stock of the situation and decide how to behave in the future. Does she want to continue the relationship? If not, this is the time to get him out of her system. She deliberately avoided phoning Ada to ask her opinion, because she knew in advance what she would say and she was liable to do the opposite simply out of petty pride. The one possible way out of the situation in which she has become trapped is so logical that it spurs her resistance. Even if she wanted to distract herself from him and to try to forget him, she sees him every day in the office, once or twice, walking past her and ignoring her completely — just as they had agreed in advance — and each time, she tries to read something on his face, in his movements, some hint, something that would help her to guess: When will we meet again? Her feelings of guilt toward him grow more and more deep-rooted, until she actually justifies her punishment, even though the last time they met, when she asked him if he was punishing her, he said: No.

On the face of things, if she had embarked on this affair not out of true love involving the hope of a life together but because she saw it as a challenge to beat him in some contest, this is her chance to put him to the test: When he asks to meet her again, if he does, she can present her conditions. And the first one will be to put an end to the strange, humiliating framework he has imposed on her. But he's liable to react by finally breaking off relations, and she knows that she won't dare risk that or the agonies of regret that would torture her afterward, and as soon as she hears him hint that he's ready to meet her again, she'll surrender unconditionally. Why keep deceiving herself? From the beginning there had been no contest here, only addiction and defeat.

After work she hurries home, switches on the television, and stares at the pictures passing before her eyes without being able to follow them. All the time she keeps weighing the different possibilities, trying to guess his intentions, if he intends renewing contact, and if so, when, and how she should react, and how it will affect their relationship in the future. Nothing is capable of distracting her from the gnawing deprivation to which she has been sentenced, and toward the end of the week, for the first time, a new idea occurs to her: He has someone else whom he is hiding in the apartment, the whole business of the delivery boy was only an excuse and his anger was only an act.

The next day, during lunch break, she takes a bus to the flat. As she stands in front of the door, the door of the bearded neighbor with the dog opens, as if he was waiting for her to come and saw her climbing the stairs. He greets her and smiles an ugly smile. His dog stands next to him and barks at her, and she, obedient to the rules imposed on her, says nothing.

"Someone was looking for you before," he says as she inserts the key in the door, afraid that Hezi may have changed the locks so as not to be disturbed in his meetings with the other woman. "A woman from the Central Bureau of Statistics talked to me from downstairs, they're doing a survey of the apartments in Tel Aviv. She has to ask you all kinds of questions. She said she would leave you a note in the mailbox."

The locks haven't been changed, and the door opens. There's nobody in the apartment. She looks around. What am I doing here? asks a voice inside her. The place feels as strange to her as if she's broken into somebody else's apartment. She checks out the kitchen, the bathroom, and there's no sign of the other woman. She goes into the bedroom, sits down on the bed, which is still rumpled — from their last meeting? Or perhaps after that? — and buries her face in the hollow in the pillow where he rests his head after making love and lies flat on his back with his eyes closed, as if he's alone in the world. And she feels no response from the cold pillowcase. On the other side of the wall she can hear the neighbor talking to his dog, she can't hear what he's saying but his voice is the voice of a lover. She wants to cry but she can't.

A ring at the door makes her jump. She goes softly, barefoot, to peep through the peephole. A stern-faced woman is standing at the door and ringing the bell insistently. Then she knocks on the door and calls: "I'm from the Central Bureau of Statistics. I left you a note. I know you're there! Someone just saw you going inside. Why don't you answer? It won't take more than fifteen minutes. What kind of way is that to behave? You think I've got nothing to do but run after you all day?"

Despairing of a reply, the woman leaves Gabi's field of vision and Gabi hears her ringing the neighbor's doorbell. The only answer is the angry barking of the dog. Gabi sees the woman coming back to stand opposite her, glaring reproachfully at her door. She feels an oppressive need to escape from the apartment and hopes she'll have the strength to withstand temptation and never come back again. After the woman disappears, Gabi waits a little longer, to give her time to get away from the building, and then she hurries downstairs. Next to the entrance, like a lioness waiting to pounce on her prey, stands the woman with her statistical papers. In order not to arouse her suspicion, Gabi overcomes the impulse to retrace her steps, opens the door, and takes no notice of her. But the woman stops her: "Are you from apartment 17?"

"I don't live here," Gabi replies and continues on her way. And the fact that she has disobeyed him doesn't bother her a bit. On the contrary, this act of rebellion fills her with confidence, a feeling that she has set foot firmly on the road to liberation.

She takes the bus back to the office. It's still early, she's hungry, and she goes into the little diner next to the office building.

He is sitting by himself at the corner table, eating with the newspaper open in front of him. With a characteristic reflex he turns his face for a second to the door, to see who has come in, and immediately goes back to poring over the newspaper. If she were to behave according to the firm resolve she felt on leaving the apartment, she would seat herself at one of the tables and order something to eat. But his grave profile in the relative gloom of the corner and the inclination of his body leaning over the newspaper dissolve all her resolutions. She turns around immediately and leaves the diner, and since she has lost her appetite, she goes up to the office.

Once she had a circle of friends, and even if she didn't see them regularly she knew they were there. They weren't many, and she wasn't equally fond of all of them, but she always felt at home among them, with all the advantages and disadvantages of home. She entered into relationships with men, none the man of her dreams, and the relationships did not last long, nor were the partings particularly painful. There were times when she liked being alone, reading a book, watching a movie or an interesting program on television, listening to music, but then too her social connections were important to her, not as a refuge from loneliness but as a kind of pipeline to the outside world. They reinforced her sense of her own existence, which was sometimes inclined to grow dim. And nevertheless, long before she knew that she would find employment in this firm, before she could have imagined the existence of this disgusting character, she had begun to let go of these connections. As if something inside her knew what was going to happen and prepared the ground for the affair. Gradually she lost touch with her friends, until the only one left was Ada. Now she decides to take her into her confidence again. In the evening she phones her.

"I think about you a lot," says Ada, "even though I don't hear from you. I have a feeling that you're not happy, I hope I'm wrong."

"You're right," Gabi admits.

"You want to meet?"

"Yes, come around to my place. When can you come?"

Ada can't come that evening, they arrange to meet the next evening.

When Gabi opens the door she is astonished to see Ada's new look: her hair, which was streaked with gray, has been dyed blond and styled by a hairdresser, her skin cleaned and treated, and her face made up in subtle shades that give it a kind of dubious freshness: her eyebrows, which are so fair as to be almost invisible, have been darkened; the eyeshadow on her eyelids emphasizes her light eyes; and her lips are shining with red lipstick. She is wearing a light, sleeveless summer dress that is not flattering to her figure. Ada has never been good at choosing her clothes.

"Is it awful?" she asks at the sight of Gabi's astonished expression.

"No," says Gabi. "But why?"

"At our last meeting, in that café, I felt so pathetic next to you."

"You did all this for me?"

"Why? Is it ridiculous?"

"Of course not! It was a great idea, it's a pity you didn't start a long time ago. I just have to get used to it. Is that why you didn't come yesterday, because you wanted to beautify yourself first?"

"Yes," admits Ada, who can't tell a lie.

"Oh, Ada, you're an expert at making me feel guilty."

Ada is carrying a little parcel, gift-wrapped in a bookshop, which she hands to Gabi.

"What's this for?" asks Gabi.

"I felt it would be right."

Gabi opens the parcel and sees a book of poems by Dahlia Ravikovitch.

"Of course," she says and gives Ada a hug of thanks, "how could I have imagined anything else? You're always faithful to your loves. The first time we sat next to each other at the university, you had a book of hers in your bag. That's when we started talking. You told me that you always had a book of hers with you."

"Right, and I've still got that book with me, in the car."

Gabi pages absentmindedly through the book. Ada holds out her hand for it and opens the book immediately to the poem she wanted to show Gabi. She gives the open book to her friend and follows Gabi's eyes as she reads the poem, to share her response.

> I don't understand why the house
> though it's heated doesn't get warm.
> It's as if the walls were flinching with pain
> inside the plaster,
> yet we keep pushing it all away
> from day to day till the end of time.
> What a fraud: to act as if we
> were the sons of gods.

"What's happening in the 'fucking' apartment?" Ilan asks with a conspiratorial smile. "Is there any action?"

"I don't know," says Aviram, "I don't think anyone goes in there at all."

It was Ilan who had dealt with the renting of the apartment, even though he argued that it would be more natural for Aviram to deal with the landlord, whom he knew from their days as neighbors, and to show interested clients the apartment next door to his own. But Aviram, who was careful to avoid personal contact with his neighbors, was unwilling, and Ilan understood. A lot of people were interested in the apartment but were put off by the high rent. When the client who eventually took the apartment appeared in their office, there was an immediate rapport between him and Ilan, mainly from Ilan's side. He spoke to the client in the language he imagined CEOs spoke to each other when alone, and when Aviram heard them talking he couldn't help sensing that there was a kind of silent agreement between them, the kind that exists between impostors. He was already only too familiar with the role Ilan was playing, but the mysterious importance with which the client tried to impress his interlocutor, his poker face and impatient grunts, did not inspire Ilan's trust. Ilan was immediately suspicious of the story told him by the client about his need for an apartment to rest in from the labors of the day, and he even remarked to Aviram afterward, with a sly wink, that he wouldn't be surprised if the fellow didn't bring a bit of work home with him anyway. Still, it was evident that he was excited by the meeting, and especially by the client's indifference to the high rent he would have to pay for an apartment where, at least according to him, he would spend only a couple of hours a few times a week. It was clear to Ilan that the man wanted an apartment in which to keep his mistress — something in accord with his notions about the lives led by top executives in the world of big business.

"So what does he need the apartment for," says Ilan, baffled by the mystery, "if he doesn't use it at all? Why is he paying hundreds of dollars a month for it? Maybe for him it's peanuts — but what for?" Ilan ponders for a moment and with his executive wisdom finds a sophisticated solution to the problem: "Perhaps he needs an address — these things are common in big business — for front companies and all kinds of transfers of capital and shady deals. He probably needs a good address in a respectable part of town. Does he get mail? Is there anything written on his mailbox?"

"No," says Aviram, "I don't think so."

Ilan smiles at Aviram despairingly: What can you expect from someone like him who shows no interest in the mysteries of the world of big business, in its intricate machinations, which might sometimes be dangerous but whose rewards are incalculable? What will we do with this Aviram given the expected expansion of Northern Star and its transformation from a miserable home realtor into a company doing real-estate deals on a big scale?

For now Ronit has not come to work, and Ilan has said nothing about it. Aviram supposes that she has stopped working for them, but he doesn't want to ask his partner the reason for her absence. And when Ilan returns at midday from various appointments outside the office he says with would-be nonchalance, trying to cover up a certain embarrassment: "Ronit won't be working for us any longer," and he examines Aviram's face for his reaction. "I expect you won't be too sorry about it."

"Why? Actually I think that she's a nice girl," Aviram surprises him.

"Yes, but you objected to taking her on from the beginning."

"I didn't object to her, I thought we didn't need any extra manpower in the office, but you convinced me. And afterward I thought that we shouldn't take her on full-time. But I've got nothing against her personally."

"All that's irrelevant now," says Ilan, "and believe me, it's no great loss to us if she doesn't work here anymore. The two of us will manage the work like we did before, and when we want additional manpower, we'll discuss it. Okay?"

So, says Aviram to himself, the affair's over, and it ended badly. And in order to fire her, the boss didn't consider it necessary to consult the lowly clerk. And what about the diabolical scheme to get him to retire from the partnership? Is that also "irrelevant" now that Ronit is out of the picture? Or has it been shelved for the moment, until the right circumstances arise once more? Now he's sorry he won't see her in the office again. He misses her presence, even though he hasn't forgotten how crude and insulting that presence was, how it emphasized his nonentity. And the touch of her bare stomach on his arm, when she bent down to see the computer screen, would have no continuation — a chance accident, almost a mishap. But who knows, very probably one day soon, when he comes into the office, Ilan will raise his head from the financial newspaper and say in a would-be casual tone: "Ronit's coming back to work for us. I'm sure you'll agree with me that her help is important so that we can devote more time to our new concerns. She'll be back at work tomorrow. Okay?"

And Aviram swears to himself that if this really happens, he won't object to employing her full-time.

Ilan answers the phone. They want Aviram. It's his father.

Aviram's mother has left home again and he has to go look for her. His father has searched the streets around their house and she isn't there. His legs are too weak to go any further afield. And she's so quick off the mark, she takes advantage of every chance to slip out of the house. This time his father went out to do the shopping and forgot to lock the door. Aviram is angry and he raises his voice: "How could you do such a thing? It's happened a few times now!" And his father replies in a low, shame-ridden voice: "Aviram, I'm also old and I forget things too."

He goes out immediately and stops a cab. The danger is that she'll get run over, because she ignores traffic lights, not to mention traffic, crosses the road without taking any notice of the cars, walks straight ahead, making for some destination of which only she is aware. The cab brings him to the neighborhood of his childhood and youth, which he rarely visits. He limits his contact with his parents as much as possible and makes do with a dutiful telephone call once a week to ask his father how they are.

He stands in the street where his parents live and doesn't know where to turn. He tries to concentrate and to let himself be guided by an inner sense, perhaps a telepathy of blood relation, if there is such a thing. He makes an effort to remember her previous escapes, when he was summoned to help search. Where had she been found then? Maybe there was some pattern in her wanderings? Experience determines the general direction in which he should go — toward Allenby Street. And at the same time he stops at every corner, going into every street branching off from the one he's walking along and scanning as far as he can. Something tells him that this time it will end badly, and the fear constricts his heart.

The area has changed beyond recognition. Whenever he comes here, he discovers that more old houses have been destroyed, giving way to buildings with banks and insurance companies, and that many of the apartments in the old buildings, whose tenants have died or moved away, have been turned into law offices and accounting firms. The occupied houses are fewer and fewer, more and more dilapidated. Almost all the remaining occupants of the emptying buildings are old, some of them veteran home owners clinging obstinately to their property, others key-money tenants paying rents that have eroded to practically nothing over the years, living in both cases in neglect and fear.

From the end of one of the streets, not far from Allenby Street, he sees her in her old blue robe, with a woman he doesn't know, who looks no younger than his mother, holding her hand and pulling her along. The weight of his fear is lifted, but instead of relief he feels anger at being forced to occupy himself with his parents, at not being left alone. He walks up to them and when his mother sees Aviram her memory clears for a moment and she calls out joyfully: "He's mine, he's mine!"

"You're the son, I remember you," the woman says.

He doesn't recognize her.

"How can you let her wander around like this?" she scolds him. "In her condition it's so dangerous, she doesn't know how to be careful."

He politely thanks the woman, who goes on her way, and walks with his mother down the streets of his childhood, which have changed beyond recognition. "I have to go home," says his mother, "there are a few things there that I have to take."

"Yes, Mother."

The faded blue robe is loose on her, because she has grown thinner in recent years. Apart from this her appearance hasn't changed, her illness has left no marks on her face. As they approach the house, his father is standing outside. When he sees them, the little man claps his hands with a groan of relief. They turn into the stairwell, and his mother says: "No, it's not here. I have to go home."

"This is home right here," says Aviram. "See, Daddy's here."

"No, no," she pleads, "first I have to go to my house to take some things."

"What things?" Aviram asks.

She reflects for a minute: "Shoes. There are shoes there that I need. Take me there, please!"

His father says: "Lately she talks all the time about her home somewhere else, and all the time she wants to go there."

"There isn't any other home, Mother, only this one," says Aviram.

"We'll go there later," says his father. "First let's go in here, to this home."

His father grips her arm and reluctantly she climbs the stairs to the first floor.

"Come in for a minute," his father requests.

"I don't have the time, Daddy, I left in the middle of work, I have urgent things to do and my partner has to go meet with clients. We can't leave the office closed."

"Come in just for a minute, I want you to see something."

He goes up to the apartment with them, and his father opens the door and says to Aviram: "Pay attention."

In the hall there is a long mirror. While passing it she steals a quick look into the glass, then turns her head to Aviram and his father and puts her finger on her lips to warn them not to talk. After they go into the room, she says in a whisper: "She's stand-ing there again."

"Who?" asks her husband.

"That poor woman."

"Why is she a poor woman?" asks Aviram.

"Speak softly, she hears every word," his mother says under her breath, "she's got nothing else to do. She's all alone, she hasn't got a father or children, she stands and watches us all the time and listens to what we say. She's very poor, you saw how she was dressed."

"I told your mother," says his father, "perhaps we should invite her in."

"What an idea!" his mother responds in an angry whisper. "I don't know her, why should I invite her to come here?"

"Your mother asked her once who she is and why she stands there all the time."

"She doesn't know how to talk," says his mother.

"Do you want me to tell her to go away, not to stand there and look into our home?" his father asks.

"No! God forbid!" his mother is horrified. "How could you do such a thing to such a poor woman?"

"This is something new," says his father, "it started a few days ago."

His mother goes up to his father and whispers in his ear: "Who is this man?"

"It's our Aviram!" says his father. "Don't you remember him?"

She examines Aviram's face. "Please, sir," she says to him, "can you take me home?"

"Where is your home?" his father asks.

She raises her hand: "Not far from here. It won't take long. Please, sir," she turns to Aviram again, "I can't get there by myself."

"I have to go," says Aviram.

"Let's go!" his mother says happily and makes for the door.

His father leads her into the other room, distracts her, and slips outside with Aviram, locking the door behind him. He accompanies him to the street.

"Did you see how sorry she is for the woman in the mirror, how she won't let anyone insult her? Even now, in her condition."

He has already told his father, more than once, that they should put her into a home where people suffering from her disease are taken care of, since her condition won't improve but only get worse. And his father says: "You want us to throw our mother out of the house and entrust her to the hands of strangers?"

"You've already been told what to expect: in the course of time she'll become incontinent, she'll forget how to talk, she won't recognize you. You're taking too much on yourself."

"Perhaps we'll be granted a miracle," says his father, and Aviram doesn't know whether to take him seriously or not. He examines his tired face, which looks like the face of a stranger, and the old man says: "I still have the strength."

"I don't think anyone else would . . ." says Aviram and the sentence refuses to complete itself.

He returns to the office and Ilan looks at him with concern: "Did you find her?"

"Yes," Aviram sighs. "I can't cope with this kind of thing. My father refuses to put her in a home, he's killing himself."

"It's a terrible disease," says Ilan. "I want you to know, Avi, that if you need help, I'll always be glad to help you."

"Thank you, Ilan, but there's nothing to be done."

A week passed and Ezra and Ruthie heard nothing about Eyal. Ezra couldn't stand it anymore and called the number he had been given. A sleepy clerk answered who didn't know who Eyal or Hagai were and who didn't understand his words, which were said in great agitation and apparently came out confused. She transferred him to another line, where he was answered by someone with an authoritative voice, apparently an officer, who knew something about the matter but neither Eyal's name nor any details about what was happening with him. Hagai, he said, wasn't on base at the moment, and he didn't know when he would be back.

Ezra said: "Ruthie, our Eyal's disappeared, I feel as if we have no child. Nobody's heard anything about him, nobody knows anything about him, the truth is nobody cares about him. Where is our son, what's happening to him?"

"I'm worried about him too, and I only hope that he won't get into any more trouble than he's in already. But we have to be strong, Ezra, and we have to have a lot of patience. This is a difficult time for Eyal and for us too. As long as nothing bad happens to him, he'll overcome his difficulties and come out of this stronger and more responsible and more mature."

"You're driving me crazy, Ruthie, how can you be so calm and talk about him as if he's a stranger, some other people's child. What are you made of, steel? I feel as if my life is ruined. I only hope that they'll catch him quickly and put him back in prison, so that at least we'll know where he is and what's happening to him. That way we'll be able to try to help him too. And if he's hiding somewhere, why doesn't he call and say something? Aren't we his parents? Doesn't he love us? Ruthie, all this isn't normal!"

"One of us has to be strong, Ezra," said Ruthie. "To hold the house and the family together. We have to think of the two little ones too, and give them a feeling of security. We mustn't let them see their parents falling apart. And I believe in Eyal, he's a strong boy. You'll see that he'll come out of it, Ezra, listen to what a mother's heart tells you."

Ezra despaired of understanding Ruthie's serenity. Sometimes he felt that not only had his son disappeared and been lost to him, but his wife too was getting more and more distant from him. And in order to entreat the mercy of heaven, he decided — without telling her, in case she mocked him — to go to a rabbi who was reputed to be a great Torah scholar and cabalist. The rabbi paged through a few books on the table in front of him, nodded his head gravely, closed his eyes, and muttered obscurely to himself for a long time. When the rabbi eventually opened his eyes, he spoke to Ezra encouragingly, assured him that Eyal was safe and sound, that he would soon return to his family and to the army, and all would end well, and to be on the safe side, he recommended the recitation of certain suitable psalms. Ezra asked to make a donation to charity, and the rabbi recommended a Talmud Torah in a nearby neighborhood. Ezra gave him the donation and also rewarded the rabbi himself handsomely for his trouble, and he left feeling more confused and despairing than when he had arrived.

A few days later, during the evening news on television, Menashe, Ezra's older brother, showed up and said that he was in the neighborhood on business and thought he'd drop in for a short visit. After drinking a glass of cold water and a little cup of Turkish coffee, he asked how Eyal was getting on in boot camp. Ruthie was silent and Ezra mumbled: "He's not getting on too well. . . . It's hard for him, he's got problems. . . . Maybe in the end he'll be okay and . . . adjust to the military framework."

"Ezra, you're not telling me the truth!" said Menashe, and

he turned to face Ruthie and demanded: "What's happened to Eyal?"

"Why are you asking, Menashe? What's on your mind?" said Ezra.

"I don't believe it, Ezra! You're hiding from your brother what's happening to your son? So let me tell you something about him. Let's go out onto the balcony." They went out of the air-conditioned room into the steamy heat outside. "I don't want the children to hear this," he explained. "Mordechai, our mother's neighbor, who's known Eyal all these years, who used to always see him coming to visit her, saw him this afternoon sitting on the pavement in the street next to the central bus station, where all the foreign workers are, and the massage parlors and the whores and the junkies, looking like a beggar. He said he's sure it was Eyal. I didn't believe him. But now, after listening to you mumbling and trying to hide the truth from me, I'm sure it was him."

"We can't afford to waste a minute," said Ezra. "We're going there right now, Menashe, we have to find him. Did he tell you the exact place where he saw him?"

"Yes, I know exactly where."

And while they drove there in Ezra's pickup, Menashe heard all about Eyal's troubles from his brother. "How come you didn't tell me straight away?" asked Menashe. "Perhaps something could have been done. I don't understand you, Ezra!"

"To tell the truth, Menashe, I was ashamed. Don't you understand? For something like this to happen to me! In our family? Where we regard the army as something sacred! The children are our display window to the world! I didn't want anyone to know, I hoped the whole thing would pass over quietly."

When they reached the area of the central bus station, Ezra parked the pickup, and the two brothers stepped into the hot, humid, sooty air of the street, walked past the bus platforms, and turned left at the cinema. Menashe scanned the arcade on both sides, apparently looking for something their mother's neighbor said was by the place where Eyal was sitting. They walked past groups of men sitting on benches in the middle of the arcade and in front of the fast-food joints, or standing in the entrances to the buildings and courtyards, under the flickering colored lights, until Menashe said: "It's here," and pointed to a kiosk whose pale neon light left the tables outside on the pavement in semi-darkness. On the counter stood a television, its screen facing the street, showing a film in a foreign language, apparently Turkish.

They passed among the tables overflowing with empty beer bottles and cans, among the foreigners laughing and talking in their language. The owner of the kiosk, a small man in an undershirt soaked with sweat and a shabby peaked cap, stood at the counter, next to the television, and behind him, on a metal shelf, a fan whirred without doing much good. Menashe went up to him, followed by Ezra.

"Did you see a soldier hanging around here today? We're looking for him."

The man shrugged his shoulders. "You see who comes here," he said and indicated the people sitting outside. "Israelis don't come here, only them."

"He was sitting here today on the pavement, I saw him," said Menashe, "in a dirty uniform, unshaven, looking completely out of it. Don't you remember?"

"Are you from the police?" asked the kiosk owner.

"I'm from security," said Menashe.

The kiosk owner examined him and Ezra, standing next to him in gym shorts and flip-flops, and shrugged his shoulders again. "All kinds of people pass here," he said, "I don't remember them." His hand drew an arc in the air. "There's a lot of places here where these people sleep," he pointed to the junction, "and places for massage and girls, you know, and all kinds of things people come here to look for. So what do I know if there was a soldier here today or not?"

They went on walking slowly down the arcade, looking at the people sitting inside the diners and outside on the pavement, turned onto one of the streets leading off the arcade, and stopped to inspect a figure leaning against the wall in the dark.

Ezra's heart froze inside him. A thin youngster, dressed in rags, stretched out his hand and mumbled unintelligibly when he saw them approaching. His voice choked, he fell silent and swayed on his feet. "From a distance he looked like my Eyal," Ezra whispered into Menashe's ear. "Thank God he's not," said Menashe. A group of men was standing at the entrance to one of the buildings, talking in a foreign language. The two brothers turned into another street, and so they continued for a long time, until Ezra said:

"Menashe, we're wasting our time. There's no chance of finding him like this. I'll come back tomorrow afternoon."

"Phone that army number and tell them someone saw him here today. Let them send MPs here to look for him," said Menashe.

"Menashe," said Ezra, "they won't look for him. They don't care about him. It's not our army, the army we once knew. I feel that we have to do it all on our own."

They returned to Ezra's house, and Menashe got into his car and drove off. Ezra went inside, and when Ruthie saw him she realized immediately that he hadn't discovered anything. "I knew you wouldn't find him," she said and burst into tears.

Ezra made haste to embrace her, feeling as if they were meeting again after a long separation. "What happened, Ruthie? You were the strong one, you were the one who reassured me all the time."

"After I heard what Menashe said, I'm afraid something terrible is happening to our son. Ezra, do you think he's on drugs?"

"That's the worst thing you can think of?" said Ezra. "I don't know anything anymore, Ruthie. I don't know our son. The more we find out, the less I understand. But nothing will stop me from finding him. Now I have to be strong. Menashe will help me. He'll do anything, and he's got connections in all kinds of places. We'll find him, and I'll bring him back to what he once was. All this will pass like a bad dream, and he'll turn over a new leaf in the army. I promise you, Ruthie, you'll see that we'll find him and everything will be okay!"

The next afternoon Ezra returned to the area around the central bus station, hung around the diners and kiosks where the foreign workers were drinking beer, went into dark little dens where people were playing backgammon and cards, peeped into the entrances of the neglected buildings and into their backyards, into clothing and shoe shops whose display windows were dusty and heaped with goods, passed the buildings housing the health clubs with three lights flickering above their doors like broken traffic lights, went into the streets branching off the arcade, stopping next to suspicious-looking groups of people, listening and trying to understand what they were saying, turning to anyone who looked as if he might understand Hebrew and describing his soldier to them — but he came up with nothing.

What is he looking for here? Even if the lad had been seen here some time before, by now he must have gone to seek shelter somewhere else, perhaps even in another town. What secret force is drawing him to this place? He walks slowly down the arcade, stopping from time to time and raising his head to scan the facades of the buildings, the shop entrances and kiosk counters, examining the people passing him, and then turning around to examine the buildings and the people on the other side, narrowing his eyes and knitting his brow as if trying to solve a riddle — and if he solves the riddle of this place perhaps he will also solve the riddle of his son, perhaps even the riddle of himself.

He stops in front of the kiosk frequented by the Romanian workers, where his mother's neighbor from Pardes Katz claimed to have seen Eyal sitting on the pavement. The kiosk owner looks at him with tired eyes, presumably not recognizing him as the man in gym shorts and flip-flops, one of the two who came by last night to ask him about the young soldier. Ezra's eyes are drawn to the big sign advertising the Little Paris health club, about twenty meters from where he stands, with a picture of the Eiffel Tower, and together with the concern for his son, an anxiety that accompanies him day and night, his heart suddenly contracts in strange longings and a shameful regret whose nature he is reluctant to explore.

He goes up to the entrance of the building that houses the health club, peers into the dark stairwell, and recoils at the stench of urine. He returns to the pavement, stands next to an adjacent shop selling roasted pumpkin and sunflower seeds and various kinds of nuts, and watches the entrance to the building. A very fat young man is sitting behind the trays of nuts and seeds arranged by type in compartments of galvanized tin, watching a little television set at his side. On the wall behind him is a picture of a famous rabbi, with the words: "Prepare for the coming of the Messiah!" together with a smaller picture of rabbis, cabalists, and miracle-makers. Next to the trays of nuts stands a box for charitable donations, it too decorated with a picture of a bearded rabbi.

Ezra catches his breath: a young girl with blond hair and blue eyes, a fresh face and soft body, in a very short skirt and flimsy tank top, emerges from the entrance to the Little Paris building and walks past the nut shop. For a second their eyes meet and Ezra imagines that he sees a hint of an embarrassed smile in her look, until she lowers her lashes. She crosses the street and disappears into one of the shops opposite, and Ezra's feeling of shameful regret is replaced by one of thrilling yearning. He senses that the fat nut vendor is looking at him with a smile.

"Is she from there?" Ezra asks him, and jerks his chin in the direction of the health club.

The fat man nods. It is strange to think of the fair, delicate girl, whose movements are so demure, as someone who works in a place like that.

"Why don't you go in there? It's good!" says the nut seller.

"Have you been there?" asks Ezra.

"No," the young man replies, "I'm not allowed to."

"Why not?"

"I'm not well."

"So how do you know that it's good?"

The nut seller smiles sadly: "Of course it's good. Everybody knows. And now they've brought girls from abroad too."

"Give me a cola," says Ezra, without taking his eyes off the door of the shop opposite, waiting for the girl to come out. He sips the cola slowly, and by the time he finishes the girl crosses the road again. She makes her way quickly to the building entrance without looking at Ezra again. When she walks past him he breathes in the pure smell of her body, fresh as a newly ripened fruit. He decides to go into the health club and ask for her there. And as he stands opposite the entrance with his back to the street, hesitating as to whether he should go in or not, he is gripped by a terrible fear that his son might be hiding nearby, watching him, and that he will see him going into Little Paris. He escapes into the stinking stairwell, climbs quickly to the second floor, and rings the doorbell of the health club.

To Mrs. Barzilai Shifra,

After the letter I got from your husband I don't want to say a single word to him anymore. It gave me such blood pressure that they took me straight to the hospital and I was going to die only they saved me at the last minute and I don't want to talk about all my other troubles and everything I have to carry on my back. I spoke to him with all due respect about our building which is your property too and he makes fun of me about how I write Hebrew and insults my daughter now a widow with two little children. You live in your villa and Shwartz has to worry for everybody and take care of the building so that it won't go to ruin. What do I need it for somebody else should have taken over long ago I haven't got the strength to do everything myself but there's nobody to do it almost everyone is a sub-tenant and the only apartment owners left are either widows who don't know what's going on anymore or invalids or strange people who're not normal there's nobody to help so why make fun of Shwartz instead of saying thank you. Now I'm writing to you Mrs. Shifra who I remember you for many years that you're a lady. Our building is in a lot of trouble. Some people we don't know people from the underworld came and bought the storeroom next to the shelter from Friedberg's inheritors they brought builders and built an apartment there in the basement and they're doing what they like in the yard as if it's their private property and not land that belongs to everybody. They destroyed the steps going down to the basement and built a bathroom there they dug a pit under the wall of the building and made a door with a terrace around it and they're going to rent it to their people. I informed the municipality and the police right away but they did nothing. The municipality arrived when it was already too late and now they're taking them to court for building illegally in a place where it's against the law to build. These people are doing the same thing all over the neighborhood and making a lot of money. They laugh at the municipality and the courts they've got a lawyer who works for them all the time. They haven't rented it yet maybe they're waiting for the court case to be over they don't want to spoil their case and they know their lawyer will fix it for them in the end. Without asking anybody's permission they moved the garbage cans to the other side of the yard so they wouldn't bother them and they're already making a garden next to the terrace on our land. And nobody can say a word the woman who bought the storeroom curses all the time and says they'll bring Arabs and gangsters to live there and that our lives are in danger if we don't let them do what they like. And now their lawyer wrote us a letter that he demands a key to the roof as if somebody who's got a storeroom is entitled to a key to the roof I suppose they want to build an apartment there too. We need a lawyer urgently to speak for us in court and stop our building from turning into a slum like Hatikva. Everybody who owns an apartment in the building has to pay 3000 shekels immediately and that may be only the beginning. It's a lot of money for us all but we have no choice otherwise our building will be ruined and not only won't we be able to live here anymore we won't be able to rent our apartments either and definitely not to sell them because who would buy a place like that. I'm sure you understand the desperate situation Mrs. Shifra we have to save our property from these people otherwise they'll take over the whole building in the end nothing will stop them and there are people helping them in certain places to laugh at the law and decency. Please send the money urgently otherwise I'm packing it in and our building can go to rack and ruin. I can't do everything by myself for everybody and nobody helps me and on top of it all I'm made fun of.

Respectfully yours,
Shwartz Ariyeh

Again she hears the low, anonymous-sounding voice on the phone, informing her from his office of the time of their meeting: "Today, at six." Even though she so longed to hear from him, a moment passes before she takes in the fact that he is renewing contact, digests the content of the message, and replies as agreed: "Okay." He has changed the time of the meeting.

She feels no excitement at the thought of meeting him again. Half an hour later he walks past the glass door of the secretary's room and she imagines seeing a promise of reconciliation in his look.

At the beginning of lunch break she takes the bus to the apartment. She feels a strange calm, as if quietly performing a daily routine. She stops to buy a few groceries to make a light supper. At the entrance to the building she sees the ginger woman, the owner of the storeroom that has been converted into a basement apartment, and her husband, in his red cap, standing in front of the door. The woman is pressing the buttons of all the apartments on the intercom panel, one after the other, and a number of voices can be heard answering together: "Who is it? Hello! Hello!"

"It's us, your new neighbors from the apartment in the yard!" shouts the woman. "Come down, we want to talk to you!"

The voices on the intercom fall silent.

"You see, miss," the husband says to Gabi, "they don't even want to talk to us, as if they're the only Jews here and we're dogs."

The woman turns to her: "What's the name of that old man from the committee? We need to talk to him!"

"I don't know," says Gabi, "I don't live here."

"So what are you hanging around here for?" the ginger woman asks and gives her a look of loathing.

"I just come to help a sick woman who can't get out of bed. You're barring my way."

Gabi takes the key out of her bag, the woman moves a little to the side, and when the key turns in the door she pushes in after her, pulling her husband behind her. "We'll ring their doorbells till they open!" the ginger woman declares.

As Gabi hurries up the stairs she hears doorbells ringing on the bottom floor, and the woman's voice echoing in the stairwell: "Come out! Come out! Listen to this. Next week you may have nowhere to live! This whole building will blow up and there'll be nothing left here. We know people who for a hundred dollars will do a clean job here. Start taking your things out of your houses before it all goes up in flames! Come out! Old maniac from the committee, where are you? Come out! Come outside before you die!"

In the closed apartment there's a smell of detergent and floor-cleaning fluid. The bed is made and covered with the bright bedspread. Yesterday the Filipino maid hired by Hezi had cleaned the place. Gabi puts some of her purchases in the fridge, places the others in the cupboard, and is about to leave when the ginger woman arrives at her door and rings the bell. "Come out! Why are you hiding in there like mice? We want to talk to you!" the woman yells. "We have an important message for you." Her husband says: "They're not at home, there isn't a sound in there." "What do you expect to hear?" says his wife. "Children playing? A mother making food? A young couple laughing in love? There are no children here, no families, only people living alone, everyone holed up by himself like in a grave!"

Gabi hears the neighbor's dog bark. She goes up to the door and looks through the peephole. The neighbor is coming up the stairs and his dog is barking threateningly at the uninvited guests.

"Take the dog away!" the ginger woman shouts at him, and she and her husband retreat to the end of the landing. The neighbor looks at them in silence. They try to shoo the dog away, kicking out with their legs and provoking him to increase the volume of his barks and threats. "We have to talk to you!" the woman calls to the neighbor. "Take the dog away!" He grabs the dog by the collar and drags him behind him.

"I don't have any business with you. What do you want of me? Go to the head of the house committee."

"Where's his apartment, what's his name?"

The neighbor doesn't answer her.

"What's he barking and jumping for all the time?" asks the husband. "Tell him to stop."

"He doesn't let strangers into the house," says the neighbor.

The man in the red baseball cap, apparently unable to stand the barking any longer, turns away and goes downstairs.

"Strangers!" screams the woman. "What are we, Arabs? Who do you think you are? A man who lives alone with a dog!"

Gabi decides to take advantage of the quarrel to beat a hasty retreat from the apartment.

"Here's another bitch!" yells the woman.

"How dare you talk about her like that?" The neighbor rushes to Gabi's defense, and a smile of reassurance and complicity peeps out at her through his beard. "Don't take any notice of her," he says to her, "that's how she talks to everybody here. She doesn't know any other way to talk."

"Oho! You've got the hots for her!" the woman laughs. "You won't get anything out of her. Can't you see she's a lesbian? She's never known a husband's love, the feel of a baby in her arms!"

"Shut your mouth!" cries the neighbor. "If you don't beat it immediately I'm letting the dog go and telling him to attack you!"

Gabi hurries down the stairs and the exchange between the neighbor and the woman goes on echoing in the stairwell.

"You shut up, you dirty pig!" the ginger woman yells. "What do you do with your dog in bed at night? We've heard of people like you. The people who live here are sick! What are you frightening me with your dog for? I know somebody who'll finish that dog off in two seconds flat for twenty dollars!"

The husband is waiting at the entrance to the building. "You see what kind of people they are?" he wails to Gabi. "The way they talk to us. We're their neighbors, is that the way to behave? Why do they hate us so much? Believe me, miss, we're quiet people, we don't make problems for anyone. But if the court says we have to destroy what we built for our daughter, we'll have no choice, everything will explode, there won't be a building left here. Like they say: We'll die together with the Philistines."

In the bus on her way back to the office, Gabi wonders why she isn't excited at the renewal of the meetings she longed for so much. Has the flame really died down? She imagines their meeting in the apartment that evening, the moments of love-making, and afterward Hezi pulling the sheet up over his waist, lying on his back and staring at the ceiling, his chest slowly rising and falling and his white hair on the white of the pillow — precisely at these moments of disconnection, when he's so distant and estranged, she loves him more than ever. And now all this gives rise to nothing more than satisfaction in her. Perhaps Ada is right: "It's not love at all, it's an infantile obsession," and this battle, to see who'll break who, is, as she says, "running away from really confronting real life." And what is real life? The lives of the people in the bus, in each of whom, if she examines their expressions, she'll discover, especially in the older ones, the fingerprints of despair? Is real life the battle of that terrible woman and her miserable husband to build a home for their daughter precisely in the basement of a building populated by people whose way of life they find so detestable?

"Love that doesn't project itself onto the future isn't love," Ada said and quoted to her from Camus's *The Plague* — another of the books from which her friend had never parted since her youth: "The plague had robbed us all of the capacity for love and even of the capacity for friendship. For love requires something of the future, and all we had left were moments."

Ada's lectures in favor of resignation and compromise with life aroused her immediate resistance. In her eyes they were no more than self-righteous attempts on the part of a friend to justify the dismal mediocrity of her own life. But at this hour of relative peace of mind, Gabi regrets not having overcome her impulse to hurt her friend on such occasions. Apparently some mysterious plague was robbing her too of the capacity for love and friendship. She reminds herself once more not to be led astray by this instinctive resistance, which stems from hurt pride and has nothing to do with an objective examination of the facts as they are.

She gets off the bus and goes into the little diner next to the office, which she has kept away from ever since seeing Hezi there. If he's there now, she decides, she'll sit at an unoccupied table, order her sandwich and coffee, and not allow it to disturb her peace of mind. He isn't there, and she is surprised by her sense of relief.

When she arrives at the apartment in the evening he is already there, chewing on something he found in the fridge. He's in a good mood, even a little jocular, and more talkative than usual. This unusual behavior on his part seems to her like a new trick in the battle whose rules she thought she already knew. There is even something humiliating in his air of relaxation in light of the mental conflict she herself had experienced since the cessation of their meetings, until she finally came to believe that she had attained some peace of mind at last. So for him the whole thing had not been a big deal. And now too, his hunger for her does not impel him to pounce on her and devour her. He sits opposite her, looks at her, and smiles.

"Are you depressed about something?" he asks.

The answer is clear and the rule is familiar and well-known, like a law of physics, the law of joined vessels, for example: whoever loves less will be loved more, and vice versa. Therefore she doesn't answer his question but tries to smile: "Me? Certainly not. Not at all!"

"What did you do when we didn't meet?"

"I lived," says Gabi, "just like the days when we did meet."

"When I saw you at work, I always wanted to signal to you: You see, there's life without Hezi too."

"That's true," says Gabi, but she can't help adding: "But it's better with Hezi."

He bursts out laughing. This is the first time she's ever seen him really laugh, and the laughter seems to her artificial.

"Nobody could say that you look depressed," she says, "and what did you do when we didn't meet?"

"I thought about you."

"I bet!"

"Don't you believe me?"

"For you I'm nothing but an occasional fuck. Until you get bored with it."

"And what am I for you?" he asks and smiles his secret smile.

She doesn't know what she should say and so chooses to keep quiet.

"Don't be silly, I have plans for you."

"And I'm not allowed to know them."

"Not yet."

He stands up, comes up to her and begins to fondle and kiss her, doing everything deliberately and slowly. She senses that his passion is growing but that he's restraining himself from falling all over her as usual, and she wonders when he'll lose his self-control. But he only puts his arm around her and leads her gently to the bedroom and begins slowly undressing her.

The neighbor's dog is already on guard behind the wall, and although the only sound in the room so far is the creaking of the bed, he breaks into angry, rebuking barks. His master can be heard trying to calm him down and silence him, but in vain. The barking is so loud in her ears, so close, that it seems as if the dog and his master are standing next to the bed and watching them. Hezi, apparently oblivious to the barks, forgets the gentleness of the skilled lover he has been demonstrating up to now and falls on her with urgent greed. Gabi presses him to her with all her strength, as if seeking shelter underneath his body, and she fails to utter a single moan of pleasure. And after he is satisfied, he doesn't move away from her as usual, to lie on his back at her side, to pull the sheet up above his waist and stare at the ceiling, but raises himself on his elbows and examines her face in bewilderment. "Didn't you come?" he asks at last, with a mixture of suspicion and disappointment.

"It doesn't matter."

"What's going on?"

"It's that dog barking there all the time," says Gabi.

"He always barks, it's never bothered you before."

"There's somebody who for twenty dollars will poison that stinking dog," says Gabi.

"Who's that?" he asks in surprise, and at the sight of the expression on her face he realizes that it's a joke and frowns in the attempt to understand what it means.

"We'll meet at different times and not on regular days," he says afterward, "it'll be better that way."

When she goes to the kitchen to make them a light meal, Hezi says: "No, no, I won't eat now, I'm not hungry. I have to go."

THREE

This morning, before the girl took me out for a walk, Pedro suddenly showed up. Why isn't he working? As far as I know he's only got one free day a week, when he comes to me. I've never liked him. I don't know what it is about him exactly that frightens me, but when he's here, sitting on the sofa and watching television, I feel tense all the time, as if he might pounce on me at any moment for no reason and attack me, like a wild animal, or get up and destroy everything in the flat.

The girl, judging by the expression on her face, was also surprised by this visit, and they argued a bit, with him all cheerful and laughing and her scolding him. When we went out he came with us. Her friends were already sitting in the park with their old men and Pedro sat down next to them. His appearance affected the girls: they talked louder, more simultaneously, and their laughter was more excited. He told them some story that apparently stirred them up. Linda laughed with them, and I understood that she wasn't annoyed about him coming with us.

The old man who used to collect junk from the street stares at his knees and sighs, and the two others tell each other about their illnesses, which disgusts me. One of them, a religious man who never takes off his hat, is called Tzarfati and talks with a Sephardi accent. And the other one, an Ashkenazi, talks with a Romanian accent, his name I don't know, one of his eyes is closed all the time, according to what he tells Tzarfati he has occasional epileptic seizures, apart from all his other diseases, and according to him these seizures don't last longer than "one or two minutes."

I know exactly what I look like even though, luckily for me, I don't get many opportunities to look at myself. And nevertheless it upsets me to be surrounded all the time by ugliness. It upsets me more than anything else. Linda and her friends and Pedro aren't attractive, even though they're young. And the old people are ugly mainly because they're old, although you can still see that Tzarfati was once a handsome man. And this park? A few measly trees and a bit of grass that goes gray in summer and two or three benches, one of them broken. And my heart yearns to see a little beauty, a little light before the sun sets for the last time.

Tzarfati's minder paints her lips red and looks as if her sexual urge is stronger than that of her friends. She brings a radio with her to the park and wriggles her body to the beat of the dance music it plays. Pedro, who's in unusually high spirits this morning, took the radio from her, increased the volume, pulled her to her feet, and started to dance with her, and all the girls shrieked with laughter. A couple of them joined in the dancing, and Linda sat on the sidelines, laughing and calling out to them in their language, apparently cheering them on. Tzarfati swayed in time to the music and clicked his fingers like the Sephardis know how to do, but there was no joy in it, there was no beauty in it. It was as pathetic as the rest of us sitting there, the old and the young.

And then, in the middle of the dance party, a boy with a dog shows up in the park. He is tall and very thin, his face blackened with a week or two's growth of beard, his eyes confused, his hair black and wild, his clothes dirty, and the dog is thin and neglected too, with a black coat and bald patches on various parts of its body. And the boy asks: "What's this, what's going on here?" And happiness breaks out in his muddled eyes, as if he's discovered treasure.

The religious Tzarfati says to him: "You're not allowed to bring dogs here. Didn't you read the sign? It says there from the municipality that it's forbidden. Take him out of here."

The boy says: "She's not a he, she's my Mammy."

Tzarfati says: "Get it out of here."

The boy takes no notice, his eyes are fixed on Pedro and the girls, who go on dancing to the music on the radio.

Tzarfati asks him: "Don't you understand Hebrew?"

The Romanian with the closed eye says to him: "Leave him alone, can't you see?" And he taps his finger on his forehead.

Tzarfati says: "I can't stand dogs, they make me sick."

The Romanian says: "I know that boy, I think I've seen him wandering around in our street. He went to a yeshiva there."

Tzarfati says: "A yeshiva student plays with a dog? It's an unclean animal!"

The Romanian calls to the boy: "Weren't you a student at the yeshiva?"

The boy approaches the Romanian and looks at him hopefully: "Do you know me?" he asks him. "Do I know you?"

"Don't you study anymore?"

"They threw me out."

"Why?"

"Unsuitability. Now I'm in the street. I haven't got anywhere to stay."

"Haven't you got a family?"

"They don't want me."

"What will you do?"

"I want to go to Eilat. I've never been to Eilat."

"With the dog?"

"Sure! She knows how to do tricks that no other dog knows. People like to see it, they pay money for it."

Tzarfati says: "Take that dog and go away. I'll tell him," he points at Pedro, "to kick you out."

"Why are you afraid of her, she's a good dog, she loves people! And she has the sense of a human being. In her last life she was a human being!"

The Romanian asks: "What does it know how to do?"

"She knows all kinds of things. If I sing Hatikva she stands to attention on her two hind legs and salutes like a soldier. Have you ever seen a dog that knows how to do that?"

Tzarfati says: "I was once in Eilat. What a place, disgusting! Blond girls from Sweden lie there naked on the beach, everything on display. Anyone can go up to some girl, look at her and have her. And little children playing on the beach see it all."

The Romanian says to the boy: "Show me what your dog knows how to do."

Tzarfati says: "No! This is a place for people, not dogs."

The Romanian says: "Show me what it does."

The boy calls his dog: "Mammy, come!" And she goes to sniff the bark of one of the trees. "Mammy, Mammy!" he calls. And when she doesn't come, he goes over to her, picks her up, and puts her down on the ground next to the wheelchairs. And he says: "Now look." And he begins to sing the national anthem.

The dog runs back to her tree to sniff the bark. The Romanian laughs and his closed eye begins to water. The boy points at Tzarfati and says: "It's all his fault, she's afraid of him, she can sense that he doesn't like her."

"I don't like you either, take that dog away from here immediately!"

"What else does she know how to do?" asks the Romanian.

Tzarfati calls to Pedro: "Hey! Get him out of here with his dog!"

The boy says: "Her name's Mammy."

Pedro and the girls take a break from their dancing. Pedro lies down on the grass, lights a cigarette, either he doesn't hear Tzarfati talking to him or he doesn't understand his Hebrew. The boy goes up to Pedro: "Have you got a cigarette for me?" Pedro sits up and looks at him.

The boy says again: "Cigarette, cigarette," and with his hand he makes as if he's smoking. Pedro gives him a cigarette and his lighter underneath it. The boy returns to the wheelchairs. He calls the dog: "Mammy! Come here at once and sit down next to me."

The dog goes to the shelter at the end of the park.

The Romanian asks him: "Why did they expel you from the yeshiva?"

"I saw God and they didn't believe me."

"How did you see Him? Did He come to you in a dream?"

"In a dream?! In real life, like I see you now."

Tzarfati is angry. "It's forbidden to talk like that! It's blasphemy what he's saying!"

"How did you see Him and remain alive?"

"Look at me, I'm alive aren't I?"

Tzarfati says to him: "Tell me, who sent you here? Are you the devil? Nothing but trouble will come of this. Go away!"

"I haven't got anywhere to go."

The Romanian suggests: "Go to Eilat. They're waiting for you there to put on a show with your dog."

"I taught her to put on shows that will drive them crazy when they see what she knows how to do."

"So why don't you go to Eilat?"

"I stood on the road for a whole day, cars passed all the time but none of them wanted to give me a lift. Now I have to put on a few shows with her in Tel Aviv first to get the money to go to Eilat."

"If you see God again, ask Him for a loan."

The boy explains: "But I can only see Him in the yeshiva, and they won't let me in."

Tzarfati plugs both ears with his fingers. "I don't want to hear what he's saying!"

The boy says: "It'll be good in Eilat, there are good people there, and they all have fun. I want to have fun too."

The Romanian says: "There are naked girls there in the sea, they'll give you a good time."

"You bet!"

The Romanian asks: "Have you ever been with a woman?"

The boy looks around and can't see his dog. "Mammy!" he calls. "My Mammy!" He starts running around the park looking for her. And we can hear him in the distance calling again and again: "Mammy! Mammy! Where are you?"

Tzarfati sighs: "Thank God he's gone. I'm not allowed to get angry, doctor's orders."

After a few minutes the boy returns. "I can't find her," he announces, "she's disappeared!"

The Romanian suggests: "Maybe it saw another dog and followed it."

"No, she only loves me. Someone must have taken her."

The Romanian says: "Who wouldn't take a beautiful dog like

that, that knows how to sing 'Hatikva' and can earn a lot of money?"

"What am I going to do now? How will I get to Eilat? Where will I get money from? Maybe you can lend me some?"

"How much do you need?" the Romanian asks.

"Seriously?"

"I can give you all the money I have here."

"God bless you. I'll give it back."

The Romanian pulls out his trouser pocket and shows him that it's empty. "That's all I've got." And he laughs and laughs and his closed eye waters. "When you see God again, ask Him for money for me too!"

The boy shouts: "Mammy! Where are you? What's happened to you? Why have you left me? There's nothing left in my life now!"

The minders stood up and began to push the wheelchairs out of the park. And when the boy saw that we were leaving he began to cry. He walked behind us and cried, until we reached the road. There he saw some people and he went up to them to tell them what had happened to him and to ask them for money.

Pedro came upstairs with us. He and the girl sat on the sofa and talked. There were moments when they laughed and moments when she was angry with him and they began to argue. Afterward she left the living room and went into her room and shut the door. He remained sitting on the sofa, drinking beer from a can, smoking and jigging his leg. Then he tried to get into her room, he asked her to open the door and banged on the glass. She wouldn't let him in. I was afraid that he would lose his temper, break down the door and attack her. Nothing good will come of this boy. But he went back to the sofa, sat down for a few minutes, then left.

She came out of her balcony room, came up to me, smiled and examined my face, as if to make sure that I hadn't noticed what was going on. Maybe she also thinks that if I don't talk I don't understand what's happening around me either. She started cleaning the house and put me out on the little kitchen balcony, which the sun had already left, so that I could look down at the playground and the children playing there. But Pedro's behavior had frightened me and I couldn't settle down. Only when she came into the kitchen to cook and I again heard her singing her songs to herself did I calm down, and the smell of her cooking filled me and gave me a good feeling of home.

Dear Mr. Shwartz,

I was very sorry to hear that my husband's letter had caused you distress. It was written with a friendly smile and in a spirit of good humor and without any intention of insulting you or any member of your family personally. Allow me to take this opportunity to send my condolences to your daughter on the death of her third husband and to express my sympathy with the family in their grief. I hope from the depths of my heart that before long a new father will be found for the little orphans.

My husband asked me to stress how much we both value your devotion to the affairs of the building and how much we admire everything you do to maintain and improve it, in spite of your poor health. Indeed, the situation which you so accurately and picturesquely describe in your letter is dreadful. I ask myself: How did things come to such a state? You are quite right, we must take a lawyer, at any price, to protect our rights and persuade the court not to allow these dubious people to rob us of our property and treat it as their own.

As for your completely justified request for money, we regret that we cannot comply with it owing to our difficult financial circumstances. To describe our humble home as a villa is to mock the poor. Our apartment in Tel Aviv is a palace in comparison to this place, and the only reason we are unable to enjoy our apartment in the big city is because my doctors have ordered me to live in the country due to respiratory problems. We are barely able to exist on our pensions and have no possibility of obtaining such a large sum of money, or even a far smaller one. Perhaps one day, if our circumstances improve, we will be able to pay our debt to the residents committee. In the meantime we can only hope that the hiring of the lawyer will not be delayed because of us, since any delay in so sacred a cause would be unthinkable.

We send you every encouragement, estimable Mr. Shwartz, and join you from here in our common struggle with hearts full of hope for success, and we thank you for your superhuman efforts on behalf of us all. We wish you good health and a long life and send our warm regards to your wife. Please read this letter to her, so that she too will know how much we admire and respect you.

Respectfully yours,
Shifra Barzilai

What's happening to me, he asks himself. Am I drunk without having had anything to drink, or is all this happening to me in a dream? The key gropes for the slit in the lock on the door and doesn't find it. The dog too reacts with strange, warning barks. Aviram bends down and discovers that there is no slit and no lock either. Someone has been at the door. They must have been trying to break into the apartment.

On Saturday afternoons he goes out for a long walk to some woods where he can let the dog roam free without fear of traffic, and he takes the weekend papers with him and sits on a bench to read them. He was away from home for about an hour and someone had tried to break in and removed the revolving part of the lock.

He goes down to Mr. Shwartz's apartment and rings the doorbell. Presumably Mr. Shwartz and his wife are taking their Saturday afternoon nap just now, but Shwartz is the only one of the neighbors with whom he has any contact. Mrs. Shwartz calls from inside: "One minute! Who is it?" Now, he knows, she'll peek at him through the peephole in the door.

The skinny old woman, whose bird face is touching in its ugliness, opens the door a crack and ties the belt of her robe. "What the matter?"

"Sorry for disturbing you. Someone tried to break into my apartment and I can't open the door. I want to use your phone to call a locksmith to come and open it so that I can get into the house."

She doesn't understand a word he's saying: "He sleep now, sick, not feel well."

"I need your telephone."

"We need telephone too. How we call doctor or ambulance if no phone in house?"

"No, just for now, for one minute, to phone from your house, it's urgent."

She still doesn't understand but she yields to his impatience and widens the opening. "Not dog! Not dog!" she whispers imploringly.

The voice of Mr. Shwartz is heard from the bedroom calling "Henya, Henya!" and asking something in their language.

Aviram coaxes the dog to wait for him on the landing, goes into the apartment, and shuts the door.

"Do you have the gold pages?"

"Gold?" cries Mrs. Shwartz and retreats to a safe distance, next to the wall. "No gold!"

Her husband calls from the bedroom in Hebrew: "Who is it? What's the matter?"

"The telephone directory, where's the telephone directory?" shouts Aviram, his impatience turning to anger.

From where she's standing next to the wall, she points to the shelf next to the telephone, where the directories are stacked, covered for some reason with an embroidery. He finds what he's looking for, calls the number, and is answered by a recorded message giving a phone number that can be called twenty-four hours a day.

Mr. Shwartz comes out of the bedroom in his pajamas and joins his wife.

A sleepy voice answers the phone.

"Someone apparently tried to break into my apartment and I can't open the door to get in," Aviram informs him and asks him to come as soon as possible.

"They removed the cylinder," explains the expert complacently, with what seems to Aviram to be a note of malicious satisfaction at his plight, and with a slowness that can only be interpreted as revenge for being woken up in the middle of his siesta. "It's not apparently a break-in, it's definitely a break-in, and not someone but two people, and they didn't only try to break in, they broke in and paid a visit to your apartment, took small, valuable things that are easy to carry, like jewelry, gold, a VCR, things that can be sold quickly to buy drugs, and afterward, when they left, they slammed the door behind them to give them time to get away before the burglary was discovered."

After Aviram puts the phone down he explains the problem to Mr. Shwartz. Gloom descends on the already glum face of the elderly head of the residents committee. "We've never had anything like this here before," he laments, "ever since those people from the underworld came here to build in the basement, all kinds of criminals are coming here, we aren't safe in our homes anymore. We wasted our money on the outside door with the intercom, it won't help us, they know how to open it. There's no law anymore and the police don't do a thing. . . ."

Aviram decides to go down to the entrance and wait outside for the expert on breaking and entering, but the dog refuses to go down with him, looking at him in astonishment at this disruption of the proper order of things and barking in indignant protest. Aviram carries him downstairs in his arms, takes him outside, and sits down on the pavement. Now he begins to grasp in all its enormity the fact that someone has broken into his apartment, searched every corner, taken everything of value, and behaved as if the place belonged to him. Apparently someone who knew his habits or had seen him going out. He scans the street and examines the few people passing by at this early Sabbath afternoon hour. Two or three of them look to him as if they may have been the burglars. He puts his hand on his back pocket, his wallet containing his credit card is there, he usually takes it with him when he goes out; at least this has been saved from the robbery. The expert doesn't arrive and Aviram wonders if he has fallen asleep again and forgotten all about him.

When the car displaying the locksmith's sign stops in front of the building Aviram waves his hand to indicate that he's the one who called, and the man slowly and deliberately parks the car and opens his toolbox to ascertain that he has everything he needs. When they arrive at the apartment the man examines the door with the expert air of a doctor examining his patient, and indeed it transpires that his telephone diagnosis was correct. He prepares Aviram for the upheaval he will shortly see in his apartment: all the contents of the closets and drawers lying higgledy-piggledy on the floor, even the freezer compartment of the fridge emptied out, because some people hide their money there, every locked cabinet smashed.

"Are you insured?" he asks, and Aviram doesn't answer, because the fear of what he is about to see is choking him.

The man sets to work, hammering on a chisel inserted between the door post and the door and kicking up a terrible din, with the dog, who tried to attack him until Aviram grabbed him by the collar, barking at the top of his voice and adding to the commotion. A few neighbors from other floors emerge from their apartments to complain about the noise disturbing their Sabbath rest, and Aviram, who has avoided any contact with his neighbors all these years, not even greeting them on the stairs, is obliged to explain what happened and apologize for the noise. When the door is finally opened he goes inside and finds the apartment exactly as he left it. The VCR is in its place and so are all the other objects of value.

The dog rushes into the living room and runs to and fro, barking furiously, perhaps he can smell traces of the intruders. The expert too is surprised at the sight that meets his eyes, and as if to save his professional honor, he pronounces: "This isn't the job of junkies looking for quick money. It's apparently the work of private investigators looking for something on you. Are you in the middle of divorce proceedings? No? Look, I don't know anything about you, and it's none of my business, but they may have been looking for documents or something incriminating against you."

The expert starts installing a new lock, which according to him will make things more difficult for burglars in the future, but, he says, nothing is one hundred percent safe, there's no door in the world that can't be broken into, even steel doors with sophisticated locks, they only prolong the work and make it noisier, and burglars prefer to break into apartments with easier doors.

After the expert leaves, Aviram walks around the apartment, trying to discover if anything has been moved or tampered with, and he can't find anything. He opens the closet and the desk drawers holding his personal documents and accounts, and there's no sign that anything has been touched. His checkbook too is in its place with nothing missing. Precisely because nothing appears to have been touched, he senses the invisible traces of the intruder everywhere (in spite of the expert's opinion, he continues to think of him in the singular), and he feels as if the touch of this foreign presence has contaminated everything in the flat, even the floor tiles on which he has tread. He's thirsty but shrinks from touching the glass. Overcome by nausea, he runs to the toilet and vomits.

After he has finished vomiting and has sat down to rest for a minute, he recovers his strength. He tries to settle down and feel at home in the apartment again, but he is still unable to touch anything, not even the handle of the refrigerator door, in order to take out the cold water and quench his thirst. He realizes that his reaction is exaggerated, even morbid, but the feeling is stronger than he is and he knows that he'll have no peace until he purifies the apartment. He washes the floors, wipes the furniture, the electrical appliances, the gas cooker, and all the kitchenware with a damp cloth, throws out the entire contents of the fridge and scrubs it inside and out, removes the soap, toothbrush, and toothpaste from the bathroom, puts the towels in the washing machine together with the clothes that were lying in the bedroom and even those hanging up in the closet or folded up in the drawers, as well as the sheets and pillowcases that were on the bed and those that were in the dresser and the duvet covers stored away for the summer months. The washing machine and the dryer work without stopping until nightfall, and then he puts everything back in its place. He cleans out the kitchen cabinets and piles their contents on the floor. He works in a frenzy, like a man possessed. All his thoughts are concentrated on the effort not to overlook anything, lest some contaminated item remain in the flat. And when his work is over, he takes a shower and emerges from the bathroom into his purified apartment. He knows that by any measure he has been acting in a fit of insanity, but he feels a profound sense of relief. He drinks a lot of water. In order to allay the hunger that now attacks him he makes himself a hard-boiled egg and opens a can of sardines. The bread, the fruit and vegetables, the cheese, and all the other unsealed edibles he threw into the trash can.

He sits at the table in the purified kitchen, his body tired from his demented labors, but his mind is too alert to think of sleep. He begins to wonder about what has happened. If nothing was stolen, why was his apartment broken into, who broke in, what were they looking for, why are there no signs of the search, who is interested in him? So few people know him, there is nothing interesting or suspicious about his life. All these questions remain unanswered.

There's no knowing how secrets escape from the privacy of the home into the public domain, but in any case, the trouble with Eyal became known in the neighborhood. People asked Ezra and Ruthie if there was any news about Eyal, if they had heard from him, and what the army had said. On the face of it, there was no trace of malice in these questions; on the contrary, sincere concern for his welfare and sympathy for the family's distress was evident in the voices of the inquirers. Nevertheless, Ezra was upset and he racked his brains as to who could have disclosed his disgrace. He considered all the people who might have heard about it in army circles or found out in some other way, and who might have an interest in spreading it about, but he was unable to point to anyone with any degree of certainty.

He always got up early in the morning, before the rest of the family, to walk to the main road of the neighborhood and buy a newspaper and fresh bread for breakfast and sandwiches for the children to take to school. On his way there and back he would greet the shopkeepers standing in the doorways to their stores and neighbors and acquaintances passing by. Sometimes he would pause to ask them how they were and to chat. He was a neighborhood veteran and generally well liked. From the day that Eyal's troubles became public knowledge and people began asking him if the lad was still in hiding and if anyone had heard from him lately, Ezra stopped going to the main road in the morning, and he stopped showing his face in the neighborhood. He only drove through it in his pickup truck, on his way to work and back or on trips out of town. He even broke off contact with Herzl, the building materials dealer from whom he had been buying his supplies for years, and preferred to buy what he needed in the center of Tel Aviv where nobody knew him. Previously he and his wife had been in the habit of doing their weekend shopping together on Thursdays, in the neighborhood stores and market. Now they drove to the Carmel Market in Tel Aviv. On more than one occasion Ruthie spoke to Ezra and told him to stop worrying about his wounded pride and concentrate on worrying about Eyal, but he said to her: "Ruthie, you're right, I know, but I can't. I can't stand for people to see me so humiliated and ask me about Eyal, and to have to explain what happened. I can't do it. I wish we could leave this neighborhood and go and live somewhere else where nobody knows us."

"Today it's not like it used to be, Ezra," said Ruthie, "the army isn't God anymore. There are lots of kids who don't want to join up at all and pretend to be crazy, and nobody makes a big thing out of it. When a soldier has personal problems, the army treats them and nobody thinks he's betraying his country. There's no reason for you to feel ashamed in front of the neighbors, you didn't meet them yesterday, they're warmhearted people who sympathize with us in our anxiety, they all know us, they know who we are and they know Eyal and know that he's a wonderful child. Everybody can slip up. It can happen in any family, and it does happen in lots of families, except that people don't know about it."

"So why does everybody know about us? Who spread the news? Ruthie, we'll never be what we were again."

"We'll get through it, Ezra. We shouldn't be thinking about ourselves now, only about how to find Eyal and how to help him. That's what's important. I'm terribly afraid that something bad is happening to him. I want him to stay healthy in mind and body. That's what's important, not whether he goes back to the army and what people think in the neighborhood."

But Ezra was not persuaded by the voice of reason in Ruthie's words. He said things to his wife that she had never heard him say before: "Once I thought that everybody was like us, that they only thought about how to help others, how to unite and close ranks, how to work for the good of the country and its security. But lately, ever since all this business with Eyal, I feel that my eyes have been opened. I see it everywhere: people think only of themselves, everybody wants to get the upper hand over the next man, to make the other person feel that he's nothing, dust under his shoe. That's what they did to Eyal, that's what broke him. Ruthie, there's evil in the world, and it's powerful. There's a lot of evil in people. I see it at work too."

Ezra continues to dwell on his gloomy reflections on human nature. Perhaps this is his refuge from the agonizing thoughts about Eyal's situation and his own inability to find out how he is and how to help him.

"There was this couple who took me to build an apartment in the basement of a building in north Tel Aviv, an empty store-room that hadn't been used for years and that they bought. Their daughter, who was an outstanding student in high school, is getting out of the army soon and going to study at the university. They want her to live in a good neighborhood, with so-called cultured people. You, who don't believe that evil exists in the world, should see how those cultured people from north Tel Aviv are fighting to keep this child from having an apartment in their building. What lengths they're prepared to go to so that she won't live there. And the way they talk to this couple, who saved and scrimped for years to give their daughter a better life, as if people from the south of the city are trash, as if they'll spoil their building for them, as if nobody will want to live there anymore. What do they care if this child lives there? What harm will she do them? But everybody wants to humiliate the next person, to show that he's worth more, that he's superior. And if that isn't plain and simple evil, what is it?"

"You're generalizing, Ezra," said Ruthie, "not everyone's like that. At any rate, not in our neighborhood, which is a warm-hearted neighborhood. We're all like one big family here, and everybody who knows Eyal wants to know what's happening with him, they're really and truly concerned for him, they want things to work out for him and for him to get back on track and bring credit to his family."

"I'm not so sure, Ruthie. I don't know what people are say-ing to each other. Maybe they're saying: It wouldn't happen to our child. Ruthie, why has he done this to us? Why has he destroyed our honor?"

These conversations could have gone on forever if Eyal him-self hadn't phoned early one evening. Ezra answered. Ruthie wasn't at home.

"My Eyal!" cried Ezra in a broken voice. "Where are you calling from?"

"It doesn't matter," replied Eyal, "I haven't got time to talk.

Listen carefully: bring my civilian clothes to Granny's house. Is that clear?"

"Eyalie! We're going crazy here, our lives are being ruined because of you. What's happening to you? Where are you? We're terribly worried about you!"

"I don't have time to talk."

"Where are you living?"

"I'm managing."

"Eyalie! We love you and we want you to be happy!"

"Then bring the clothes to Granny's as soon as you can. Someone will come and pick them up for me. I have to hang up now."

"Wait. Just one more thing . . ."

The line went dead.

When Ruthie came home, she found Ezra sitting pale-faced and breathing heavily. "He just phoned," he said.

"How is he?"

"He didn't say anything. Just for me to bring civvies to my mother's house for him. Someone will come and fetch them. What does it mean, Ruthie?"

"We'll do as he asks," said Ruthie, "let's go there now."

"Don't you understand?" demanded Ezra. "This means that he's going to go on running. In civilian clothes it will be harder to identify him as a soldier. Or maybe his uniform is already torn and dirty and he wants clean clothes so as not to attract attention. Ruthie, it's not over yet by a long shot."

"What difference does it make?" said Ruthie. "If he needs those clothes, we'll bring them to him. He has to know that we're with him, on his side, that we'll always help him."

Ezra called Menashe to keep him in the picture, as he had promised, and to consult him as to what they should do: Inform the army, as they had been told? Or do as Eyal asked?

Menashe listened to the details of Eyal's phone call and his conclusions were the same as his brother's. He said that they shouldn't bring him the clothes, so as not to facilitate his escape and to make him call again, but at the same time not to report

back to the army phone number they had been given, in order
not to help them trace the boy. "In any case they're not really
interested in him," said Menashe, "you know that yourself.
They've got more important things to worry about than Eyal.
Before they catch him, if they ever do, we have to make contact
with him, talk to him, meet him if possible, hear from him what
his problem is, and persuade him to give up this silly escape."

"Ruthie thinks we should do what he asks, so that he feels
we're behind him, that we're always there for him, whatever
he does."

"Ask Menashe if your mother's heard from him," said
Ruthie. "I wouldn't be surprised if he got in touch with her."

Menashe overheard her question. "I was around there this
afternoon and she never said anything to me," said Menashe.
"But I don't have to tell you, it's impossible to get any sense out
of her."

Ezra said: "Menashe, I'm desperate! And the whole neighborhood's talking about it."

"Don't talk nonsense, Ezra, you've got nothing to be
ashamed of. I'm beginning to respect that boy more and more.
I'm telling you, he's a real man! I never knew him. I never imagined he had the endurance and resourcefulness to manage on
his own like this, and what perseverance and determination! It's
just a pity it's wasted on negative things, it would be a lot better if he invested all that in excelling in the army. But I have to
tell you that he's got the right stuff, and when this whole affair
is over, and believe me it will be over soon, you'll get a strong
man back."

"Did I wake you up?"

She switches on the light next to the bed. It is half past twelve.
This is the first time he has phoned her at her apartment.

"No, I'm reading in bed. Where are you calling from?"

"A public telephone."

"What are you doing wandering around the streets at this
time of night? Haven't you got a family, a home?"

"I went out to get gas. In the morning it's a whole performance. But mainly to call you. I have to get back now, but I want
to tell you that when I walked past your desk today and you
had your hair loose, like when we're alone, you looked so cute
that I felt like jumping on you right there in the office."

"It's not easy for me," Gabi says. "When I'm not with you I
don't know what to do with myself except to think of you and
long for you."

"It's hard for me too, I think of you all the time too. Don't disappear on me, hang in there, because we both want the same
thing. I don't want to lose you. You're important to me. Don't be
sad. Try to lead a normal life as far as possible, go out, meet people, women friends, men friends, it makes no difference, don't
stay at home all the time, it's no good for you. Be strong. I have
to be careful now, I can't afford to make mistakes. You can help
me by being strong. I want you to know that I love you."

This is the first time he's actually said the words "I love you,"
and they move her so much that she forgets her superstitious
belief originating in a literary quote and she is no longer afraid
to ask the dangerous question:

"So when will we meet again?"

"I don't know. I'm going abroad next week. If I can, I'll
phone you from there, but don't expect it. And when I come
back too, everything will depend on the situation then. It will
take time. I'm counting on you. If we want our plan to succeed,
the next stage will require us to be patient and keep our heads."

And Gabi very much wants their plan to succeed even though
she has no idea what it is.

The words "I love you, I want you to know that I love you,"
go on echoing in her ears afterward, in his voice, and she
doesn't wonder why he never said them to her before, not even
in the first, passionate period of their meetings. He himself had
once said: "In any case if I stop loving you you'll know right
away," and in fact she had agreed with him. So why had he said
it this time and repeated it for emphasis, and why precisely
now? But the excitement at the statement itself is stronger than

any question, any memory, pushing aside all the suspicions and nit-picking interpretations to which she was usually susceptible. These three words had always seemed hackneyed to her, cheapened by overuse in novels and movies, a ritual declaration with something perfunctory about it, as if lovers had nothing more original, unique, and personal to say to each other about their love than this statement of fact that was presumably already known to them both. When she heard this slogan repeated in a movie, she sometimes said to herself that even silence, a certain kind of silence, would be capable of expressing more precisely and more richly the feeling in the hearts of the lovers in this moment of grace and their certainty of its uniqueness. But the belief in happiness apparently distorted the power of observation. For these hackneyed words in the mouth of a man she still knew next to nothing about, and next to nothing of his intentions toward her or the depth of his feelings for her, were enough to smooth out all the difficulties, as if they were charged with the power to bring about the future and even perhaps to change the events of the past.

The next day she goes to work with her hair loose, rather than combed back and gathered in a dancer's bun on her neck as usual, and waits for him to walk past her desk, but he doesn't put in an appearance all day. As soon as she gets home she calls Ada.

"When I don't hear from you for a while," says her friend, "it means that you're either in very good shape or very bad shape. Which is it now?"

"I don't have to tell you. You already know. Let's go to a movie. I haven't seen a good movie for ages."

"We've never been to a movie together."

"I have to get out of the house, see people. I can't go on like this."

"Do you mean this evening?"

"If you can."

"I haven't been to the movies for ages either. Hang on a minute, I'll ask Gadi."

Ada puts the receiver down and Gabi feels sorry for her friend, who has to ask her lord and master to graciously consent to give her an evening off.

"Let's go to an early show," says Ada when she comes back, "then we can sit somewhere afterward." Gabi agrees. Ada goes to fetch the newspaper. "Did you have a particular movie in mind? I can't see anything interesting here, only American movies I can't stand. Just a minute, they're showing *Jules et Jim* at the Cinematheque at an hour that suits us."

"I've seen it," says Gabi.

"So have I, more than once, but it's such a great movie, I always find something new in it."

Gabi was actually thinking of an American movie with famous movie stars, one of the latest hits that were drawing big crowds of simple, unpretentious people. This seems to her the right way out of her confinement into the fresh, healthy air of ordinary life. She is reluctant to go back so many years, to the time when she had first seen this movie — at the Cinematheque then too, in the company of a small clique of intellectual snobs, which is how she sees the people who go there — as if it would mean encountering herself in a previous incarnation, an unpleasant experience in itself, and one that would only lead her further back into herself. But she can't resist the quiver of enthusiasm she hears in Ada's voice. They arrange to meet at the entrance to the Cinematheque.

Gabi, expecting to see her friend looking like she had at their last meeting, with her hair smoothly set and rinsed in a pale color and her face freshly and delicately made up, is taken by surprise this time, too, when the old Ada appears, with her prematurely worn complexion, her hair dulled by threads of gray, and her dreary clothes emphasizing the breadth of her hips. And Ada, who caught the expression crossing Gabi's face as they went to buy tickets, says as they climb the stairs to the small hall: "Are you disappointed?" Gabi pretends not to have understood the question, and Ada goes on: "Gadi doesn't like it. He thinks it's better to look natural, to be what we really are at each stage of our lives. It really was stupid, some weird, perverse impulse. I felt ridiculous. It still embarrasses me to think about it. Why should I try to compete with you? You look the way you look, and I look the way I look. I was never pretty, I've learned to live with it."

"That's not true, Ada, it's not a question of natural or unnatural. We're the ones who decide these things. Our appearance is what we choose to signal. The question is what signal each of us wants to send to others, to her surroundings, to the world."

"In that case, what do I signal?"

"You signal: Don't pay attention to me, I'm not worth a look. I'm just someone of no importance who has nothing to offer."

"You may be right," says Ada, "that's really how I feel."

"Then that's your problem, that you don't know what you're worth — and not whether you dress this way or that way, or take care of your face and hair or not."

"Do I look terrible?" Ada asks.

"You look like Ada, and that's quite a lot."

They go into the small hall, and before they find seats Gabi takes a quick look at the audience and immediately hates them: apart from a handful of youngsters, most of the men look to her like the man with the dog who lives next door to the secret apartment, and most of the women like Ada, and on all their faces she imagines she can read the signs of loneliness and despair.

The shabby black-and-white look, and the monotonous sound of the narrator's voice accompanying the film, make her feel depressed from the word go. Even Jeanne Moreau no longer seems as beautiful and thrilling as she once did. This femme fatale is nothing but a screwed-up pain in the neck who doesn't know what she wants. And the two men she torments now seem ridiculous and pitiful. How could she have been so foolish as to be thrilled by the movie when she first saw it, how could she have thought it the height of happiness for a woman to play with the love and the lives of these two men, who were more interested in each other than they were in her, who didn't compete for her love at all and weren't required to sacrifice their friendship for her? From time to time Gabi steals a look at Ada, who is gazing intently at the screen, participating in the emotions of the characters, mimicking their expressions, smiling with them, looking sad when they look sad. Ada remains faithful to her old attachments — in literature, cinema, friendship — as if time and change have no effect on her.

Even before the lights go on, Ada takes off her glasses and puts them back in her bag, takes out a tissue and wipes her eyes. They go downstairs in silence, and in the lobby Ada says: "Should we go and sit somewhere?"

"As long as it's not here," says Gabi.

"You can't stand this place, can you?" says Ada. "Neither the movies nor the audience."

Gabi has decided not to distress her friend by sharing her poor opinion of the movie with her, and Ada, who knows what she thinks, decides to content herself with this general remark and leave it at that.

"There are nicer places near here," Gabi says.

They cross the road and go into a pub that is less dark than the others, and where the music is less loud, and sit down next to the glass window facing the street.

"I hope Gadi doesn't know about my story," says Gabi. "Please keep it just between the two of us."

"No, he doesn't know. Not that I have secrets from him, but things like that simply don't interest him. He's only interested in what happens in our family, in his work, and in politics. Nothing else. But it's strange you should have said that. Why do you care? Are you ashamed of something?"

Gabi says: "No, I don't know. But suddenly I thought . . ."

She doesn't finish the sentence, and her friend assumes that she can't find the right word to express her thoughts, but Gabi grabs hold of her arm and stares at the street outside the glass window.

"Ada, I don't believe it, it's him!"

Next to the sidewalk on the other side of the street he parks his car, gets out, opens the back door, and leans inside and examines the seats, as if to make sure that he hasn't forgotten anything there. Afterward he relaxes, locks the doors, and glances around as if looking for an address or someone he has arranged to meet. Then he turns his back to the car and scans the shop fronts, restaurants, and pubs lining the pavement. In the end he crosses the street, and Gabi, still clinging to Ada's arm, as if trying to draw support from it, increases her pressure and says quickly: "Listen, if he comes in here, we go on talking and I act as if I don't know him. No one must know of the connection between us." They both sit in silence. And he steps onto the sidewalk and walks past them without looking through the glass window.

Gabi suddenly announces: "The movie was so interesting!"

"Yes . . ." mumbles Ada, her face turning red in sympathy with the suspense and tension gripping Gabi.

Gabi's eyes wander from the sidewalk to the entrance to the pub and back again, but he has already disappeared from view. After a moment of silence, Ada says: "Would you like to go somewhere else?"

"Not now!" says Gabi, her eyes still scanning her surroundings. Ada is silent.

"You must be ashamed for me," Gabi whispers.

"What's happening to you?"

"I don't know. I don't even know if I'm happy or unhappy, there's only one thing on my mind all the time, like an obsession: I want him, all of him, for myself. I do what he tells me, and he does as he likes. Lately we haven't met at all, he keeps saying that he has to be careful. Sometimes he phones to tell me that he loves me, and says that he has plans for both of us. That's how he keeps me from leaving him."

"You sound completely desperate and at the same time you say that you don't know if you're happy or unhappy. You have to break it off."

"He was the one who said it wasn't good for me to stay home alone all the time, that I should go out with friends, men or women friends, lead a normal life. That's why I called you and asked you to go to the movies with me."

"To free yourself of your situation you have to free yourself of him. Maybe that's what he wants too?"

"I don't know. Maybe what he's really saying to me is: If you want to prove you love me, then stop loving me."

"What about that apartment?"

"I haven't been there lately."

"Where does he get the money to rent an apartment like that and not use it? Is he so rich?"

"I don't know. Is it so important? It doesn't interest me."

"It's a good thing you're still living in your own apartment and not there."

"What on earth made you say that?" Gabi asks in astonishment.

"I remembered a movie I saw years ago, I was only a child and it was already old then. A Hollywood melodrama, a real tearjerker, which would probably seem ridiculous to me today. But I can't forget the impression it made on me then. I think it was called *Backstreet* in English. It's about a young girl who comes to the city and goes to work in some firm. One day the director, or the owner, sees her and takes a fancy to her. He invites her on a date, they start having an affair, and he buys her a little apartment in one of the back streets of town, and he comes to her there whenever he can. Later on, either he gets tired of her or it begins to endanger his marriage or his business, I don't remember the details, in any case he asks her to wait until he sorts things out and then he'll come back and marry her. And her youth passes, her middle age passes, her whole life passes, alone in that back street, waiting for him to come back to her. I don't remember the end anymore, I only remember the tears."

"It's a good thing you didn't take me to see that movie tonight," says Gabi.

"It's weird that he turned up here and walked past next to us," says Ada. "I don't like that kind of coincidence. It makes

me feel as if we're cogs in a machine that we don't know anything about."

"How does he look to you?"

Ada says nothing for a moment and looks at her friend in
embarrassment. "Gabi, he's really old," she says.

"No," Gabi protests, "it's only his hair. It's not a sign of age,
Ada, his hair went white when he was a young man. He's our
age."

"I don't know," says Ada and her face turns red again. She
tries to change the subject: "I keep thinking of what you said
about the way we look and the signals we send to other people.
And I'm trying to work out what signal you send."

"And what's your conclusion?"

"It seems to me that you signal: I'll stay young forever."

The next day, in the office, Gabi hears his voice on the phone,
brisk and dry as always in these circumstances, announcing:
"Lunchtime today."

When he arrives at the apartment he seems impatient and preoccupied, and she smiles at him with a smile that apparently
annoys him.

"What are you looking at me like that for?" he demands
angrily.

"You surprised me today. I didn't believe it would happen."

"If you like I can go."

"Did you come here to fight with me?"

"I came here to love you."

"So why are you angry?"

"I can't stand it when people look at me the way you looked
at me when I came in."

"I don't know how I looked at you."

"As if you were stripping me naked with your look."

"I've already seen you naked. Why should I undress you with
my look?"

"You know exactly what I mean."

Gabi doesn't know. "Please, let's stop this," she says.

He is appeased and tries to smile, he embraces her, his hand slides under her blouse, strokes her back and shoulders, passes to her breasts and throat and nape, then he tightens his embrace, and when they kiss he keeps it up for a long time and prevents her from turning her face away.

When they get into bed and he leans over her, she hears him say, again in the same angry voice, "Don't yell, you hear?"

And she, as if some principle of honor is at stake here, some last stronghold of her independence that she will not allow him to conquer, when their lovemaking approaches its climax, screams more shockingly than ever. The dog on the other side of the wall bursts into loud, furious barks of protest. Hezi immediately puts his hand over her mouth to silence her, and she struggles with him and tries to push it away, grunting as loudly as she can with her mouth gagged, and refuses to let him penetrate her. The dog doesn't stop barking. They roll from side to side and his grip is stronger than her resistance, and the more passionate they become, the more violently, savagely, and stubbornly they wrestle, as if they are fighting to wrest from one another a piece of life that cannot satisfy the infinite hunger of either. Thus the moments of climax are prolonged, until she feels that she is dropping slowly from a vast height into the blissful weightlessness of total surrender, and she kisses his hand that is still clamped over her mouth, although its grip has weakened. Now she hears his heavy breathing. He doesn't move over to the right side of the bed or pull the sheet up to his waist but slides his arm under her shoulders, embraces her gently, and whispers in her ear: "You're bad, you're so bad," and in his breathless voice the words sound like words of love. He looks at his watch and says: "I don't want to go. I want to stay with you all the time, joined to you, not to move from you." And he kisses her on the cheek, very close to the lobe of her ear, and breathes in her smell.

"Why were you cross with me before?"

"I don't know. What do you think, that you're the poor deprived victim in this story and I'm the bad guy with all the power having a great time in his life? You might find it convenient to see it like that, but there are things that hurt me too and things that frighten me. You think I don't know that this arrangement between us is difficult for you? But I don't have any other option. And until I do, try to be strong. I've already told you: If you're strong it will help me and advance our common plans. I'm sorry I spoke to you like that before."

Afterward, in the kitchen, he asks her casually: "Who's that girl you were sitting with in the pub on Ha'arba'a Street yesterday?"

"So you did see us."

"Of course I saw you, and I saw that you saw me too."

She tells him about Ada and about their long friendship.

"Such long friendships are rare among women, right?"

"What nonsense!" protests Gabi. "Who told you that? Where do men get all the nonsense they invent about women from?"

"I just thought so," he laughs. "I hope she doesn't know about us."

"Because women are gossips and you can't trust them to keep a secret!"

"Does she know or doesn't she?"

"She doesn't know."

Before he leaves, next to the door, she puts her arms around his neck, clings to him and says: "I love you."

"I know," he says.

"I want to move in to live here."

"Are you serious?" he extricates himself from her embrace.

"Yes, this is our home."

He looks at her in surprise and disbelief, comes back into the living room, and sits down. "What's gotten into you all of a sudden?"

"I'll always have something left of you here, even when you don't come to me."

"Is it so important to you?"

"Yes."

He thinks for a minute, studies her face, he can't understand her. "But you'll keep our rules, you won't talk to anyone in the building, not the neighbors or anyone else who comes here, you won't bring anyone here and you won't tell anyone where you live, not even your best friend, you won't use the telephone, except to answer me, according to our signal, you won't get mail here, you won't put your name on the door or the intercom. Do you agree to all that?"

"Yes."

"How can you live like that?"

"I can."

"It would be better for you to lead as normal a life as possible, to go out, meet people, not wait to hear from me all the time. It's not healthy."

"It won't stop me from leading a normal life."

"Every Sunday afternoon the Filipino girl comes here to clean. I gave her the key. Don't come home before five, half past five. She'll see your things in the flat and she'll know that there's a woman living here, but she doesn't have to know who you are."

"When are you going abroad?"

"In three days' time."

"I'll move in after that."

"I'll call you here."

FOUR

From the moment he enters the waiting room he feels an inexplicable sense of oppression. He sits down in one of the two unoccupied spaces on the bench closest to the door. Among the people sitting on the two benches a lively conversation has already developed — a sign that they have been waiting a long time — and he can't make up his mind whether to leave or stay. The woman sitting on his right is describing how her purse was snatched on the bus. No doubt she will repeat this story several times. At the left end of the bench is a tough-looking man with a bald head, silent and withdrawn, holding a cast-iron ashtray in his left hand and filling it with the stubs of the cigarettes he smokes one after the other. On the right-hand end of the bench against the opposite wall is a gray-haired man in a gray suit with reading glasses hanging on a cord around his neck and a newspaper open on his knees. His car was stolen in the night and he is full of complaints against the police, who, as he sees it, are failing to do their job properly. Next to the gray man is a middle-aged tourist pouring his troubles in a mixture of Spanish and English into the ears of anyone willing to listen, to the accompaniment of despairing gestures with his hands, describing how his wallet with all his papers was snatched from him in a park when he was on his way back to his hotel late at night. On the tourist's left is a young woman covering her bruised cheek with her hand, and next to her a good neighbor who has come with her to give her support and to corroborate her complaint against her violent husband with eyewitness evidence. On the solitary chair between the two benches sits a prostitute who claims that she was robbed and beaten in the course of performing her job. At a desk barring the way into a wide corridor sits an elderly policeman with a few sheets of paper in front of him, making sure that nobody cuts in line and directing the waiting people to the appropriate rooms. In the corner, next to the passage leading to the toilets, a young couple sit close together like two frightened birds, keeping themselves demonstratively apart from the others, whispering to each other and casting looks full of impatience and distress in the direction of the policeman sitting behind the desk. A strange young man is pacing up and down the room and muttering unintelligibly to himself, as if pondering the solution to some difficult problem.

The waiting room opens onto offices and corridors leading to more offices. The doors are painted in dark green oil paint, peeling here and there and exposing the former color, a pale brown. The walls too are painted in oil paint, the lower half the same dark green as the doors and the upper half white that has gone gray over the years. From time to time the room is crossed by policemen and policewomen and people dressed in civilian clothes, emerging from one of the corridors and turning into another corridor or into one of the offices. From a hidden room a woman's voice can be heard calling: "Sammy! Where's Sammy? Has anyone seen Sammy?" Nobody answers her question. After a moment the voice calls Sammy again, and a man's voice shouts from the corridor: "He's gone out to eat!" and the door to one of the invisible rooms slams shut.

"I saw him, the thief, I can recognize him," says the woman on Aviram's right, once more describing what happened to her, as if reciting a spell that may have the power to make time run backward and put things right. "If they show me his picture, I'll recognize him at once. He was standing at the exit all the time, and he pressed himself against me when I wanted to get off the bus. I thought he was some pervert taking the opportunity to press up against a woman. And then when I got off the bus I saw that my handbag was open and my wallet was missing. The bus drove off and I didn't even have time to write down the number."

"And how would it have helped you if you'd gotten the number?" asks the owner of the stolen car. "How would that help to find the pickpocket?"

"They could make an identikit picture according to my

description," says the woman, "and show it to people until somebody recognizes it."

"What are you talking about, ma'am," the man in gray says grimly, "they don't do anything. They're not interested in all these things that make the citizen's life a misery. What do they do except hand out parking fines and lie in wait for someone to run a yellow light or cross a white line? That's all that interests them!"

Someone comes out of one of the rooms and makes his way to the exit. The young couple brace themselves and go up to the desk occupied by the policeman, who turns to look at the open door as if waiting for a signal, and then instructs them to go inside.

"Stop walking up and down like that, up and down, up and down, you're making me dizzy!" The voice of the bald, silent man, hoarse from cigarette smoking, suddenly thunders from the corner of the bench where he is sitting and holding the ashtray, which is already brimming over. The policeman, whose desk is next to the bald man, starts from his chair at the unexpected sound, and in order to cover up his reaction, unbecoming of a policeman of his seniority, he too scolds the strange boy: "Yes, what are you walking around all the time for, sit down already, you're disturbing my work too," and he points to the papers lying on his desk, for who knows what. The boy runs in alarm to the empty place on the bench, to the left of Aviram, and goes on muttering. The prostitute, who is wearing a very short skirt, crosses her legs and brings the conversation back to the question of police inefficiency: "When you need them, they don't come. What's that one hundred number worth? Nothing!" She laughs bitterly. "Once someone came into my house, took out a knife and tried to kill me. I dialed one hundred for them to come and rescue me — you hear some music playing there and a machine says over and over 'All the lines are busy' — what's that supposed to be, a joke? And when someone finally answers they say: 'There's no patrol car available, you'll have to wait five minutes.' What's that supposed to mean? I'm supposed to tell a criminal

who's going to stick a knife into me that he should wait five minutes for the patrol car to come and get him?"

The policeman at the desk interrupts her: "That's enough!
Stop it! You're starting again? You promised that today you'll
sit still and wait your turn without opening your mouth. If you
keep on talking I'll kick you out of here, you hear?"

The prostitute waves her hand accusingly in his direction and
looks around grimly at the people sitting in the room as if to
say: There you are, what did I tell you?

"Haven't you got anything better to do than come here every
day and make a nuisance of yourself? I'm sick of the sight of
you!" says the policeman, and he shakes his head in despairing
resignation.

The woman whose purse was snatched looks anxiously at the
prostitute, who is sitting opposite her on the chair between the
two benches, and the latter responds with a friendly smile,
takes a pack of Marlboros out of the large handbag resting on
her knees, lights a cigarette, inhales with short, rhythmic puffs,
and blows out the smoke, pursing her lips. She looks around for
an ashtray. But the only ashtray is in the tough guy's hand and
is so full that there's no room in it for even a speck of ash. She
glances quickly at the policeman and the people sitting around
her, hides her hand behind her back, and drops the ash on the
floor under her chair.

"I don't know what she's going on about," says the battered
woman's neighbor to the man in gray, who has put on his
glasses and picked up his newspaper, and jerks her head in the
prostitute's direction, "and without any connection . . . but
she," and now she points to the woman at her side, "went to
the police a few times already to tell them about her husband,
and they didn't do anything to him. She doesn't want to go on
living. I had to drag her in here today to make a complaint.
What are they waiting for? For him to kill her?"

"For her to kill him," the prostitute breaks the silence. "Why
not? The law says she's entitled to!"

The gray man drops the glasses from his nose and puts the

newspaper down again. "They say about everything that they haven't got the manpower and the resources because they're busy with other, more important things. I ask you, if they haven't got the time to deal with the car thefts, what have they got the time for? Have they stopped traffic accidents? Have they solved the problem of drug abuse? Have they put an end to organized crime? Have they caught all the terrorists? I'd like to know what the other important things are that they have succeeded in doing."

The boy on Aviram's left gets up suddenly and resumes pacing up and down the room. The policeman, presumably for fear of the reaction of the tough guy, who has already raised his head with an ominous look in his eye, gets up and goes over to the boy, puts a hand on his shoulder, and stops him. "Why are you walking around like that?" he asks in a gentle voice. "What's the matter with you? Why don't you sit down like everybody else and badmouth our country's police force with them?" And he leads him back to his seat and pats him reassuringly on the shoulder.

A woman emerges from one of the rooms, and the tourist, whose turn has come to go in, stands up, but the policeman signals for him to sit down again, goes into the room, and closes the door behind him. The tourist protests at the delay and returns to his seat. And the policeman immediately comes back out, sits down at his desk, and sends in the battered woman and her neighbor. After a while the neighbor emerges, returns to her seat, and says: "They won't let me stay there with her. They're going to mess around with her again."

The longer Aviram waits, the more his sense of oppression grows. And it isn't the troubles of the other people sitting there that depresses him, or the seedy air of the place, which looks like something in a television program about a third-world country, that bothers him, or even the waste of time and the pointlessness of coming here, but the feeling that he has given himself up and come to serve his sentence, and these are his cellmates.

The battered woman comes out of the closed room crying

and turns quickly to the exit, with her neighbor running behind her. The policeman goes into one of the rooms to consult someone again, and on returning he sends the tourist into the room vacated by the battered woman and the muttering boy into another. The prostitute gets up and goes over to his desk: "I was here first, what's going on here?"

"You only come here to sit and talk to people anyway, there's nothing for you to do at home at this hour of day," says the policeman, "so sit still and wait!"

She hangs her big bag from her shoulder and walks up to the corridor.

"Where do you think you're going?" demands the policeman and he gets up to return her to her place.

"To the toilet!" announces the prostitute. "What's the matter? You want to come with me?"

"It's your turn next," the policeman says to the tough guy holding the iron ashtray in his hand, who raises his angry eyes for a second to confirm that he has received the message.

The woman whose purse was snatched looks impatiently at her watch. "By the time they see me he'll get away and they'll never catch him," she says. "I'll never see my money again. And it's not just money, my ID's there too and the picture of my granddaughter abroad, and after he takes the money he'll throw the purse away and leave it lying in the street."

"If your ID card's inside it," says the man in gray from behind his newspaper, "maybe someone will find it and send it to your address."

"Damn him to hell," says the woman, "people like that should be sent to jail for the rest of their lives!"

Again a woman's voice is heard calling from one of the invisible rooms: "Sammy! Where's Sammy?" And Sammy's voice answers: "I'm going to my office, what do you want?" "I'm going out to eat!" "Okay, I'm here." A few policemen and women pass through the waiting room on their way out, apparently for lunch. A man in a hat, holding a big plastic bag, enters the waiting room and goes up to the desk to sign in. Up to now

Aviram was last in line, but now that the line has shortened and there is somebody behind him, he feels more acutely that his turn is approaching. He realizes that his sense of oppression is nothing but fear, an obscure fear gripping his guts and demanding to emerge from obscurity and become concrete.

Presently a voice is heard from the end of one of the corridors, where one of the doors has opened, a very familiar voice, bursting into shrieks of laughter: "You think I don't know you, Sammy? You maniac, you can't fool me!" And the laughing voice of her interlocutor saying: "I'll bring it tomorrow and you can see for yourself." The door closes and after a while the ginger woman who owns the storeroom comes into the waiting room.

She goes straight to the elderly policeman's desk. "How's things, Baruch?" she asks. "Didn't Saul come to work today? Sammy says he hasn't seen him."

"How's that? I saw him this morning," says Baruch. "Maybe he went out."

"I can't find him," says the ginger woman, and she heads to the toilet at the start of the corridor. On the bench next to the corridor the only person now left is the owner of the stolen car, reading his newspaper.

"Hang on a minute, Yaffa, there's someone in there," says Baruch. And he gets up, goes over to the toilet door, and bangs on it with his fist: "What are you sitting in there for an hour for, what are you doing in there?" he shouts at the locked door. "Get out! There are other people here who need to go!"

"Okay, okay, there's no need to yell," says the voice of the prostitute. "I'll be out in a minute."

The ginger woman, who has been standing until now with her back to Aviram, turns around and sees him. "Neighbor!" she cries gaily at the top of her voice. "Here's a neighbor! Wonderful! What are you doing here? He's our neighbor!" she informs Baruch. "Have you come to press charges against us?" she asks Aviram and bursts into loud laughter. "He doesn't talk to me, the maniac. He's a dog maniac, he lives alone with his dog, instead of a woman he uses a dog," she explains to the policeman. "Don't worry, neighbor, we know everything that goes on here, we know everybody, right, Baruch?"

Baruch is silent.

"Send him in without waiting in line, Baruch," she instructs the policeman. "I'll wait for you," she says to Aviram, "you'll get a ride all the way home in my car. Why not? A neighbor's a neighbor after all, right?"

The prostitute emerges from the toilet and occupies her seat on the chair between the two benches. The ginger woman enters the toilet and Aviram takes advantage of the opportunity to escape. He looks behind him to make sure that there are no policemen running after him to take him back inside. His throat is dry and raspy. He stops a cab and rides to the office.

Before going up to the office, he goes into a café and orders a cold beer to quench his thirst and wet his throat. Gradually the alcohol dispels the weight of the oppression.

Ilan is talking to a client, and Aviram sits down at the computer to make up the quota of work he set for himself for the day. But he finds it difficult to concentrate, and he doesn't know if this is due to the influence of the alcohol, which he is unaccustomed to drinking, or if it is the old fear, nourished and strengthened by the memory of the break-in at his apartment and by the wait at the police station, tightening around his neck like a noose.

After the client leaves, Ilan asks: "Well, how did it go? You see, it's not so terrible."

"Actually," says Aviram, "I didn't go in. I couldn't wait any longer."

"Because of work?"

"Not just because of work. I was fed up with sitting there and waiting for my turn, and for what? To get the money for changing the lock back from the insurance company?"

"You've got the wrong attitude, Avi," says Ilan, "it's a question of principle. You're insured, aren't you? You should get them to pay you what you're entitled to, never mind how small the sum. Wasn't there any other damage to the house?"

"No, they didn't even make a mess. The problem is that a stranger entered my home and touched all my things. You can't imagine what it did to me. I was up all night cleaning the place and washing everything in the closets. The thought of it disgusted me so much, it drove me crazy. The insurance doesn't pay for that."

"Perhaps it was a girl?" Ilan smiles the smile he reserves for telling dirty jokes. "Today women break into houses too, to get money for drugs. It doesn't need much strength, all you need is special pliers to turn the cylinder and pull it out of the lock."

"I never thought of that," Aviram tries to smile.

"It really is strange," says Ilan. "Breaking into the flat and not taking anything. What were they looking for?"

"I have no idea."

Ilan racks his brain to solve the riddle. When he concentrates like this, his plump face, which is always shiny, winter and summer, from sweat or some oily lotion he smears onto his skin after shaving, shines even more than usual. Aviram imagines how he would feel if he knew that it was the young woman on the other side of the wall, about whom he thinks so much and whom he wants to reach so badly, who had broken into his apartment.

"Listen!" says Ilan. "They broke into your place by mistake. I'm telling you that they were sent to break into the apartment next door and they broke into the wrong apartment, and when they discovered their mistake they got out fast. That's why they didn't search the place and turn it upside down. They didn't come for money for drugs. They were sent to look for something else. After they left your place, either they broke into the other apartment straightaway, or else they thought that two apartments in one go was too risky and they beat it. What do you think?" Ilan looks smug.

"What were they looking for?" asks Aviram.

"Documents, Avi, letters, contracts, accounts, all kinds of papers connected to what goes on there, and maybe, who knows, to attach a bugging device to the telephone? I told you already, that apartment isn't for fucking, like we thought at first, it's a secret address for some kind of business, and somebody who wants to know what's going on there sent the burglars."

Ilan's spirits, encouraged by his success in solving the mystery, soar to the realm of his longings — the world of big business, with its dark, convoluted intrigues, skillfully and cunningly conducted in the twilight zone between the legal and the illegal, between loyalty and treachery, a world with no morals or feelings. "Maybe the firm he works for found out something and they suspect he's operating on his own against their interests, maybe competitors discovered the address, maybe the whole operation's illegal and they're looking for evidence against him? Maybe it's the police, who in certain cases prefer to use private professionals to do their breaking and entering for them instead of getting a search warrant from a judge? There are all kinds of possibilities. You don't know if they broke in next door too?"

"No."

"Interesting. Try to find out."

Menashe called: "Come to Mother's, bring the clothes."

"Is he there?" Ezra shouted.

"Yes."

Ezra put down the receiver and looked at Ruthie wordlessly.

"Ezra, what happened?" she cried in alarm.

His voice returned: "He's at my mother's. We're going there now."

"So why are you making such a tragic face? Come on, let's go and see him!"

"Ruthie, he wants his civilian clothes."

"So we'll take them to him. Enough, Ezra, we've been through all this already."

"He isn't going to turn himself in, Ruthie, it isn't over yet."

Ruthie went to fetch the clothes.

"It's strange, Ruthie. When I spoke to Menashe after Eyal called, he agreed with me that we shouldn't take him the clothes," said Ezra, "and now he's telling me to bring them."

"You see, he understands too."

They drove to Pardes Katz. All the way Ezra was silent, sunk in thought, he neither put on the radio nor lit a cigarette, only gazed at the road ahead of him, his face tense with worry. Ruthie didn't break the silence. Before getting out of the car Ezra said: "For the time being we'll leave the clothes here. We'll see what happens." Ruthie didn't answer him.

Menashe opened the door and with pounding hearts they entered the little ground-floor apartment where Ezra and all his brothers had once lived with their mother. Eyal was sitting on the couch, next to his grandmother, barefoot, in gym shorts that were too big for him, apparently Menashe's. When they came in he remained seated and looked at them with a strange indifference. Finally he asked in a dry voice: "Did you bring the clothes?"

"Eyalie!" cried Ezra in a broken voice. "What's happened to you?"

"Don't shout at him like that," his mother scolded him.

"It's so long since I saw you," Ezra's voice trembled and his eyes filled with tears. "My life's ruined." He turned to the wall and wiped away his tears.

"Didn't you bring the clothes?" asked Eyal.

"They're in the car, I'll get them for you," said Ruthie.

"What do you need them for?" asked Ezra.

"Where's your uniform?" asked Ruthie. "I'll wash it for you."

"It's already on the line," said the grandmother, "getting dry."

"I don't need the uniform," said Eyal.

"Why don't you need it!" shouted Ezra.

"Why are you yelling?" his mother scolded. "Did you come here to yell at him? If you didn't bring the clothes, I'll get clothes for him. I know where to get them."

Ezra gave Ruthie the car keys and she went out to fetch the clothes.

"What happened to you, Eyal?" asked Ezra. "What happened to screw up the army for you? You were so keen to enlist, you wanted to get into a commando unit."

"What did they send you to jail for?" Menashe, the more practical of the two, interrupted his brother.

"There was some maniac of an instructor in boot camp who kept picking on me all the time. I hit him."

"For that they send you to jail?"

"He's a sergeant."

Ruthie returned to the room with a plastic bag containing the clothes.

"Give it to him," said the grandmother. "He needs it."

She gave him the bag and he put it on his lap.

"What are you going to do?" asked Ezra.

"I'm going to get dressed," said Eyal, and he stood up and left the room.

His grandmother followed him with a satisfied look.

Of all her many grandchildren she was most attached to Eyal, even though he was not the first. The bond between them had lasted since his infancy, and their intimacy had not diminished when he grew up. He visited her frequently in her apartment in Pardes Katz and sat with her for hours at a time. What did they have to talk about? Why should a boy like him, who grew up in a modern society, spend so much time with an illiterate old woman whose world was so remote from his? Ruthie puzzled over this question and shared her bewilderment with Ezra, but Ezra couldn't see anything wrong with it, regarded it as an expression of the respect the boy felt for his grandmother, and was gratified by his frequent visits to her.

Eyal returned to the room in his civilian clothes and took his seat next to his grandmother.

"When are you going back to the army?" asked Ezra.

"I'm not going back to the army," said Eyal.

"You'll have to finish your jail sentence first. At the moment you're regarded as a deserter."

"I don't intend to go to jail."

"Menashe has connections in the army, Eyalie, he can fix it for you to finish your jail sentence and go back to boot camp," Ezra informed his son.

"I'm not going back to jail or to the army," said Eyal.

"So what are you going to do?" asked Ruthie.

"I'll manage," said Eyal. "Don't worry."

"Where have you been hanging out all this time? With the whores and the junkies at the central bus station?" asked Ezra.

"I know that Mordechai saw me. And what was he doing there in the first place? I got out of there fast. I knew he'd tell and you'd come to look for me."

"And you didn't want us to find you?"

"No."

"Why not?"

"Because I wanted to be alone."

"Why? What were you doing there?"

"Learning about life."

"That's not life the way people like us live it."

"So what?" Eyal looked at his watch.

"Are you in a hurry?" asked Ezra.

"Yes."

His father suppressed his anger. "Tell me, don't you think about us at all? Don't you understand what you've done to us?"

Eyal said nothing.

"What are you living on? Have you got money for food?"

"I get by," said Eyal.

"How? Where do you get money from?"

Eyal was silent. His father looked suspiciously at his old mother. "You're not taking money from your grandmother! You know that she won't let us help her and she lives on social security! You know how much that is? You're not ashamed to take money from her?" demanded Ezra.

The old woman answered for the boy: "What do you want of him? He doesn't take money from me, and if he needs it, I have it to give him."

"Why are you sticking up for him all the time?" demanded Ezra. "He ran away from the army, he has to go back there."

"If he isn't happy in the army, he doesn't need to be in the army."

"What will he do now?"

"He knows what to do, he's got brains and a lot of strength."

"He's like you," said Ezra.

The old woman laughed. She put her arm around Eyal's shoulder and hugged him.

"Why didn't you come home at all?" asked Ezra. "So that we'd know you were alive at least."

"I knew they'd look for me at home."

"Who'd look for you?"

"The military police."

"Nobody's looking for you, Eyal! The army's not interested in you. They don't care about you. You're running away and nobody's chasing you. I wish they would look for you and catch you and put you back on the straight and narrow, and all this mess would be over! But it's not the army we knew, everyone there only thinks about themselves, and not about the country."

"And if they catch you, what will you do?" asked Menashe.

"I'll run away again."

"They won't let you get away with it twice," said Menashe.

"There are ways of getting out of the army," said Eyal.

"What do you mean?" demanded Ezra.

"I can pretend to be crazy, or get religion and go to a yeshiva, or say I'm a homo."

"I can't believe I'm hearing this!" cried Ezra. "Did you hear what he said?" he asked his old mother. "Did you hear him? And you stick up for him. He's not my child!"

"He's my child," said his mother.

Ruthie said: "Eyal, I want to talk to you for a minute in private."

The boy stood up reluctantly and went outside with her. They stood on the sidewalk, facing the house with their backs to the street, leaning on Ezra's pickup.

"Eyalie, can't you explain what's happening to me? I don't understand anything."

"What's there to understand?" asked Eyal. "I don't want to be in the army."

"Why? Everyone goes to the army and gets through it somehow."

"So I'm not like everyone. It doesn't suit me."

"Don't you want to be like everybody else?"

"No, I want to be like myself."

"Tell me, when you were hanging around in all those places, didn't you get involved with drugs?"

"I don't even smoke cigarettes."

"You have to be careful not to come under the influence of people like that, junkies, perverts, criminals. Are you strong enough to look after yourself?"

"It's all right. Don't worry."

"Know that whatever happens we love you, that we're always there for you."

"Okay," said Eyal.

"And give us a sign of life every now and then, as long as this thing lasts, so that we'll know at least that you're all right."

"Okay."

When they returned to the room Ezra and Menashe, who appeared to have been quarreling, immediately fell silent. Eyal took his seat on the couch, next to his grandmother, and Ezra looked at him solemnly. "Look, Eyalie, I understand. I realize that you're already eighteen years old, you're grown up, you have the right to choose your path in life, we can't force you to follow in our footsteps. Okay. But I want to understand, just to know what's going on in your head. Don't you feel any obligation to serve like everybody else? Don't you have any feeling for our army?"

"Fuck the army."

Ezra opened his eyes wide and looked at Menashe, as if to ascertain whether his brother had heard what he had heard. Menashe put his hand on his shoulder, as if to prevent his brother from getting up and attacking the boy. "How can you talk like that in front of your parents? In front of your grandmother!" yelled Ezra. "In all our lives we never even came close to talking like that in front of our mother. Haven't you got any respect for anything? That's what you learned from those criminals and junkies where you've been hiding out, those are your pals now. How dare you dirty your mouth about our army? Aren't you part of this country?"

"Fuck the country," said Eyal.

Ezra stood up, breathing heavily and red in the face. "Come on, Ruthie, let's go home. I don't want to hear another word from him. He's not my son, he's a piece of trash! I've got nothing to do with him anymore."

"No," said Ruthie, "I'm not prepared to leave like that. I want to talk to Eyal, to understand him. He's my son, I love him even if I don't agree with everything he says or does."

"You're still sticking up for him, after what he said about the army and the country? I'm not prepared to stay here with him for one more minute. If you won't come with me, I'm going home alone."

From his place next to his grandmother, Eyal watched them arguing; he watched with the same strange indifference on his face, as if it had nothing to do with him.

She had already tried all hours of the day, and apparently she had decided to try at night as well. It is after eleven o'clock when the intercom buzzes, interrupting a moment of menacing silence in the television movie and waking the sleeping dog, who hurries to the door and begins to bark. Her voice rises from the receiver, charged with suspense and hope.

"Are they home?"

"Who?"

"Apartment 17; don't you know my voice yet?"

"This isn't apartment 17."

"I know, but they never answer there."

"What can I do for you?"

"Don't they have a phone? Doesn't anyone live there? It says Neuman here, where are the Neumans?"

"I don't know. I don't know the neighbors."

He hears a nervous creak from the apartment next door. "Hello! Hello!" her voice cries impatiently in the receiver. "You see," she says, "there's no reply."

He replaces the receiver, silences the television, goes into the bedroom, and puts his ear to the wall. There's no sound from apartment 17. Recently the young woman has moved in. In the morning she leaves for work, and Aviram times his departure to coincide with hers, waiting to hear her lock the door before he leaves so that he can meet her on the landing and go downstairs with her on his way to work. On a number of occasions he has tried to start up a conversation with her, but without eliciting a response, although it seems to him that he discerns a suspicious interest in her expression. They both come home for their lunch break at about the same time. For some time now he hasn't heard the man's voice in the apartment. In the evenings she is alone, and through the wall he can hear music, or voices on the television. Now there's nobody there, or else she's keeping quiet in order to hide her presence from the statistician.

The intercom buzzes incessantly again and the dog barks.

"What is it now?"

"Open the door, I want to come in."

He presses the button to open the door to the building and looks through the peephole, waiting to see her. When she reaches his landing, she looks around and makes for the apartment next door, leaving his field of vision. This wasn't how he imagined her when she spoke to him before. He grabs hold of the dog's collar and tries to silence his barking, even though he knows it won't do any good. She rings the bell next door, knocks on the door, rings the bell again, comes back into his field of vision, and stands next to the banister, looking at his door. In spite of the distortion caused by the lens in the peephole he can see that she is an attractive woman. For a moment she seems at a loss, then her expression changes to one of resolution and she steps up to his door and rings the bell.

In order to conceal the fact that he has been looking through the peephole, he returns to the living room, with the dog behind him, waits a minute, and then returns to the door and opens it a crack, to keep the dog, who doesn't stop barking, from getting out. She glances doubtfully, albeit affectionately, at the dog, and then looks curiously at his owner. In a gesture that takes even him by surprise, he invites her in, keeping a firm hold on the dog's collar. She ignores his invitation.

"It's very strange," she says. From the big bag hanging on her shoulder she removes a clipboard with yellow sheets of paper attached. "How come there's never anybody in the apartment?"

Definitely an attractive woman, in her forties, tall, not too slim, short hair, restrained makeup, just a black line to emphasize her rather sunken eyes.

"I've already told you more than once that I can't help you. I don't have any contact with anybody here."

"Excuse me, sir, I have no personal interest in these people. I have to fill in a statistical form with them, for the government."

Something in her stubbornness touches him, as if she's fighting for her life.

"There are other neighbors here," he says, "maybe somebody else will agree to do it for them. I'm prepared to do it myself. If the dog bothers you, I'll shut him up in the other room."

"No!" she laughs despairingly. "I'm afraid that's impossible. Everything has to be done in the framework of the sample. And this apartment came up in the sample. Don't you understand? We know there's a couple living here, but we can't find them or reach the owner of the apartment. All the work on the sample's been done and this apartment is the only one left."

"If you like, you can leave me your phone number, and if I find anything out I'll let you know."

She hesitates for a moment and finally jots something down on the corner of one of her yellow sheets, tears it off, and hands it to him: Shula, and a phone number in Ramat Hasharon.

"What's the deal?" she complains, "why don't they answer? Have they got something to hide? They've ignored all the notes I left in their mailbox and on their door. Don't they understand that they're obliged by law to cooperate?"

"Maybe you should send someone to break in and see what's

going on in there," he suggests, and she examines his face as if to see whether he's joking or talking seriously.

He closes the door, peeps through the hole, and sees her turning again in the direction of the apartment next-door, disappearing from his field of vision, but she doesn't knock or ring the bell, presumably she's writing another note to stick in the crack between the door and the door frame.

Before going to bed he takes the dog down for a walk, and in the yard, at the side of the building, he sees a figure standing in the dark and looking up at apartment 17. He approaches the figure, and the dog, who doesn't like changes in his route, barks loudly in surprise and disapproval and refuses to budge from the sidewalk. The woman shows no sign of embarrassment like a person caught red-handed, but on the contrary, as if continuing her previous line of argument, she points up at the window of his next-door neighbors. "Look, you can see the light on in the room through the blinds."

"Your name isn't Shula, is it?" he says.

"Yael — is that better?"

"Definitely. And this devotion to the Central Bureau of Statistics, working at this hour of night?"

She doesn't answer. He returns to the sidewalk and sets out with the dog on their usual route. In the little streets they pass through, most of the apartments are already dark and their blinds are down. From time to time he can hear a car passing on the boulevard. There is hardly anyone about. When he reaches the boulevard he sits down on a bench and watches the dog running between the trees and the bushes. These are his favorite moments of the day. After about twenty minutes he stands up and walks back home by the same route with the dog at his heels.

And she's still standing there, next to the building, looking up at the windows of apartment 17.

"How long are you going to go on standing here?"

"Until they switch off the light."

He climbs up to his apartment, goes into the bedroom, and

begins to undress. The telephone rings next door, it rings three times and stops. Then it rings again and he hears her voice clearly saying:

"Yes! Where are you speaking from?"

"What's the time there now?"

"When are you coming back?"

Hezi's voice comes over the line as strong and clear as if he's standing next to her. "I don't know," he says, "it depends on all kinds of things connected to my work, and also on my plans for both of us."

"I miss you," says Gabi.

"I miss you too. How are you getting on in the apartment?"

"I feel at home here, because this is where I wait for you. That's all that's important to me."

"Are you being careful? Any mistake on your part could ruin everything for us."

"Don't worry, everything's okay. I haven't forgotten anything."

"If I don't contact you from here again, I'll see you in Israel. I love you."

As usual she goes to sleep on the left side of the bed, with his empty place on her right, like the moments after they make love. Love cannot exist without being nourished by projecting itself into the future, and Gabi's heart tells her that he will come back to her different from when he left, since he has said again: "I love you." And in her last moments of wakefulness she imagines how he will stay with her all night, and she will fall asleep in his arms, surrounded by the warmth of his body while he whispers words of love to her, and afterward they slowly and unconsciously drift apart into their separate sleep, but then too his presence behind her radiates warmth and his quiet breathing caresses the nape of her neck in a steady rhythm coordinated with the beating of her heart, and she promises herself that she will wake up at daybreak to see him sleeping, covered with the sheet up to his waist, his head turned to the left, to her, his white hair on the white pillowcase, his cheek crushing the pillow, a captive to forces stronger than him, defeated and helpless.

The building is on the corner of two streets: one of them, bigger and wider, is the commercial center of the neighborhood and sees a lot of traffic; the second, a small, quiet street, has only residential buildings. The front of the apartment, the bedroom and the living room, overlooks the little street, and the big street passes in front of the kitchen and the bathroom. When we bought this apartment, we could have bought a place on the top floor of a building opposite the sea instead. She didn't want it, she found all kinds of things wrong with it. There was no elevator, and it was difficult for her to climb stairs even then. And there was another disadvantage: it was an old building, the salty wind from the sea corroded the walls and ruined the furniture, and the apartment would have to be painted every year. She didn't need beauty, she didn't know what it was. She wanted an apartment in a new building. She was interested in the furniture, the carpet, the fridge, the stove. And the main thing was for it to be in "a good neighborhood." I let her have her way. Today, when I sit on the little kitchen balcony looking down at the playground, the bank, the supermarket, the houses visible on the other street, I ask myself what it would have been like to sit like this and see only the ocean, without buildings, without people, without life. Perhaps it would have been pleasant to feel the salty breeze, which eats the walls, gradually eating my body too, until there would have been nothing left of it but bones. But how long could I have gone on looking at the sea? Perhaps I would have grown tired of it, and then I would have been obliged to admit to myself that my longings for beauty were an illusion and a lie, that people aren't shadows, like I think, that I need to see them moving about in their houses, walking in the street, going into the bank and the supermarket, talking nonsense, looking at girls, dreaming that something will happen in their lives that has never happened to anyone before, or at least nothing worse than what they think happens to other people. And so I can go on living in a world of shadows and longing for true beauty.

The girl isn't here now, she went to do the shopping and didn't want to take me with her. She said she didn't have the time, but I know that she doesn't like having me with her there. An ambulance sounds its siren. Ambulances often come here. From the living-room balcony it was possible to see the whole of the little street and part of the big street, and see to where they were going. But now that the living-room balcony is the girl's room, I sit only on the kitchen balcony and from there I can see the ambulances only when they pass by in the big street, next to the bank and the supermarket and the playground, or when they turn into the little street and pull up next to one of the first houses. They often come to the corner building opposite my house. A fat woman lives there whom the ambulance has been coming for ever since I've been here. Even then it was hard for her to walk, and in recent years she hasn't gone out at all. There's no elevator in the building and she lives on the top floor. She calls an ambulance, and two people carry her all the way downstairs in a chair. I don't know where they get the strength to carry that weight. Outside, next to the ambulance, they pick her up from the chair and put her on the bed, and she yells: "Gently, gently!" You can hear her yelling all the way from where I sit on the balcony. A few hours later the ambulance returns, they take her out, and before they can seat her on the chair that they have to carry all the way up the stairs, she's already yelling: "Gently, gently!" People say that she takes the ambulance to go to the hairdresser to have her hair done, but I don't know if it's true. People say all kinds of things.

This time the ambulance turns into the little street and stops at a house I can't see. I won't see it when it comes back either, because it's a one-way street. Once something strange happened to me, I must have been half-asleep, I heard the siren and saw the ambulance turning onto our street, and suddenly I was sure that they were coming for me, that I was already dead. I felt no sorrow, no pain. Only the hope of getting through it as quickly as possible. Let them put me on the stretcher, cover me with a sheet, take me wherever they like, what difference does it make? Maybe it will really happen just like that, and that's just fine with me. Maybe the girl will come in and find me dead on the chair on the kitchen balcony. At first she'll be alarmed, she'll be so frightened she won't know what to do. Then she'll phone my daughter to come right away. She has her number and also my son's, but she knows that she has to phone my daughter if anything happens. She'll find work with somebody else.

I remember this incident now, and I wait for her to come home so that I can pretend to be dead. When I hear her opening the door I close my eyes, let my head fall to the side, on my shoulder, and not on my chest like it does when I'm sleeping, I don't have to make my face crooked because it's crooked anyway since the stroke, I only stick my tongue out a bit. That's how you look when you're dead. I hear her coming into the kitchen, the bags of groceries rustle on the counter, and when she comes out to the balcony and approaches me, I don't breathe. She stands in front of me, I can feel her looking at me, I can hear her breathing, and there's a moment of silence. Afterward, "Hey, hey!" she tries to wake me up and I don't move, "Hello! Hello! You sleep?"

She shakes me and my head falls further down and my entire tongue comes out of my mouth. I hear her sigh. I imagine how she looks, maybe she's crossing herself in her fear, the way they do. I can't see it, but I can imagine it. I enjoy the thought so much that I can't control myself anymore, my body starts to shake and I laugh. My eyes open. When she sees that my eyes are open she's angry and she begins to hit me with her fists on my shoulders, and this makes me laugh even more. "You are bad, very bad!" she shouts at me. "I hate you!" And she goes back into the kitchen in a sulk.

Why was she frightened? Was it just the fear of seeing death, or perhaps she has some feeling for me? Why does it give me so much pleasure? Is it my natural meanness? Later on she's still cross with me. She puts my food down in front of me and immediately turns her back. I say to her: "Linda, Linda," which invariably brings a kind of feminine expression to her face, even a certain charm, which she does not usually possess. But now she doesn't turn to look.

"What the matter with him?" says Mrs. Shwartz. "He can't lie quiet in bed?"

She hangs onto her husband's arm and they slowly descend the stairs. Aviram bumps into them as he leaves for work after his lunch break. Mr. Shwartz, who has grown very thin and whose face has shrunk and turned a yellowish color, is wearing a thick, dark blue dressing gown over striped flannel pajamas whose wide pants come down to the bottom of his calves, exposing beige long johns clinging to his skinny legs and stuck into thick gray socks emerging from a pair of woolen slippers.

"I have to talk to you," says Mr. Shwartz and he bars his way.

"I'm going to work now."

"I'm going to work too!" replies Mr. Shwartz angrily.

"He need to stay in bed, don't want. Not sleep even. All the time only house, house, house. I say: Enough, you finish already with committee, twenty years not enough? Now somebody else do committee. He sick, no strength left."

"There isn't anybody else!" says Mr. Shwartz. "They're all subtenants. How many apartment owners are left here? Three or four sick old women or not normal and if there are one or two normal people they don't want to do it. Why work for others? Everybody thinks only of himself, and Shwartz can do the work for everyone. If only someone would take it from me! Do I have the strength for it?" He tries to pull up his gown to show Aviram the urine bag again, but his wife hurries to remove his hand. "You want to be on the house committee?" he asks as they reach the bottom floor, and Aviram doesn't answer the question, in his opinion rhetorical, and steps back to allow Mrs. Shwartz to lead the old man outside. Mr. Shwartz stations himself outside the door to prevent Aviram from getting away.

He grabs him by the sleeve. "I want you to come there with me now to see something," he says.

"What's to see?" complains his wife. "A thousand times he goes there and nothing to see."

"She doesn't understand nothing," Mr. Shwartz explains to Aviram as they make their way to the backyard at the pace of the old man's shuffling slippers, "she doesn't know nothing. She can't even read the newspaper."

"Polish I can," says Mrs. Shwartz.

Mr. Shwartz stops, turns to face Aviram, looks him in the eye, and shakes his head from side to side to refute this claim: "No she can't. Nothing, nothing."

His wife does not stand up for herself and drops her eyes. The three of them reach the new basement apartment and stop at the corner where the trash cans once stood, surrounded by a low, crumbling concrete wall, until they were moved, without the permission of the house committee, to the other side of the building, leaving only a cracked concrete floor behind them. Mr. Shwartz approaches the basement wall, which has been painted white, and bends down to the two closed windows in order to see the dark inside of the room through the glass panes. After he has despaired of discovering anything there, he goes on shuffling with his wife's assistance to the new facade of the basement and stops next to the steps leading down to the new sunken porch.

"Go down there and ring the bell, maybe someone will open the door," he says to Aviram.

Aviram descends the steps and presses the buzzer next to the door. Nobody answers.

"Maybe they're inside and they don't want to open," says Mr. Shwartz.

"There's nothing there," says his wife. "You can't see?" She turns to Aviram. "All the time — where they are, where they are? What he care about them? They can go to hell! Just we come in ambulance from hospital, instead to rest, to sleep in bed, a sick man, again and again he have to see here inside it and ring them on the door."

"There's nobody there," says Aviram.

"So where are they?" Mr. Shwartz demands a satisfactory explanation from Aviram. "They suddenly disappeared? What happened? All day and all night they were here, why don't we see them anymore?"

"I don't know," says Aviram. "As long as their court case with the municipality lasts they're not allowed to use the apartment or rent it to anyone else."

"You know how long cases like that can go on? Years, years!"

"So what do you care? The longer it lasts, the better. In the meantime the apartment's empty. What do you need them here for?"

"These are people who worry about the law and the courts? You think a law court makes an impression on them? They came to shout through my door that if they lose the case and they have to pull down what they built, they'll blow up the whole building. You think they won't do it? You don't know these people! But they won't have to blow up the building. They won't lose the case. They've got a lawyer to look out for them, and he'll do a deal with the lawyer for the municipality, and everything will come out in their favor. Maximum, maybe they'll have to pay some fine. And believe me, they're not short of money. And we haven't got the money to pay a lawyer to look out for us. I asked all the apartment owners to pay three thousand shekels each so we could take a lawyer too to take care of our property. Did you pay, sir?"

"I meant to tell you that I can't possibly give you the money. Not now."

"Nobody paid! Nobody! Everybody voted for it at the meeting, but they all thought the others would pay. You voted for it too."

"Yes," said Aviram. "In the meantime what's certain is that they're not coming here."

"Really? They're not coming!" Mr. Shwartz plays his trump card: "And who's watering their plants? You? Me? Look, it's still wet!"

Indeed, the plants around the sunken porch show signs of having been recently watered.

"A terrace, with a garden, on our land, you see their plan!"

Mr. Shwartz begins to tremble with rage, and his wife cries anxiously: "You see, now he gets attack of blood pressure again and have to go in ambulance to hospital!"

Aviram beats a hasty retreat and escapes to the street. When he reaches the pavement he turns his head and sees Shwartz, supported by his wife, stopping next to the basement windows, where the old man bends down and presses his face to the windowpane again, in the hope that this time he might discover his enemies hiding there in the dark.

The new girl, Mali, returns from what Ilan, presumably inspired by his experience in the army reserves, likes to call a "properties patrol," returns the keys of the empty apartments she has been showing to clients, and sits down in her corner.

"What's happening?" Ilan asks her.

"They said they want to think about it," Mali replies. "They're probably working with another firm too and they want to see what they've got to offer. And the old woman in Ein Gedi Street is suddenly saying now that she hasn't yet decided if she wants to sell or rent. I have the feeling that she isn't going to move out at all."

"I'll call her nephew and tell him to get it sorted out with her first and come back to us only if she's serious."

"And she's so deaf that you can hardly communicate with her even if you scream at the top of your voice," says Mali. "In my opinion we're wasting our time on that apartment."

Ilan met Mali when they were both working in another agency, before he went into partnership with Aviram. "She's a single mother," he told Aviram when he informed him of their decision ("Okay with you?") to employ her. From his tone Aviram understood that she wasn't a divorcee or a widow bringing up her children alone, but an unmarried mother.

Mali is about forty, pleasant-looking but not attractive. The marks of time — and the troubles of being a single mother, so Aviram assumes — are evident on her face and she makes no attempt to conceal them. She is hardworking and experienced, and she knows how to talk to clients and inspire their trust. "A true professional, a serious contribution to the firm," said Ilan, "unlike Ronit, who may have been nice to look at sashaying around the office with all her goods on display, but who was completely useless, except when it came to using our phone for interminable private conversations and demanding pay raises."

With time Aviram forgot his resentment against Ronit and her humiliating behavior toward him, and the charged atmosphere her relations with Ilan had created in the office. Now he remembers with longing her youthful, sensuous presence, so full of freedom and spontaneity, and not a little vulgarity as well. Even the memory of her bursts of coarse laughter and provocative remarks to Ilan now give rise to longing in his breast. Aviram does not deny Ilan's real need for help in the "property patrols." Their whole burden falls on his partner, who released him from sharing the task either because at the time he enjoyed going out with the clients himself or because he didn't think that Aviram would make a good impression on them.

Bringing Mali into the office was therefore a reasonable step that did not appear, on the face of it, to be prompted by any ulterior motives. But who could guarantee that Ilan was not, in fact, back to his old tricks again, and that behind the apparently innocent step lay the plan, dormant for a while, to make him feel so redundant in the office that he would dissolve the partnership of his own free will? But this possibility no longer insults and angers Aviram as it did before, for ever since Mali came to work in the office her attitude toward him has been consistently genial and friendly, and he can find no signs in her behavior or personality of participation in a conspiracy against him. Besides, his heart has lately been full of the uneasy, but also exciting, feeling that his life is approaching a decisive crossroads, in comparison to which his partnership in the firm pales in insignificance.

When he is about to leave for his lunch break, and Mali has already returned from showing clients the apartments on the firm's lists and finished her half-day's work, she always offers him a lift in her red Fiat Uno, even though it lengthens her journey home, where her daughter is waiting for her after coming back from school. They go to the parking lot and join the crawling lines of traffic filling the road. He could have reached home a lot faster by walking, but he doesn't want to hurt her feelings by consistently refusing her friendly offer of a lift.

"Ilan's a good guy, it's a pleasure to work with him, no?" she said the first time she drove him home. The conversation between them was rather artificial and the need to participate in it embarrassed Aviram.

"Yes," he said, "you can always rely on him."

"He's always in a good mood and there's a nice atmosphere in the office, without any pressure. He really likes you, he says you're very special."

"I think he would prefer me to be less special and more like him."

"On the contrary!" said Mali. "He says it's a good thing that you're not the same and that in the office you complement each other."

"I'm sorry that you're taking the long way home and keeping your daughter waiting because of me."

"She's a big girl now, she can manage until I get there. It's no big deal, and besides, I offered you a lift, nobody forced me. What do you do on your break, do you have lunch at home?"

"Yes," said Aviram, "and I take my dog out for a walk. When I'm at work he's shut up alone in the apartment, and he expects me, he knows when I'm supposed to come."

"So you also have someone waiting for you to come home at lunchtime."

"Yes."

After a while, when they had already driven home together a number of times, they conversed more freely, and Mali talked to him about her personal life as if it were the most natural thing in the world. Once she even talked about being a single parent. Aviram thinks about her with affection, and also with sorrow and concern. He senses that she's interested in him, perhaps even thinking of a relationship between them. She may very well have been pretty and attractive once, he could easily imagine her resembling Ronit in her youth. But today she looks like a faded, defeated, and worn-out version of her. She's intelligent, good-natured, frank, she radiates a pleasant and confidence-inspiring simplicity. But he is not interested in having a relationship with her, not for her will he sacrifice the secret dream that absorbs his entire being — the dream about the cat moaning behind his bedroom wall and the desire to win her, to conquer her if only for once and once only, thereby redeeming his life, which up to now has dragged on without purpose or hope, from its dullness and pointlessness, never mind what happens afterward.

The women he has gone to bed with up to now, all for a fee, were generally younger than Mali, but not all of them were prettier and more attractive. It was the thought of their corruption that attracted him to these women, an attraction that turned, after he had satisfied his lust, into disgust and hatred for them and for himself, so that he had never gone back to any of them again. He knows that even if his relations with Mali become intimate and he goes to bed with her, he will feel the same toward her, he won't be able to stand her closeness or even her friendship, he'll deny her and hurt her. Working together, too, will become a problem for both of them and spoil the atmosphere in the office.

The agitated siren of an ambulance sounds behind the column of cars advancing at a snail's pace and blocking the road. A few of the drivers in front of them stop, apparently in obedience to some law giving priority to emergency vehicles and the column comes to a halt. "Idiots!" sighs Mali, honking her horn and waving her hand to signal them to move ahead. "Why are they stopping? How do they think he's going to get through? They should move until he has room to pass us."

"In emergencies they should use helicopters," says Aviram.

"People should know how to drive in the city," Mali asserts.

Independent, self-confident, and domineering, Aviram notes to himself.

And indeed, the ambulance driver's voice comes over a loud-speaker calling on the cars in front of him to advance to the intersection as quickly as possible. The column starts moving again and the ambulance passes them with earsplitting wails.

"Do you like going to the movies?" Mali asks even before the siren subsides. "If you like, we could go and see a good movie together one day."

"Yes, one day," says Aviram, "but I usually stay at home after work."

"With the dog."

"Yes."

Did he only imagine hearing a note of irony in her voice when she said "With the dog"? Is the rejected woman already beginning to take her revenge?

"Mali really likes you and respects you," Ilan says to him one morning. "You should get to know her better. She has a heart of gold."

"Yes," says Aviram. "She's okay. Not exactly my taste," he adds, "from the point of view of looks, I mean. But she's really okay."

"What's wrong with the way she looks?" asks Ilan in surprise, and Aviram hears the unspoken words behind the question: And how do you think you look yourself?

Has Ilan been to bed with her? Aviram wonders. Could he be the father of her child? For some reason this possibility gives rise to an irresistible curiosity in him.

"Who's the father of her daughter?" he asks.

"I have no idea," says Ilan, and he looks at him for a moment and asks with uncharacteristic resentment: "Is that what bothers you about her?"

"No, of course not. I actually respect her for it very much."

No doubt about it, Ilan is the matchmaker, he's the one who encouraged her to make a move, and now he's feeling out Aviram.

"By the way, her daughter's a very nice girl," Ilan adds and buries his face in the financial paper again.

"How old is she?"

"Eleven."

"How does it work, in fact?" asks Aviram. "After all, a woman who's decided to have a baby out of wedlock doesn't just walk down the street and choose someone and say: Let's have a child together, I want to be a single parent. It must be a friend of hers, or someone who went to bed with her and got her pregnant and doesn't want to or can't marry her. So is there any contact between the child and her father?"

"What's the matter with you, Avi? Why are you asking me all these questions? What am I, an expert on single parents? Why are you so interested?" Ilan asks impatiently. "And if she was a widow, would it be any better?"

Now he has no doubt that Ilan is the father.

"Just curious," says Aviram. "I have no personal interest in the matter."

She was about thirty, prettier, fresher, and more attractive when she and Ilan worked together in the same office. Ilan was already a married man with a family then and he got her pregnant, perhaps in one of the empty apartments they were showing to clients. He knows the girl's exact age and he knows that she's nice, apparently he goes to see her from time to time, and now he's looking for a father for the little family. This is typical of Ilan and not at all to his discredit — at work too he doesn't like leaving unfinished business.

To Mrs. Barzilai Shifra,

I'm writing to you with my last drop of strength I can hardly hold the pen I'm so sick and weak. This letter I'm writing privately as an old neighbor and not representing the committee which I've resigned from. Everybody knows that the whole committee was only me by myself nobody wanted to help me and now there's nobody to take over from me a sick man of eighty. Everybody only worries about himself and now there's no more house committee finished. There's nobody to collect the dues no money for the boy who washes the stairs and cleans around the trash cans none for the person who cuts off the branches in the garden and clears the thorns none for the repairs that have to be done all the time on the sewage pipes that rot after so many years none for changing the light bulbs in the stairwell to see at night and not even to pay the tax to the office in Jerusalem every year that we have to pay by law. There's only a few owners left but all the rest that live in the building pay rent they're young they don't care it's not their house here today tomorrow somewhere else they laugh at anybody who talks to them, they make noise at night throw papers and cigarettes on the stairs and the rubbish they throw on the ground and not in the cans. Soon our building will be such a fine sight that everyone will come and look. After a few months the branches will grow like a jungle and close the path everything will be full of big thorns so a person can't get into the entrance or the yard darkness and dirt on the stairs the whole yard and garden flooded with sewage and stinking up the whole street the intercom door broken all the time open which is very dangerous and rats come from the garbage get into the building and into the house. The renters go to live somewhere else anybody who can escapes from a place like this. Who stays is only a few apartment owners with nowhere to go old men and women most not normal. Who profits from this is criminal people from the underworld who came to build here in the basement and yard and make money from our land that they stole from us. Now the municipality is taking them to court it can go on for years. They have a lawyer to fix it for them so everything comes out in their favor. We have no lawyer to look after us. Whatever comes out in the case is no good for us. If they make them a deal or give them some fine they'll build in all the storerooms and the yard and on the roof and rent to criminals and people who take drugs and the few sick old people still left in the building won't be able to live here anymore. But who'll buy an apartment from them in such a building so what can they do, they go to those thieves and sell them their property for pennies that's not enough to live or die on as long as they can get out of here. And then the new owners take the whole building and fix it up nice and modern money they're not short of and then they rent and sell all the apartments for millions of dollars. And what if they lose the case even with their lawyer and connections in certain places, even then it's no good for us. They already shouted outside my door that if the court tells them to pull down what they already built there they'll blow up our whole building. Liars that they are I believe them they're capable of anything. But at least we should do what we can not wait for the municipality and this case that can take years but get a lawyer of our own to take them to court not sit and wait for all these things that I wrote to happen. And if the lawyer is an expert he can stop them from doing all the things I said they'd do. But the apartment owners don't want to give money for a lawyer after they themselves voted for it at the meeting they all want the others to give and Shwartz can break his head alone what to do. Nobody gave money everyone says why he can't nobody wants to help in this terrible situation. This is the end Mrs. Shifra this is the end of our building that was always so nice and there was order and good people lived here and even if there were quarrels sometimes never mind it happens between people but it was nice to live here and there was peace and quiet for everybody. Now it's all finished. That's

why Mrs. Shifra I resigned there's no more committee
the apartment owners already know from the telephone
that I told them and now I'm telling you in this letter
and also to say good-bye because I remember you as a
good and educated woman I always have respect for
you and I'm not cross with your husband either a
respectable and educated man too even if he said things
about me that I want to forget now. I don't know how
long I've got to live my situation is not good this letter
took me a week to write to you and I haven't got any
strength left.

Respectfully yours,
Shwartz Ariyeh
former Head of the House Committee

"Where are you? What's going on? You're never home. I'm terribly worried. Just call and tell me you're all right."

Ada's voice on the answering machine in her apartment in Givatayim. Her fourth call on the tape. And a few other, unimportant messages. After listening to the tape and going quickly through the mail she found in her mailbox, she stands and looks around. The furniture she acquired in her years of living here, the pictures hanging on the walls, all chosen with care and taste, the carpets, the bookshelves and records and knickknacks scattered about — all the things intended to set her personal stamp on the apartment, and which she had stopped noticing in the course of time. All this now arouses her hatred and disgust, makes her nauseous. She even shrinks from going up to the shelves and taking a few books and records, as she had intended doing, and hurries out of the apartment.

Outside she walks to the bus stop as the summer dusk fades into the night and waits for a bus to Tel Aviv. The cleaner hired by Hezi must have finished her work in the apartment ages ago and she can go home now. As she waits a feeling of weariness spreads through her body, accompanied by an oppressive sense of futility. Suddenly a car stops next to her and the driver, his features blurred in the darkening air, calls: "Gabi!" in a voice she doesn't recognize. She approaches the car warily and sees Oded smiling at her from the window. "Can I give you a lift?"

The car radio is playing preclassical music, and Oded turns down the volume when Gabi gets in and sits down beside him. "Where do you want to go?"

"Malkhei Yisrael Square, if it's on your way."

Oded starts the car. "And if it's not on my way, can't I take you where you want to go?" he says, and as he drives he keeps turning his head to look at her. There is a hesitant smile in his eyes, or maybe it's an ironic smile that he is trying to suppress.

"Go where you need to go," says Gabi, "and I'll get off at a place convenient for me to get to where I have to go."

"It's okay, I'm passing Malkhei Yisrael Square."

The sound of the singers' voices, one female and two male, accompanied by antique instruments, fills the car with boundless longings for harmony and peace of mind.

"Strange meeting up with you today," says Oded. "On Friday night I was over at Ada and Gadi's place, just like that evening when you were there, and I asked Ada about you. She said that she hadn't heard from you for a long time. Did anything happen between you?"

"No," says Gabi. "I work all day and when I come home I'm worn out. And on the weekend I have a million things to do. I never manage to get anything done. I'll phone her soon."

"I went there in the hope of seeing you."

"What's that music we're listening to?"

"Do you like classical music?"

"Yes."

"It's Monteverdi, 'Nisi Dominus.'"

Since Gabi is silent, he goes on to explain: "Psalm 127. 'Except the Lord build the house, they labor in vain that build it: except the Lord keep the city, the watchman waketh but in vain. It is in vain for you to rise up early, to sit up late, to eat the bread of toil: for so he giveth his beloved sleep. Lo, children are a heritage of the Lord: and the fruit of the womb is his reward. As arrows are in the hand of a mighty man so are the children of his youth. Happy is the man that hath his quiver full of them: they shall not be ashamed, but they shall speak with their enemies in the gate.' That's the whole Psalm."

"And you remember it all by heart?"

"It's not strange to me. I come from a religious home. And Vivaldi wrote a marvelous piece of music for the same psalm too. I've listened to it lots of times with the Hebrew text in my hand, so it's remained etched on my memory. If you like classical music, you should hear Vivaldi's 'Nisi Dominus.' I've got a beautiful recording of it with a wonderful contratenor."

He waits for her reaction, and when it fails to come, he adds: "If you liked, I would be very happy to invite you to my place to hear it."

"Thank you," says Gabi, "one day, when I have the time."

"Okay," he says, and in spite of the skeptical tone of his voice he takes a calling card out of his jacket pocket and offers it to her.

"For the time being I really haven't got a minute to spare, but maybe later." She studies the business card for a moment, out of politeness rather than any curiosity about where he works (a law firm; this is apparently the connection between him and Ada's husband), his address, or telephone number. The tape comes to an end, he removes it from the deck, and the "Voice of Music" comes over the radio: a Mozart piano concerto.

"I go to concerts a lot," he says. "I have a subscription for two to the Philharmonic, so if you're interested, I'd be glad . . ."

They pass the Northern railway station and go on driving up Arlozorov Street. At the corner of Bloch she says: "This is fine for me. I'll get off here."

"Do you want me to take you to the door? It isn't a problem for me."

"No, thank you, this is fine."

"As you wish."

He stops the car, she thanks him, and before she gets out he says softly: "Get in touch, okay?" And his voice sounds like a call carried on the wind from far away. "Give me a chance, you don't know me."

She crosses the street and glances back over her shoulder. His car is still standing in the spot where she got out, and she knows that he's watching her. After she turns onto Bloch Street and then onto one of the streets leading off it, she looks back again, to see if he's following her.

The next morning, when she arrives in the office, she finds a letter from her boss on her desk, informing her of the termination of her employment due to unsuitability and cuts in manpower. She decides not to wait until the end of the month, as the letter proposes, and without saying good-bye to the other girls in the office, who appear to be more absorbed in their work than usual, she leaves immediately.

The elevator is slow in coming and she is in a hurry to get out of there. She feels no disappointment or anger or worry, or even surprise. The whole thing seems of no significance to her. Just as she is about to turn away and go down the stairs, the elevator suddenly stops and Hezi steps out of it, walks quickly past her, and goes into the office.

By the time she recovers from the surprise, the door closes and the elevator continues on its way.

Gabi walks down the five flights, emerges onto the street, and gets on a bus. On the seat opposite her are two women. One of them is a young girl in jeans and a black sweater, and the other is older, Orthodox judging by her clothes, and wearing a hat.

"For weeks she sat at home and cried," says the younger woman, "she didn't want to go on living. They told her: You're young, beautiful, there will be someone else who'll love you and treat you well. It's lucky it ended this way, what would have happened if you married him, if you had children, and suddenly he left you without saying a word. And all she could say was: Only Remmy, Remmy, and Remmy, I never had another man and I never will, if I can't have Remmy I'd rather be dead. And after a while she finds out that she's pregnant."

"Didn't they see him, know what kind of a man he was?" asks the older woman.

"And how they saw him! He would come to the house, like one of the family, a nice guy, open and aboveboard, they all loved him. They were already talking about a wedding. And all of a sudden, he doesn't want to hear about her anymore. And she, poor thing, doesn't know why, can't understand what happened, keeps on calling him, and the minute he hears her voice on the phone, he hangs up. And now she's pregnant. The father went to talk to him where he works, and the guy says to him: It's not mine. It's someone else's. I don't love her anymore. She can forget me. And she swears on her mother's and her soldier brother's life that she's never been with anyone except Remmy.

And after a bit he leaves his job and moves away, nobody knows where he is anymore. And she, even after he trashed her like that, still went on loving him, praying for him to come back, not listening to anything anybody said. She stopped going to work, she didn't leave the house, she didn't even want to watch TV, all the time she just cried and called him: Remmy, Remmy, come back to me. And from all her crying and misery in the end she had a miscarriage, so she didn't have to have an abortion."

"God forbid!" says the Orthodox woman.

"To save her future and her family's honor," the young woman hurries to explain.

"What kind of honor is that, getting pregnant and wanting to have an abortion on top of it!" the older woman protests.

"For about six months she just stayed at home, she didn't go to work, she didn't go out, just sat and cried and called him to come back to her. They didn't know what to do with her. In the end they forced her to go back to work and they thought it would bring her back to life and she would gradually forget him."

"They should have taken her to the mental hospital," says the older woman. "If they didn't know how to look after her and bring her up to behave properly. It's all a question of education, of family."

"No, they're a good family, clean people. My parents still live next door to them. We grew up together, ate from the same plate. But she had no luck, maybe because she's so pretty. So she went back to work, and one day she was coming home from work on the bus and looking out the window, and suddenly in some courtyard on Herzl Street she sees written on the wall: 'RETURNS LOST LOVES. Entrance from the courtyard.' She never noticed it before. The next day she sees it again, and the next day again, and it stuck in her head. In the end she got hold of the money and she went there.

"Nobody knows what he did, that magician, and what went on there. He told her that if she revealed the secret to anyone, the spell wouldn't work and she'd be wasting her money. But when she came home she was quieter, she stopped crying, she started acting like she used to. Her family said that if all he did was get Remmy out of her head it was worth it.

"That night she already slept better and the next morning she went to work in a good mood. And after work she wants to buy something and gets off the bus in Allenby, and suddenly she sees that Remmy is standing in front of her on the sidewalk, as if he was waiting there for her to pass him. She stands still, she was in shock. She couldn't get a word out of her mouth. And he says to her: 'I love you, Riki, only you, I can't live without you.' And she asks him: 'So why did you leave me like that, where have you been all this time, why didn't you get in touch?' And he says: 'I wanted you to forget me, to find someone much better than me, someone who would give you a good life, like you deserve. All this time I've suffered and missed you, but I hoped that you'd forgotten me, that you were happy, and that gave me the strength to carry on. But a few days ago something happened to me that never happened in my life before. I'm sitting in my room in the afternoon and suddenly there's like an explosion in my heart. I thought I was going to die. I lost consciousness, and when I woke up, I felt that I had to see you, that I couldn't go on living without you, I loved you and missed you so much. I wanted to phone you right away, but I was afraid that maybe you'd already forgotten me and you were happy and I'd ruin it all for you. All night I couldn't sleep, and after work today I didn't want to go home. I didn't know what was happening to me, I started wandering around the streets without knowing where I wanted to go, and my feet brought me here, as if somebody was pushing me in this direction, and suddenly I see you in front of me.'

"'When did you feel that explosion in your heart?' she asks him.

"'Yesterday afternoon, at about five o'clock,' he says to her.

"And that was exactly when she was with that guy that returns lost loves."

The Orthodox woman, who up to now has been listening attentively and patiently to the story, can no longer keep quiet.

"How can you believe in such nonsense, how do you know that all that really happened, were you there?"

"She told my sister herself," the young woman replies.

"So she made it up."

"Why should she make up something like that, what good will it do her?"

"Beats me. All those magic spells are nonsense, and they're against the Torah too. Why do you believe those stories? Maybe they really did meet in the street by chance, and as soon as he saw her he felt like starting with her again, after everything he did to her, so she made up all that rigmarole to tell them at home so they would forgive him and agree to receive him again."

"It was exactly the opposite. Listen," the young woman says.

Throughout the journey Gabi is afraid the two women will get off the bus before the end of the story. And then the bus reaches her stop, and although she wants to get home as quickly as she can in the hope of receiving a telephone call that will explain everything, and perhaps hold out some kind of promise as well, she can't tear herself away from the riveting story and she continues the journey, not knowing where it will end.

"He says to her," the young woman goes on with her story, "'Let's go sit in a café and talk.' So they go to a café and talk, he asks her what happened to her all the time she didn't see him and tells her what happened to him, and she looks at him and says to herself: It looks just like Remmy, talks just like Remmy, knows all the details of their story, but nevertheless it isn't him, it's like somebody else. Everything's exactly the same, except for the look in his eyes, as if somebody else is looking out of them. He speaks to her lovingly and asks her to forgive him for what she went through because of him, he wants them to get back together and start all over again, he wants to marry her, and she, she sees something bad in his eyes, which was never there in the real Remmy's eyes, who she remembers as a good man even though he did what he did to her and dirtied her name. And she feels that she doesn't love him at all, she doesn't want to see him again, only to forget him forever. He asks her when he'll see her again, and she says: 'I don't know,' but he keeps at her, he won't let her go. He says to her: 'You're my woman and I'm your man. We can't live apart.' In the end, when they leave the café, she goes to take the bus home and he gets on after her and sits on the opposite bench and looks at her all the time with that evil look in his eyes. She goes home and he goes with her, talking to her all the time, he won't leave her alone, and she goes into the house and leaves him outside. He stays there all night, sitting on the ground and waiting. She doesn't say anything at home and they see that the happy mood she was in that morning is over, and she's sad again.

"In the morning she's afraid to go to work, because he's still there, waiting for her. In the end she gets up her courage and leaves the house and walks past him. He follows her and says to her: 'If you don't marry me I'll kill you. I've got nothing to lose, without you my life's not worth living.' And she says to him: 'I don't love you, you're not the Remmy I once knew, you're somebody else, and I don't want anything to do with you. I'll complain to the police that you're threatening me.' And he says: 'What do I care, let them throw me in jail. Without you my life's not worth living.'

"And he kept on following her all the time and waiting outside her work, outside her house, crying and cursing and threatening, not giving her any peace. She told her family, and they saw what was going on, that she was in real danger. Her soldier brother wanted to go and beat him up, but she wouldn't let him. They said they'd go with her to the police to complain, but she didn't want to. Maybe in spite of everything she was still a little sorry for him. She told them to wait one more day, because she was going back to that magician.

"And he followed her there too. When he saw where she was going he started to cry: 'Riki, don't do this to me, don't go there, it will kill me, don't kill me.' And he held onto her by force, he wouldn't let her go in. She nearly started to take pity on him when she saw how he was suffering and crying tears. But a minute before she gave in she managed to free herself from his grip and she ran into the magician's building. When the magician saw her coming to him again, he got a fright, and she told him what happened. He said to her: 'Maybe it's not the real Remmy, but some demon disguised as him who wants to take you on an evil path from which there's no return. Lucky for you that you didn't listen to him and fall into terrible danger. I'll do what has to be done now and everything will be all right, don't worry.' I don't know what he did, she won't tell anybody that either, in case something happens to her, but when she came out, that person wasn't there anymore, and she never saw him again. Two days later it said in the newspaper that he was killed at work. He worked with electricity and he was careless and on the spot he turned into coal. Nobody knows if it was an accident or on purpose."

The Orthodox woman bursts into nasty laughter and asks mockingly: "And the one who was killed, who was it, the demon or the real Remmy?"

"I don't know," the young woman mutters and falls silent, and her face suddenly clouds over with worry and doubt.

The two women get off at the next stop and Gabi sits rooted to the spot. From one stop to the next the bus empties until she's the last person remaining. From time to time the driver examines her in his mirror until he finally calls out: "Where do you want to go?"

"To the last stop."

Now that I don't speak and can't walk, it may be that I have less chance of making mistakes, because the less I interfere in what happens to me, the closer I come to my real situation. So why are there things that make me angry? Why do I care? My daughter goes on trying to persuade me that I'd be better off in a home for invalids (an "institution," she says, as if that makes it more dignified, more tempting) than at home with the girl. I'm not worried about the girl, she'll find work somewhere else.

But I've grown used to her. My daughter says it's not good for me to be alone, I should be with other people. But I'm not interested in other people. I was never interested in other people. They're like shadows to me. I can't even understand myself, all I need now is a crowd of shadows around me.

This afternoon my daughter came and brought Vicki with her — a social worker, is how she introduces the tall young woman. First of all Vicki looked the girl over with an expert eye, and it was obvious that she was looking for shortcomings. That already annoyed me. Even before she opened her mouth, I knew that I would do the opposite of whatever she said. And then she opened her mouth:

"Can you hear me?" she yelled. "Do you understand what I'm saying to you?"

I nodded my head at her: Yes, yes. But she kept on shouting. And my daughter sat on the sidelines and kept her mouth shut, she didn't tell her that she didn't have to shout. I let her yell herself hoarse.

"What's his name?" she asked my daughter in her normal voice, which I wasn't supposed to hear.

"Jacob," said my daughter.

"Jacob! How do you feel?" yelled Vicki. "Are you happy at home like this?"

I nodded.

"Does she know how to look after you? Is she a good girl, does she do everything you need for you?"

I nodded.

"You don't lack for anything?"

I shook my head.

"Jacob! Do you know that she's not a nurse and she doesn't understand anything about medicine, and if something happens she won't be able to help you?"

I nodded.

"So it would be better for you to be in place with medical supervision, with a doctor and nurses there all the time."

I shook my head.

"Jacob!" yelled Vicki. "You know that your physical condition isn't good. When you're in pain she won't be able to do anything for you. And if you have another stroke, by the time you reach the hospital it will be too late."

In her normal voice she asked my daughter: "Has she been with him long?"

"Almost a year," says my daughter.

"He's grown attached to her," said Vicki in a worried voice. And then she started yelling again: "Jacob! And what will happen when she goes back to her country, maybe then you'll want to move into an institution appropriate to your condition?"

I shook my head.

"So what then, you'll want someone else like her?"

I nodded.

"Jacob!" yelled Vicki. "You and only you will decide where you want to be. But I want to make a logical suggestion to you that I'm sure you'll accept. We'll take you to the institution for a week or even a few days, just so you can see what it's like and make an informed decision."

I shook my head.

"What do you have to lose, Jacob? You can always come back home and the girl will be here waiting for you. Just so you can see what it's like."

I shook my head.

"Jacob!" yelled Vicki. "Do it for me! Just go there for a visit, to see what it's like, and then come back home."

"It won't work," my daughter said to her. "He's as stubborn as a mule. Daddy!" She started yelling too, she learns fast. "Nobody wants to force you to do anything you don't want to do. If you don't want to go, stay home with the girl. I was only thinking of your own good, to be under medical supervision, to get the proper care, so that you don't suffer if anything happens. But if you prefer staying the way you are, that's all right."

I nodded in agreement.

"I want to talk to her," said Vicki to my daughter.

We were in the living room, and during the entire visit the girl sat passively on her bed on the covered balcony, as if waiting for her sentence. I had the feeling she understood what was going on: she looked tense, perhaps she was going to be fired and she would have to leave the house immediately. Now Vicki went onto the porch and began to question her in an English that was no better than the girl's: what she knew how to do and what she didn't know how to do, how long she had a permit to stay in the country, what her connection was with the agency that had brought her to the country. The girl answered quietly, as if under police interrogation. A little child-of-a-woman, not pretty, and poor, living in a strange land with an old invalid all day and night, instead of living her own life, and opposite her a big, strong commander.

The bell rang. My daughter went to open the door. It was Pedro. Lately he's been coming often to see the girl. Apparently he isn't working, except for Sundays, when he takes her place here. He shares the food she cooks for herself, and once I even saw them talking in her room and she went to the place where she hides the money she sets aside and doesn't send home and gave him some of it. He probably told her it was just a loan, but she won't see a penny of it again. I won't be surprised if he steals the lot one day.

The commander examined him with an expert eye. "Who's he?" she asked my daughter.

"He takes her place here on Sundays, when she's off."

"Today isn't Sunday," said Vicki, "so what's he doing here?"

I couldn't stand it any longer. I pushed my chair up to the commander, I shouted and waved my hands to shoo her out of the house. At first she pretended not to understand, and my daughter said: "Daddy, what's the matter, why are you angry?"

I did it again, and it was quite clear. I don't know if that woman was really from the social services, or if she was just a friend of my daughter, who brought her here under false pretenses to try to get me to go into a nursing home, which would oblige me to sell the apartment. The two of them beat a hasty retreat, and the girl got off her bed and looked at me questioningly — perhaps she didn't know what was going to happen to her now. I beckoned her to come to me. When she approached me, I took her hand in mine and pressed it hard, looked her in the eyes, and said: "Linda, Linda." And in my heart, without making a sound, I called loudly to her: I want you to stay with me always. And then I kissed her hand. When I raised my eyes, she smiled, and her face, which is usually expressionless and therefore looks so sad even when she's not sad, took on a feminine charm, like when she was angry with me after I pretended to be dead.

Pedro said: "You love Linda?" And he burst out laughing. "You know what is Linda? Linda is beautiful." He'd already said this to me before.

She scolded him in their language and I beckoned him to come closer, took his hand and pressed it, too.

"But please you don't kiss me," said Pedro, and he laughed again.

The girl and Pedro sat on the sofa and talked, and I remained opposite her balcony, with my daughter's and her friend's promises that what lay in store for me was suffering and pain. There are words that creep like worms straight into your heart. All the other things they said sank slowly like dust and only these words remained, together with the fear they brought with them. And I had already grown accustomed to thinking that one day I would simply go out like a candle. The thought of a healthy man and not one in my position.

The girl got ready to go do the shopping and agreed to take me with her. We went down in the elevator and set off, Pedro pushing my chair and the girl walking next to me, and I wanted it to be like this always, with the three of us together. We reached the supermarket, she went in and he stayed outside with me, standing behind me with a cloud of smoke from his cigarette over my head. We waited for her to come out, and then I signaled to them to continue to the playground. When we got there they put my chair next to a bench and sat down next to two young women keeping an eye from a distance on their children. And before I had a chance to see who the children playing there were — I had seen some of them before and some were new to me — the boy who had seen God came into the playground, leading his dog on a piece of rope tied around her neck.

One of the two young women sitting next to us, who was in an advanced stage of pregnancy and had her hair cut short like a boy's, said to her friend, the young woman with the blue eyes: "Just look at that." And she stood up and called out to the boy: "Don't come in here with the dog, there are small children here, it frightens them."

"No," said the boy, "don't be afraid, she's a good dog, she loves children."

The girl and Pedro smiled, they remembered him from the last time, in the park.

"That dog of yours looks terrible!" said the pregnant woman in a shocked voice. "Where did you find her? Maybe she's got rabies? Take her away! Anyway, dogs aren't allowed in here."

Her friend stood up too, approached the dog and inspected it. "How can you drag her around like that, with a rope?" she shouted at the boy. "Can't you see that it's made a cut on her neck? Poor thing! Take it off at once! Haven't you got any pity for her?"

"You don't know her. She has the soul of a saint," said the boy. "In a previous life she was a famous saint who performed miracles for our forefathers."

The boy tugged at the rope, walked up to the smoking Pedro, and asked for a cigarette. Pedro pretended not to understand.

"Take her out of here and undo that rope," said the young woman.

"She'll run away," said the boy.

"Of course she'll run away, if that's how you treat her."

"She's suffering," the pregnant woman explained to him. "It hurts her. Do you understand what I'm saying to you? You have to take her immediately to the SPCA so they can look after her."

"Can you spare me a cigarette?" the boy asked Pedro again.

The blue-eyed woman whispered something to her friend, and she asked the boy: "Where do you live?"

Pedro gave him a cigarette and lit it for him with his lighter. The boy took a few puffs, left it stuck between his lips, and bent down and tied the rope to the bench. He sat down on the ground at our feet, concentrating on his cigarette, and the dog came and lay down beside him. I saw the wound on her neck, it was full of flies and she turned her head from side to side to get rid of them.

"It's awful, I can't bear to look at it!" said the pregnant woman.

She and her friend went up to the swings and seesaws, collected their children, and left the playground.

It began to get dark and the playground emptied out. In the end the only people left were us, with the boy and his dog at our feet. The noise of the traffic and the voices from the street and the houses sounded far away, as if the dark, empty playground was a world unto itself. The swings and seesaws and jungle gyms now looked like shadows of frozen giraffes and giant birds that had fallen to the ground and were unable to rise again. A light breeze, maybe from the sea, freshened the air after hours of heat and humidity, caressing our faces. This time the girl did not hurry home. She and Pedro sat next to me and talked quietly, exchanging brief, matter-of-fact remarks, with long pauses of agreement between them. The way people talk when they've been together a long time and understand each other. My heart filled with love for them, and like a shadow, the fear of losing them accompanied this love. When had I ever experienced such moments before? I felt my soul longing to detach itself from my body, from its fetters, from its weight, to take off and drift through the air like a feather, to wherever the wind bore it.

The boy who had seen God stood up and turned to face us. The dog tied to the rope stood up too. He seemed unsteady on his feet, he looked at us with suspicion and fear, as if he had fallen asleep and didn't remember where he was.

"Maybe you could give us some food?"

He stood swaying on his feet, waiting for an answer, but none of us could answer him.

"I haven't got any strength," he sighed and sat down on the ground again at my feet, and the dog lay down next to him. His head dropped as if he had fallen asleep again.

I put out my hand and pointed to the little bag the girl always wore on her shoulder when she went out, with its strap crossing her chest. She didn't understand what I wanted. I repeated the gesture, and she pointed at the bag and said: "You want it?" I nodded. She removed the bag from her shoulder and gave it to me. I struggled with the clasp, unable to open it. She helped me. There's a little compartment inside it, closed with a zipper, where she hides her purse. She saw me trying to open the zipper, understood what I wanted, took the bag from me, removed the purse, and gave it to me. Pedro looked at me with a curious smile and said something to her, and she shook her head at him. I took out a banknote and returned the purse to her. I tapped the boy on the back. "I can't," he groaned, "I can't now. Leave me alone. Do me a favor."

I tapped him on the back again. He started in alarm, raised his head, and looked at the dark playground in front of him. "Where are they?" he asked. "They're waiting to come out already." Then he turned around, undid the rope tied to the bench, and stood up, and the dog stood up too. He stood still for a moment to steady himself before setting off. Pedro took the money from me and offered it to the boy, but he took no notice and stared into the darkness. The girl stood up and started pushing my chair. Pedro called out loud, to attract the boy's attention, and tried to give him the money again, but he took no notice. Pedro put the money in his pocket and she didn't say anything. The confused boy looked at the three of us for a moment in silence, as if waiting for us to return to the darkness from which we had emerged, and then he turned around and walked to the playground gate. We followed him to the street. He was swaying like a drunk, I imagined that he had nowhere to go, and in that hour of grace I couldn't help loving him too, and his dog tied to him by a rope, with the wound of love on her neck.

Dear Mr. Shwartz,

My feelings after reading your letter can be summed up
in one word: shock. First of all, the concern for your
health, and the heartfelt hope that perhaps you are
exaggerating, that in spite of everything your situation
is not as bad as you describe it. In any event, my husband and I wish you well from the bottom of our
hearts, and hope that you will recover and enjoy good
health and a long life.

We thank you very much for taking the trouble to
write to us in spite of your weakness in order to report
on the state of the building in Tel Aviv and to describe
the grim developments possible in the future. The
prospects are indeed dark and we are very concerned,
even supposing that the true situation is not as grim as
the horrors you described in your letter — for we cannot imagine that the picture is as unrelievedly black as
you describe, without a single ray of light.

In your letter you stress the financial problem again,
and there is no doubt that it is indeed a source of concern, but money, dear Mr. Shwartz, for all its importance, is not the main thing in life. The main thing is
man! The crucial and urgent question to be answered, as
we have already hinted in our previous letter, is this:
How did things reach such a state? Why was the deteri-
oration not halted before it was too late? Who fell
asleep at his post? First of all these questions must be
clarified, so that those responsible can be called to
account.

In spite of your weariness and poor health we do not
think that this is the time to let go of the wheel and
allow the ship to sink, but on the contrary, not to
despair, not to surrender, to gather the vestiges of your
strength and continue the struggle until we reach safe

harbors. We cannot, therefore, accept your resignation from the important role you have been performing for so many years to the best of your ability. There is no doubt in our minds that you took this hasty decision in a moment of despair and anger, and knowing you as well as we do we are sure that you have already recovered from this moment of weakness and are ready once more with renewed strength to embrace your important and difficult mission. We wish you a speedy recovery and assure you of our moral support in any step you take to correct the shocking situation you described so vividly in your letter.

My husband and I send our warmest regards to your dear wife and to your daughter and her family.

Shifra Barzilai

Mali stops the car next to his house and before he can thank her, say good-bye, and get out of the car, she says:

"Don't people ever ask you why you never married?"

"When I was younger they did. Not anymore. They could ask you the same question."

"Right."

An ambulance enters the street, and Mali, skillful driver that she is, immediately moves over to the left, drives up onto the sidewalk, and makes way for it. The ambulance stops in front of Aviram's building. The driver and the paramedic sitting next to him get out of the ambulance, take a stretcher out of the back, and go up to the entrance to the building. From the window of Mali's car Aviram sees them standing outside the door for a few seconds, then pushing it open and going inside.

Mali switches off the engine.

"Things didn't work out for me," she says. "The men I wanted didn't want me, not to start a family at any rate, and the men who wanted me I didn't want. And that went on until I began to worry that if I waited any longer I wouldn't be able to have children anymore, so I decided to become a single parent. I've never regretted it. I did the right thing."

"And the little girl's father?"

"That's not something I talk about," says Mali.

"The same with me," says Aviram, "if I wanted anyone she didn't want me, and if someone wanted me I didn't want her. The way I look, which isn't exactly Paul Newman, I never had much of a chance of finding someone I wanted who would want me too."

"Why do you say that? You look just fine. If only you'd shave off that beard."

"What has everyone got against my beard?" asks Aviram, half-insulted, half-amused.

Mali looks at him appraisingly: "It's like a mask, you hide behind it. Without that beard you'd probably feel naked."

"No, it's a part of me, like my hands and feet."

"Maybe you're attracted to women you know in advance you have no chance with?"

"I could say the same thing to you, but I don't believe in psychological bullshit."

"People who don't get married remain children all their lives," says Mali.

"And people who do get married don't remain children?"

"Not the women. The men do remain children as long as they live."

Where does she get all these truths from? The conversation is beginning to get on his nerves. He looks at his watch.

"The dog's waiting," says Mali.

"Yes."

Before opening the front door, he sees the ambulance men coming down the stairs carrying Mr. Shwartz on the stretcher, covered with a blanket, with his wife behind him holding up an infusion bag attached to a tube that disappears under the blanket. Aviram opens the door for them. Mr. Shwartz's eyes are closed, but his face, covered with white stubble, is wrathful, like the face of a man who had fought many battles in his life and hasn't given up yet. When they pass him, Mrs. Shwartz looks at Aviram accusingly and nods her head as if to say: Yes, yes, yes.

He stands in front of the door to his apartment and the silence freezes his heart. He presses the bell a few times to arouse the joyful barks that always greet him when he comes home from work, but nothing happens. His hands are trembling so much that he can hardly fit the key into the lock.

There's a bad smell in the closed apartment. The dog is lying in his corner, and next to him is a dark puddle of urine and diarrhea. Aviram bends over him, he raises his head a little, opens his eyes, utters a short, strangled whimper, and drops his head.

Aviram phones the vet, who reassures him and tells him to put a bowl of water in front of the dog and coax him to drink, and to bring him to the clinic. "Drink, sweetheart, please drink," Aviram begs the dog. He strokes his head. "Drink, it will do you good," he says and brings the bowl closer, dipping his snout into the water, but in vain. With the last of his strength the dog turns his head away from the bowl, half-opens one bleary eye that seems to contain all the sorrow and helplessness in the world, and looks at him as if to say: Why bother, nothing will help me now.

Aviram phones for a cab, picks up the dog, and carries him downstairs in his arms. Coming up opposite him is the pretty woman from next door, holding a plastic shopping bag. He greets her with a nod, and she, as usual, ignores him with a blank look on her face. When he steps aside to let her pass he gives her a look of protest. "My dog's been poisoned!" he says, and after she climbs a few stairs he calls after her: "Somebody poisoned my dog!" He himself is surprised by his words: Why did he say that? What gave him the idea that his dog had been poisoned? But the moment the words are said they turn into a firm fact that fills his heart with rage against his persecutors and pity for himself. Now all he has to do is discover the identity of the poisoner.

He stands on the pavement waiting for the taxi with the dog in his arms. The ginger woman who owns the storeroom emerges from the yard. She and her husband have not been seen there for some time. When she sees him, she comes up, bursts out laughing, and shouts in the direction of the backyard: "Moshe, come quickly, get a look at this!"

Aviram now has the answer to his question. He remembers how she once threatened to pay somebody twenty dollars to poison his dog.

The man in the red Olympic cap comes out of the yard and joins her. "Leave him alone, Yaffa," he pleads. "You promised not to talk to them anymore."

"What's the matter with you? Who's talking to him? I'm talking to you," she says, "get a look at him holding his baby. A pity there isn't someone from the television here to take a picture."

"Stop it, that's enough," says her husband. "Come on," and he pulls her back into the yard.

The cab driver asks him if there's something wrong with the dog. "He's sick," says Aviram. "Look here," says the driver, "don't let him puke on the upholstery. Something like that happened to me a while ago and you can't get if off with any cleaning agent. I had to change all the upholstery in the car."

"If he dirties the upholstery, I'll pay you whatever it costs," says Aviram.

In the mirror he sees the worried face of the driver, inspecting the backseat to see if the dog is already vomiting.

"Someone poisoned him," says Aviram, and he doesn't know why he said it. He has never gotten into a conversation with a taxi driver before.

The driver doesn't react. From time to time Aviram sees his face in the mirror, watching him anxiously.

"And I know who did it."

"That dog looks dead," says the driver.

"He's not dead."

The vet too does not take seriously the suggestion that the dog has been poisoned but says nothing in reply, out of respect for his client, and satisfies himself with a routine diagnosis of a virus causing dehydration of the digestive system. "He's getting old," he says to Aviram, "you'd better get used to the idea. He's becoming weaker and he'll get sick more often."

But Aviram persists in his claim, which fits into a wider range of signs that have appeared in his life recently.

"Your theory has no basis in logic. You're being hysterical," Ilan says to him. The dog, which Aviram brought with him to the office from the vet's, lies at his feet and seems to be asleep, apparently under the influence of the drugs administered by the vet.

"Who would break into an apartment, and twice too, in order to poison a dog?" asks Ilan.

"Some junkie who needs drugs and gets money from those people to do it."

"And why should those people pay for a thing like that? Why should they take the risk? If the junkie's caught, he'll turn them in without thinking twice about it. Why on earth should they take the risk?"

"It's a fact that she said they'd do it," insists Aviram, "and today when she saw me waiting for the taxi with the dog, you should have heard how she laughed. Like someone who'd succeeded in carrying out her plans."

"Avi, you slay me with your naïveté. They've got enough problems with their illegal building, and they have to make a good impression in court, so you think they'd risk getting into trouble for such nonsense?"

"You don't know those people. If you heard the way she yells and curses all the time — she's not sane. She's capable of anything."

"Look here, Avi, there's no need to get carried away. Maybe they're not very nice people and their manners aren't exactly to our taste, so what? What have they done that's so terrible? What's the big catastrophe if a storeroom that was empty and disused is turned into a little apartment for somebody to live in? And what if it's not for their poor daughter, like they say, and they're building like that in all kinds of places in town to rent or sell, and making good money out of it — so what? Good luck to them! I wish a lot more people would do the same. Those neighborhoods in the north of town, four stories with a garden in front that nobody uses and that silly arch they cut in the hedge at the entrance, and a backyard full of weeds and thorns and garbage bins. All that may have been appropriate for the old days of the British Mandate, when they decided that Tel Aviv was going to be a garden city and laid down that style of building for everyone. But today when there's such a terrible parking problem, and people come home from work and there's nowhere for them to park their cars — who needs those silly gardens? Instead of the gardens in the backyards there could be proper parking for the residents' cars. And why shouldn't people build fifth and sixth stories on their roofs, and find a place to put in an elevator? And who needs all those storerooms and basements? Why shouldn't people live there? Believe me, if it's done in an orderly and aesthetic way this city will be much better adapted to our times and it will be a far more pleasant place to live in."

And while Ilan is describing his urban vision to him, Aviram looks at his dog and sees the rhythmic movement of its breathing.

"I think he's feeling better," says Ilan, sensing that Aviram's attention is not on his words but on the dog. "He's sleeping."

"I was terrified," says Aviram. "I thought he was going to die."

A client enters the office, Ilan turns away to attend to him, and Aviram tries to concentrate on his work, but the dog's quiet sleeping fails to dispel his master's anxiety. The dog is old, and this is what he has to look forward to now. In this whole city, he says to himself in a new, unfamiliar voice — or perhaps it's an old but long-forgotten voice — in this whole happy, hedonistic city, with its pubs crowded every night, with its pretty, radiant girls, with its strong, healthy youngsters, its rich, successful men who can get whatever they want, its theaters and concerts and exhibitions and intellectuals and journalists and soldiers and athletes — wherever I look, as if some evil spell has been cast upon me, always, at every turn, all I see is misery and old age and illness and filth.

At night the fear and despair banish from his heart the belief he cultivates during the day that he can break the spell. Till midnight the radio next to her bed quietly plays classical music, and these sounds bathe and caress her smooth, white, catlike body, the mysterious shadows kissing the secrets of her ripe, haughty nakedness before penetrating the wall and reaching his ears. Sometimes he hears a sigh or complaint rising from her sleep, little grunts of objection or pampered mews. And in the morning, the electronic beeping of her alarm clock sends a cold shiver down his spine, and then the radio comes on again with the news. The man's voice hasn't been heard there for a long time, and the phone hasn't rung ever since that call late at night from abroad. Only a few centimeters of a rather flimsy wall separate them, but the road he has to travel to reach her is interminably long.

Menashe called them a few minutes after they came home: "After you left I talked to him. I told him: 'Your father loves you so much and he's terribly worried about you, and that's why he lost his temper and spoke to you like that.' And he said: 'Bullshit, he loves the country and the army, that's what's important to him, not for me to be happy.' After what you said to him I was afraid he wouldn't want to have anything more to do with you, and we have to keep the 'channels of communication' open, as they say. If Mother had a telephone he would probably call her directly, because she's the only one he trusts. But he can only contact her through me, so I can keep my finger on the pulse, and if there's any problem and he needs help, he'll have to contact me."

Ezra listened tensely to Menashe's explanations, but they did not seem to satisfy him. "We have to get him back into the army, Menashe, that's the best solution for him personally, and it's also the right thing to do. There's no other way. Where is he now? Did he stay at Mother's?"

Menashe said nothing.

"You're hiding things from me, Menashe. You promised him you wouldn't tell me."

"Ezra, I need him to trust me, in order to know what's really happening to him. Don't you trust me? We have the same goal, we have to reach it in a more intelligent way."

"I know I shouldn't have spoken to him like that, it wasn't right. But I was in shock, you understand, Menashe, I've never heard him use words like that before. Who talks like that in our house? And about the army and the country! And how dare he talk like that in front of his grandmother, in front of his parents. I don't understand. I can't believe I heard it."

"Look, Ezra, that boy knows exactly what he wants and what he doesn't want, and fighting and yelling won't get you anywhere."

"What will?"

"He has to come to it by himself."

"In other words, let him hang around and hide and wait for him to break?"

"Yes."

"He'll get into trouble in the kind of places he hides out in, with junkies and pimps, he'll become a criminal, he'll ruin his life and ours."

"Ezra, he's not a child, he's not a fool, he's got a strong character, he'll do only what he wants to do."

"He's got no respect, no conscience, you heard how he talked about pretending to be a homo to get out of the army."

After he put down the receiver Ezra sat down and buried his face in his hands. Ruthie, who had been standing next to him during the phone conversation, thought that he was devastated by some new detail his brother had given him over the phone.

"What is it, Ezra," she said, "what's wrong?"

"Ruthie, I said terrible things to Eyalie, things a father should never say to his son. You were right. I'll never forgive myself as long as I live. It's because he's trampling on the things that are most sacred to me. And the words he used — I was in shock.

But the love of a father for his son is sacred too. He's not a child anymore, he's a man, and I'm not used to it yet."

"So what are you thinking of doing, Ezra?" asked Ruthie.

He raised his head with a resolute expression on his face: "Tomorrow morning, first thing, I'm going to call the army number they gave us and I won't get off their backs until they find that Hagai that spoke to me, and I'll tell him where Eyal's hanging out, in that mall next to the central bus station. I won't tell him that we saw him at my mother's, so as not to involve her and Menashe. And I'll ask that Hagai why the army isn't doing anything to find him. Ruthie, it's their duty."

"And what does Menashe think about it?"

"He thinks we should let him break, wait until he gets sick of hiding and wants to turn himself in. Ruthie, if he has to break, I prefer him to break in military jail and not among whores and junkies. It's much better for him that way."

"And I think, Ezra, that you shouldn't do it. We have to stand by Eyal, not take sides against him. You yourself said that he isn't a child anymore and you're not used to it yet. If he wants to keep on running away from the army, he knows what's best for him. And even if he's wrong, it's his right to do what he thinks best. All we have to do is help him when he asks for help, to let him know that he can rely on us."

The next morning, Ezra again called the army number he had been given. This time Hagai himself answered, he knew at once who the missing soldier was and listened to Ezra's story about how he had been seen next to the central bus station and how he and Menashe had gone to look for him there.

"Tell me, are you trying to make fools of us?" asked Hagai. "Why did you wait so long to let us know? What good does it do us now? You have to report something like that immediately. From the point of view of the law, you're aiding and abetting a deserter, because you knew where he was and you didn't report it immediately."

"Listen here, Hagai," Ezra explained, "I want him to be found more than you do, but you're not doing anything."

"You think the IDF's got the manpower to conduct house-to-house searches in Tel Aviv or go chasing all over the country after every soldier who goes AWOL or escapes from jail and goes into hiding? That's why we need the cooperation of the families. The next time you have any contact with him, report it at once, and if there's no reply on this line, then report it to the civilian police."

Ezra promised to do as he said and expressed hope that the affair would be concluded soon and Eyal would return to jail to serve his sentence, and then rejoin his unit.

Ruthie said: "I'm very angry about what you're doing, Ezra. You don't listen to me and do only as you see fit. I don't want to get into that whole argument again, but I'm telling you that what you're doing is a betrayal of our Eyal, a betrayal of his trust. I promised him, in both our names, that we were on his side, that he could trust us. And now he'll never believe us again."

Ezra was silent, it was evident that he was wounded by his wife's words, but he restrained himself in order to avoid any more arguments.

A few days later the boy phoned. Ezra picked up the phone and as soon as he heard his voice he cried: "Eyalie, I'm sorry for what I said to you at Grandma's house. You're my son and I love you and I only lost my temper like that because of those words you used."

"Okay," said Eyal. "Can I speak to Mom?"

"Where are you?" asked Ezra.

"I have to speak to Mom," said Eyal.

"Why don't you answer me, Eyalie?"

"My phone card's nearly finished."

Ezra handed the phone to Ruthie while cupping his hand over the mouthpiece. "He doesn't want to talk to me," he said to her, "ask him where he is."

"Mom," said Eyal, "I need a bit of cash. Bring it to Menashe, I don't want to . . ."

The conversation was cut off, the card was apparently finished. Eyal's voice disappeared into thin air and Ruthie's heart froze in fear. She held the receiver out to Ezra so that he could hear the staccato signal, and there was a look of despair in her eyes.

"What did he say to you?" demanded Ezra. "Why are you so pale?"

"He needs money. He probably hasn't got anything to eat."

"Where does he want us to take it?"

"To give it to Menashe."

"He didn't say where he was."

"No."

"If we don't know where he is, I've got nothing to report to the army. Ruthie, you heard, I said I was sorry, and he, instead of also saying he was sorry for the words he used, wasn't even prepared to talk to me," complained Ezra.

"What are we going to do, Ezra?" asked Ruthie. "He needs money for food. And if he hasn't got money for a telephone card, how is he going to get in touch with us?"

"You're saying that we should help him to go on being a deserter?"

"Yes, Ezra, I'm saying we have to help him in any way he asks."

And she wondered about the words Eyal had said to her before they were cut off, trying to decipher their meaning, as if they held a clue to the future: "I don't want to . . ." What was it that he wanted to say and didn't have time to say — what didn't he want?

In the mornings, after his master goes to work, the neighbor's dog howls behind the bedroom wall. She sits on the bed and listens tensely to its howling, like a music lover listening to a new performance of a familiar work. A high wolfish howl of longing and loneliness bursts out and rises and subsides with the loss of breath, and then comes a moment of silence, and then another howl, long and piercing, and sometimes there are lengthy silences with only an occasional choked whimper interrupting them from time to time. And as in the poem that Ada showed her, it seems to her then that the walls of the house are wincing in pain inside the plaster.

At midday the howls suddenly give way to grateful, joyful barks. The door of the adjacent apartment slams, and she hears her neighbor showering words of love on his dog. Some time later the door slams again and the stairwell echoes to the proud, triumphant barks of the dog going out for a walk with its master, after which the sounds die down and silence descends on the building.

After the telephone has been silent for days, it suddenly rings and startles her from her place: three rings, a pause, and then another ring.

"How are you doing?"

"I'm doing all right," she replies in a voice colder than she had intended.

"Why are you so sour?" he sounds surprised, if not disappointed.

She suppresses her instinctive retort. Better to play his game and not appear as the offended, rejected one: "No, not at all! I'm happy to hear your voice. How was your trip?"

"Okay, but it was a lot of work. And ever since coming back, too, I haven't had a moment to give you a ring."

"Never mind," says Gabi, "we're all very busy people. The main thing is that everything's okay with you. Are you speaking from the office?"

"No, from a phone booth. Listen, I've just heard that you've stopped working for us."

"Yes," says Gabi. "It didn't suit me."

"Pity. Look, there's a problem with the apartment. We have to vacate it by the end of the month."

"All right," says Gabi.

"So when are you leaving?"

"It's still two weeks till the end of the month, what's your problem? Is it so urgent for me to leave right away?"

"No, but what difference does it make to you? You still have your apartment. You didn't rent it, did you?"

"No, but I still have all kinds of arrangements to make."

"What arrangements?"

Silence.

"You're angry. Believe me, this is the last thing I would have wanted."

"I'm not angry, why should I be angry?"

"I'll come around and we'll talk about it in a friendly, civilized way, okay?"

"There's no need. You're busy and I don't want you to waste your time. I'm busy too."

"What are you busy with?"

Silence.

"Okay. I'm coming now. Make something nice for lunch, you're such a good cook."

"Perhaps some other time? It's not very convenient for me today."

"I'll see you in a little while."

She sits down again and in her mind's eye she sees the sequence of pictures that have come to haunt her before, when she sensed that she was losing him and that she wouldn't be able to go on without him:

Without warning he shows up at their secret apartment like someone escaping from his persecutors. Pale and gasping he falls onto the bed, burning with fever. Chills shake his body. "I'm so cold," he murmurs. She takes off his shoes, lifts his legs onto the bed, pulls him by the shoulders until his head is resting on the pillow, and covers him with her down quilt. He tries to sleep but his body continues to shiver with cold. She adds woolen blankets to the quilt. It seems to her that he has stopped shivering and is about to fall asleep. She sits down opposite the bed and looks at his pale, bewildered face. Suddenly his eyes open — narrowed and glittering strangely. He turns his face toward her and looks at her suspiciously, as if wondering what she has to do with him, until his eyelids grow too heavy to stay open. She sits looking at him like this for a long time, she has no idea how long, until he grows restless and pushes the blankets down to his waist. She bends over him to see what the matter is. The smell of his body, which by now has become the smell of her love, breaks out sharply and aggressively and floods her head. He is bathed in sweat. His clothes are wet, as are the pillowcase and sheet he is lying on. She fetches a towel and wipes his face and neck with it, removes the covers, and takes off his sweaty shirt. With his eyes closed he helps her and shifts his body from side to side. When she pulls his undershirt over his head he sits up, raises his arms obediently, opens his eyes and looks straight into her eyes. After that she takes off his trousers and his underpants and wipes the sweat off his body with the towel, moves him to the other side of the bed, next to the wall, which is still dry, and covers his nakedness with a clean sheet and a single woolen blanket. "I'm thirsty, do you have a cold beer in the fridge?" he asks. She goes to the kitchen and brings him a can of beer. He sits up in bed, opens the can, and sips the beer slowly. "Ah, that's good," he says. After a few sips he holds out his hand to her and she comes closer and takes it. He pulls the back of her hand to his mouth and kisses it and doesn't let go. He looks around the room. "We'll stay here until we escape overseas, to a place where they can't find us. We'll be far away and free." — "When will that be?" she asks. — "Sooner than you think, I'm working on it all the time." He finishes the beer and hands her the empty can. "Come, get into bed," he says with a smile, "I'm ready now."

The key rattles in the lock without opening the door. Is he using the wrong key by mistake, has he forgotten to bring the key to the apartment with him? He rings the bell and she waits a moment, then goes to the door, looks through the peephole, and sees his face. Beads of sweat are visible on his upper lip. She opens the door and he gives her a friendly smile, which disappears as soon as the door closes. "Why is everything shut up? The whole place smells of cooking." And he goes immediately to open the windows in the rooms and the kitchen. When he comes back into the living room the polite smile returns to his face. Gabi is glad that she didn't make herself pretty for him and stayed in the same clothes she put on in the morning. He sits down on one of the two easy chairs on either side of the table and inspects the room, as if to ascertain that everything is still in its place. She stands opposite him on the other side of the table. A man with a blank face and white hair is sitting in front of her and smiling in an attempt to hide his fear that he has lost control of the situation.

"Why didn't you want me to come?" he asks with a questioning smile.

"And why did you want to come?"

"What kind of a question is that? I wanted to see you!"

"You came to throw me out of the apartment."

"We agreed that you could stay here until the end of the month."

"Don't worry, I have no intention of hanging onto you against your will. You won't see me or hear from me anymore."

"Why? I want us to keep in touch."

"But I'm not interested. The only connection I had with you was physical. But I don't feel any attraction to you any longer. You don't interest me anymore. I can't even think of having sex with you. It revolts me."

"You want to punish me."

He gets up, comes over to her, pulls her to him by force, and embraces her. "I don't want to," she says, "leave me alone, I don't want to." She tries to push his hands away, but he struggles with her and won't let go. The smell of his body envelops her. And like an alarm bell the cry rises inside her, spreading and echoing through her body: I can't resist it, I can't resist that smell! He buries his head in the hollow between her neck and her shoulder and his hand gropes under her shirt, strokes her back and waist, his breath warms her neck, and his voice, commanding and imploring at once, sounds as if it is coming from her throat: "You do want me, you want me now."

On the other side of the wall a wolfish howl of longing and loneliness suddenly breaks out, a single howl lengthening and dying away as the animal's breath runs out, and afterward silence. She feels the rage rising inside her, and she begins to struggle to free herself again. Surprised by her renewed resistance, he stops caressing her and raises his head. For a moment he examines her face, and then he puts his hands on her shoulders and pushes her violently away. She recoils and retreats to the end of the room, and he sits down on the armchair again, panting and averting his face from her, and goes back to inspecting the walls and the furniture. She remains standing in the place to which he pushed her and looks at him curiously. In the end he raises his face to her:

"Maybe you'd like me to hit you. I won't do you that favor." Then he says with a forced, affected laugh: "What's gotten into you today?"

"What do you take me for, some pathetic little bimbo?"

"Get real. One little smile from a bimbo in the street excites me a lot more than anything I can get from a cultivated old maid like you."

"So you've decided to throw me out and bring some little bimbo here instead, or is it simply that you can't go on stealing money from the firm to pay the rent for this apartment?"

"You're completely out of your mind, what the hell are you talking about?"

"Don't worry. I'm not going to tell anybody about it. Or about your bank accounts abroad either. You're in no danger from a vindictive mistress here."

He looks at his watch.

"Are you in a hurry? I'm not keeping you."

"No, I have time."

"You know, when I started working at the firm, they told me to beware of you, to keep away from a shit called Hezi. In those words."

"And do you think so too?"

He looks insulted, she is surprised that he should care what she thinks of him.

"Do you care?"

"You really hate me," he mumbles.

"The truth is I don't." She comes and sits down in the armchair opposite him: "Look, what happened is that I got involved with a man that I never really loved, and that I have nothing in common with."

"And wasn't it ever good for you with me?"

"I suffered more than I enjoyed myself."

"This moment always has to come," he says softly, to her or to himself, "there's no way of avoiding it." There is a hurt expression in his eyes, and for some reason this embarrasses her.

"There is something about you that I loved," she says.

His face asks: What?

"The smell of your body."

"And that's not enough?"

"The cultivated old maid needs more than that."

He gets up to go, stands still for a minute looking at her with a questioning expression, perhaps he's waiting for her to get up too and come over to him, make some kind of farewell gesture. But she stays where she is, averting her face and waiting for him to go. The neighbor's dog breaks into joyful barks in anticipation of his master, who is climbing the stairs on his way to their midday meeting. Hezi leaves and slams the door behind him, and Gabi hurries to the peephole. She gets there in time to see him standing on the landing for a few seconds and looking thoughtfully at the door, and then he leaves her field of vision and disappears. And only his head of hair, for the briefest of instants, like a shooting star in a dark, hollow sky, leaves a trail of whiteness on the fish-eye lens before it blurs and vanishes without a trace. She knows in her heart that she will never see him again. And in the split second between his being there and his disappearance, she realizes that only now is she beginning to really know the meaning of love.

The barking of the dog has muffled the sound of Aviram's footsteps on the stairs. In front of her door he sees the man and doesn't know if he's coming or leaving. The man gives him a worried look, as if he has been caught red-handed, and hurries away. I know that guy with the beard from somewhere, Aviram imagines him saying to himself, but I can't place him. After an hour, after a day or two, perhaps the man will suddenly remem-

ber the insignificant clerk sitting behind the computer in the corner of the Northern Star offices, while Ilan came forward to
greet the client with the expression he reserved for such occasions, that of an important CEO up to his neck in complicated
international business deals. From Aviram's corner the two of
them had looked then like a couple of impostors trying to con
each other. Ever since the apartment next door had been rented
to serve as a meeting place for the lovers, Aviram had not set
eyes on the man. And now, after his voice has not been heard
there for weeks, Aviram has suddenly bumped into him on the
landing and revealed his identity as the neighbor on the other
side of the wall.

Any incident of this nature, which to a casual observer might
seem nothing more than a coincidence, served as another sign-
post to Aviram, one more sign on the road leading to the trap.
The road went around and around in ever-diminishing circles,
each circle bringing him closer and closer to the trap into which
he would inevitably fall.

Mr. Shwartz, in a thick dressing gown and woolen slippers,
steps out of the taxi that stops outside the building and his wife
helps to steady him on his feet. The taxi drives off and they
shuffle slowly to the entrance. Before Aviram, who is taking the
dog out for a walk, can escape and slip away by the path at the
side of the garden, Mr. Shwartz sees him and waves. The dog
begins to bark, and Aviram has to grab hold of his collar to stop
him from pouncing on the old couple. He asks Mr. Shwartz
how he is, but the old man ignores the polite question and goes
straight to the matter preoccupying him:

"What's going on over there, have you seen them?"

"Have I seen who?" Aviram asks ingenuously. "What are you
talking about?"

"You don't know what I'm talking about?"

His wife opens the door for the old man and urges him to go
inside, but he refuses.

"Come there with me now!" he commands Aviram.

"I have to take the dog for a walk."

The old man says nothing, his face flushes with anger.

Aviram sees the pretty neighbor coming down the stairs and approaching them. She greets them, stops next to them, and strokes the dog, who stops barking and responds to her stroking. The old man struggles with his wife, who is trying to push him inside, and the neighbor asks: "Can I help?"

"What do you want?" demands Mr. Shwartz. "What are you doing here?"

"Just now comes in taxi from hospital," his wife laments to the young woman.

The old man scolds her in their language, but she ignores him and goes on telling Gabi her story:

"He nearly died there in hospital, now must to be in bed, and he — only to go in yard, to see Friedberg's storeroom. He want to die? I die first. I got no more strengths for him, I sick woman too." Her birdlike face twists and her mouth gapes as if she wants to scream and the scream is stuck in her throat.

Gabi puts her hand on the old woman's shoulder to encourage her. Mr. Shwartz gives her an accusing look and his lips tremble: "What are you doing to this building, eh? What do you want of our poor building? Are you happy now? Everything's ruined!" He grabs hold of Aviram's arm and hangs on to it. "Come there with me, help me to get there, she won't let me go. She doesn't understand anything. Did you see them? What are they up to?"

"They haven't been here," says Aviram. "Don't worry."

The old man shakes his head and his face expresses disbelief and despair: "Did you go even once to see what they're doing there? Ever since they moved the garbage to the other side, did you ever come here? You're not interested. Maybe someone moved in to live there? But what do you care? Our whole building can go to hell!"

"There's nobody there!" Aviram insists. "They don't come here anymore." He looks at Gabi, scrutinizing her face for the hint of a smile of agreement as to the old man's craziness. She goes on stroking the dog. "He doesn't let just anyone stroke him," Aviram says to her.

"And why does he let me?"

"Maybe he thinks you're a part of his territory."

Mr. Shwartz raises his eyes to the sky, which is full of dark, heavy clouds. "I hope it rains and rains and doesn't stop raining all winter," he say to Aviram. "I hope there's a flood! You know why? Not just for our country and for the agriculture and the water supply" — he looks suspiciously at the young woman stroking the dog and pulls Aviram closer to him; a sly smile lights up his dull eyes and he whispers the secret in his ear: "In the years when there was a lot of rain, Friedberg had trouble in his storeroom. You know what groundwater is? If there's a good winter and it rains a lot, the ground fills with water and it rises under the floor there and the whole storeroom fills up like a pool. What didn't Friedberg do: he brought all kinds of experts, they dug everywhere, poured in concrete, put down tar, plastic, they tried all kinds of things, and nothing helped. You know how strong water is? Nothing can stop it. And now that those people opened the wall down below too, and made a terrace under the ground, the water will come in from there too, under the door. Oh God! Please let there be a good winter, let there be a flood!"

Like an elixir of youth this vision rejuvenates Mr. Shwartz. Again he pushes his wife in the direction of the yard and she resists and tries to push him to the front door, but the power of his obstinacy overcomes her resistance, and she gives in and leads him slowly to his goal.

Aviram whispers to Gabi, who has remained standing there: "How do you like that? I was sure he was already in the world beyond. And suddenly he pops up again, as obsessed as ever. With one foot in the grave he still won't let go. That's what keeps him alive — his war against those people."

"Hatred gives you strength," she says.

Aviram's voice rises and grows more confident: "It's not that I feel sorry for those crooks who built there in the basement; don't get me wrong: I hope they force them to pull down what they did there and that they'll go away. But with him it's become a real obsession. As if it's his way of fighting death."

"And his poor wife, what's she guilty of?"

"Nobody's guilty. Not even those crooks, they're not to blame either — everyone is what he is, and that's all there is to it."

She strokes the dog again. "When he's left alone at home," she says, "I hear him crying he misses you so much, really crying."

"I've never heard that," he says. "When I come home he senses me in the distance and barks for joy. I miss him too when he's not with me. Sometimes I can hear myself crying too, deep down inside."

The dog raises his head and his sad eyes say to them: What's all the fuss about?

They go out onto the street and Aviram says to her: "I'm taking him for a bit of a walk."

"I'm going to the store."

"We'll walk you there."

But the dog breaks into barks of protest and refuses to go with them. Aviram talks to him coaxingly and pulls his collar, but to no avail.

"What's the matter with him?" asks Gabi.

"He can't stand changes in his regular route. We only pass the store on our way home. It's always the same with him, he's stubborn as a mule, like all old creatures."

"Is he old?"

"In human terms, he's nearly eighty."

"Like the old man from the house committee," she says.

"Yes," says Aviram, surprised: this comparison has never occurred to him before, and he doesn't like it.

"I'll walk with you a bit," she says, and they set off in the direction in which the dog is accustomed.

"How come you're suddenly talking to me and behaving so freely?"

"I'm leaving soon."

"No!"

"What difference does it make to you?"

"Everything's changed for me since you started coming here, and even more after you moved in to live here."

"I don't understand what you're talking about."

"When are you leaving?"

"At the end of the month."

"I don't even know your name."

"Gabi."

"I'm Aviram."

"So what changed for you because of me?"

"Knowing that you were there on the other side of the wall, so near and yet so far."

"That sounds almost like a declaration of love."

"That's exactly what it is."

She smiles and looks at him with disbelief. The sky is getting darker and an evening dusk invades the midday light. They walk in silence, and suddenly a deafening thunderclap interrupts their silence. The startled dog begins to howl. Aviram kneels down beside him, puts his arm around him, and speaks to him affectionately to calm his anxiety, trying to coax him to go on walking. A barrage of deafening thunderbolts follow each other in close succession, the dog howls in terror, trembles all over, and refuses to budge. Aviram loses his temper. He kicks the dog, which refuses to get up. Aviram pulls him by the collar and drags him violently along the pavement. The dog's claws scratch the pavement and his belly scrapes against it.

"What are you doing to him?" Gabi asks, more in wonder than in protest.

It starts to rain, and he picks the dog up and carries him in his arms. They run to the entrance of one of the buildings to take shelter from the shower. The thunder has stopped and the rain is coming down harder. He puts the dog down, his belly on the floor tiles, his body shivering and his eyes closed. Aviram bends down, strokes his head, and says: "I lost my temper, I don't know what happened to me. Sweetheart, what have I done to you." Gabi looks at him with curiosity and pity. For a long time they stand silently in the entrance to the strange building. Around them everything looks veiled, as if in a dream, a place that doesn't actually exist. Suddenly they are talking to each other, and more than that, being silent together with complete naturalness, like old friends. He doesn't dare to believe that it's true. The screen of rain and the evening darkness at noon dim his sense of the reality of the present moment. Sadness crushes Aviram's heart, like the sadness that descends on him when he drops his guard and exposes himself to the picture of failure and lost opportunities that pierces him with its sharp clarity.

"What do you do for a living?" she breaks the silence.

"I'm a clerk."

"Where?"

"In an office."

She doesn't ask for details.

"What about that woman, the statistician?" she asks. "Have you heard from her lately?"

"No, she stopped coming. She must have given up."

"Where can I find her?"

"Now, when you're leaving, you want to get into her statistics?"

Gabi says nothing and sinks into a thoughtful silence.

"I had her phone number," says Aviram, "she wrote it down for me once."

"Will you try to find it?"

"I hope I didn't throw it away. You never showed much interest in her visits at the time."

"Look for it please, okay?"

The rain subsides and they step out into the street. The dog stands up and follows them, raising his eyes questioningly to Aviram, as if to ask, what now? His gait is slow, and after a while he stops and lies down on the pavement, breathing heavily. Gabi is in a hurry to get to the store. She says good-bye and quickens her pace. Aviram says to the dog: "You old hag, because of you I won't have time for lunch." He pushes the toe of his shoe under the animal's belly and shakes him: "Get up!" The dog gets up, steadies himself, walks a few yards, and lies down on his stomach again, looking at the pavement beside him, as if at some obstacle that has impeded his progress.

Aviram says to himself: I know that nothing happens in vain, but I don't know how to read this sign language. The trouble is that instead of trying to decipher it and finding out what it's telling me, I behave like someone who's reading a difficult text and who, instead of making an effort to study it and understand it, crosses out the hard sentences and writes in new ones, never mind what, as long as they're in a language he can understand.

It starts raining hard again. Aviram picks the dog up in his arms and runs home. On the paved path leading to the entrance, he puts him down, and the dog follows him through the door into the stairwell, but instead of bounding up the stairs as usual he stands in front of the first step and looks at Aviram as if to say: So far and no further. Aviram carries him upstairs.

SIX

Ezra screamed in his sleep. Ruthie switched on the bedside lamp and saw that his face was twisted in pain and that he was panting for breath, as if he had been running. She shook him and he opened his eyes with difficulty, looked at her for a moment, put his hand on her shoulder, and said in a broken, breathless voice: "I had a terrible dream, Ruthie. I saw our Eyal dead." He burst into tears: "My son was lying dead on the pavement."

He got slowly out of bed and went to the toilet, washed his eyes and face in the bathroom, filled a glass with water in the kitchen, got his cigarettes, and returned to the bedroom. He pulled up a chair next to Ruthie's head, sat down, and sipped the water. Ruthie sat up in bed and looked at him without saying a word. Ezra lit a cigarette and gradually his breathing returned to normal. "I went to look for him in that street next to the central bus station, and I saw him lying on the pavement, face up, and people walked past him and nobody noticed that he was there." Ezra groaned: "He was dressed in rags, his hands and face were black with dirt. I bent down next to him and shook him, I thought that maybe he was drunk, or drugged, or maybe he had fainted from hunger. I took his hand and it was cold and his eyes were open, and they were a dead man's eyes." Ezra buried his face in his hands and Ruthie was afraid that he was going to burst into tears again. She put out her hand and gripped his arm.

"I sat down next to him and shouted at the people: 'This is my child, he's dead!' And they went on walking, Ruthie, they walked past us without taking any notice, they didn't even look at us, as if they hadn't seen us or heard my shouts, as if we didn't exist at all. I got up and stood in front of them and called out: "I'm the murderer! I killed my child!' And then you woke me up. Maybe something terrible has really happened to our son! Psychologically speaking, what does that dream mean?"

"The dream means that you feel guilty, Ezra. But you shouldn't feel that way. Even if you're mistaken, whatever you do is motivated by your wish to help and save him," said Ruthie.

"No, Ruthie, I'm fighting against him all the time: I didn't send him money when he asked for it, I wanted him to do what suited me, not what suited him. I thought about our honor, about the country and the army, not about his suffering. I didn't listen to you. You were right. I betrayed our child. I'll never forgive myself. Who knows where he is now and what he's going through. I'd like to go to somebody who knows how to interpret dreams to tell me according to my dream how Eyal is, where he is, if he's safe and sound, and how all this is going to end."

"Eyal's all right, Ezra, don't worry," said Ruthie. "He's safe and sound and he knows how to get by. Listen to me, a mother's heart knows far more than all kinds of fortune-tellers who interpret dreams and read coffee grounds and all that nonsense. Don't go running after all that rubbish."

"I already went to someone like that, Ruthie. I didn't tell you, I was so ashamed. When this whole business with Eyal began, I went to a certain rabbi with a reputation for being a famous cabalist and being able to see things that we can't see. And he paged through his books and closed his eyes and told me that he saw Eyal, that he was fine, and that soon everything would end well. That's what he told me. I gave him a lot of money and made a contribution to a Talmud Torah that he recommended too. All that's nonsense, I know. But perhaps there's something serious, scientific, that can tell from dreams what's happening in reality."

"Go to sleep, Ezra," said Ruthie, "you're too upset by your dream to think straight now. When you get up in the morning in a calmer, more rational mood, we'll think about what we should do."

"Yes," said Ezra, "we have to do something! We have to find a way to help him, to give him what he needs, so that he can live the way he wants to. From now on I'll do what he wants, I won't try to force him to do what I think is right. Early tomorrow morning I'll try to catch Menashe before he goes to work. I can talk to Menashe, I'm not ashamed to tell him I was wrong, terribly wrong." He lit another cigarette. "Ruthie, listen to me now, I want to swear an oath: I swear that if Eyal comes back to us safe and sound and the whole thing blows over, I'll quit smoking and I'll never touch another cigarette as long as I live!"

It had been a long time since Ezra slept as soundly as he did that night after he fell asleep again. After his terrible dream and self-accusation, he recognized that he had been wrong, and he made up his mind that from then on he would love his son unconditionally. He felt that he had finally embarked on the right road that would bring his son back to him, and already he could taste the blissful relief in store for him when the whole thing was over with no harm done.

The next morning he got up earlier than usual and called Menashe, waking him from his sleep.

"I'll call you in the evening," said Menashe. "Before that I won't be able to get in touch with him."

"Menashe, where is he, is he okay? Just let him tell me what he needs, I'll do whatever he wants."

"I haven't been in touch with him lately," said Menashe, "but don't worry, he's all right. You know, Ezra, that if you help him to desert instead of reporting immediately to the police or the army, you're breaking the law and they can take you to court."

"The same goes for you, Menashe. And in comparison to what he's taken on himself, I can certainly take that risk."

Now that he had stopped fighting Eyal and made his love for him unconditional, Ezra decided not to be ashamed of his son any longer and to hold his head high. And he got dressed and went out to the main road to buy a newspaper and fresh bread. He had always loved this hour, when some of the shops were not yet open, there was hardly any traffic, few people in the streets, and everything was quieter and cleaner. At the Sharoni brothers' restaurant they had already washed the floor and the sidewalk where Menahem, the older brother, was now putting out the tables and chairs, and the meat was already turning on the electric spit, ready for the first customers of the day. Ezra called out to him: "Good morning, Menahem!" And Menahem called back: "Good morning, Ezra! How are things with you? We haven't seen you in the neighborhood lately."

"I wasn't in the mood for hanging out. There's a bit of a problem with our son."

"Yes," said Menahem, "what's happening with him now?"

"He ran away from the army and he doesn't want to go back, he's confronting them head-on."

"I had a few run-ins with the army too when I was his age," said Menahem. "Don't take it to heart. If he's confronting them head-on he must be a strong character. He'll survive."

Alkalai's barbershop was still closed, and the meat delivery van was parked in front of Shirazi's butcher shop while the driver carried the heavy, bleeding joints into the shop and put them down in front of the butcher, who lifted them up and hung them on the hooks in his huge refrigerator. Ezra hesitated at first, reluctant to disturb Shirazi from this laborious work, but he immediately overcame his scruples and went into the shop. The butcher turned around, surprised to see him. "What's up, Ezra?" he asked. "I haven't seen you for ages."

"I've got trouble with my son. He ran away from the army. He quarreled with his officer, went to jail, succeeded in getting away, and now he's hiding. Didn't you hear about it?"

"No, I didn't know," said Shirazi. "What can you do, things like that happen in every family with children making trouble, but with God's help everything works out in the end, they grow up and bring honor to the family."

In the grocery store the fresh, warm bread was already there, and the newspapers were lying in the entrance still tied up with string. Avram opened the first parcel for him and gave him a newspaper. "What's happening with Eyal?" he asked.

"Nothing new," said Ezra. "I don't know where he is and I'm worried. I hope he knows what he's doing."

"He was always a good, quiet child, what got into him?" asked Avram.

Instead of going straight home from there as usual, Ezra went on to the next store, Herzl's building materials and hardware shop. Herzl was sitting behind the counter, talking to a customer on the phone. His assistant, Eliyahu, was busy taking out rolls of wire netting and poles for a fence, apparently to await delivery. Since the telephone conversation was dragging on, Herzl asked the person on the other end of the line to wait a minute and asked Ezra what he wanted. Ezra told him he wanted to order building materials and that he would wait for him to finish his conversation, but when it dragged on even longer, he said that he would come back later. Herzl quickly concluded the conversation and turned to Ezra.

"I haven't been here lately," said Ezra.

"Did you take a trip abroad?"

"No," said Ezra, "I've been having problems with my son, you must have heard about it."

"No, what happened?" asked Herzl, and Ezra didn't know if he was pretending because he felt embarrassed or if he was the only person who still hadn't heard of his trouble.

"He got into trouble in the army, he was sentenced to jail, he ran away, don't ask. I was so depressed, I didn't have the heart to hang out in the street."

"And what happened in the end?" asked Herzl.

"It isn't over yet. He's hiding out somewhere. We're not in touch with him."

Herzl shook his head. "That's hard," he said, and immediately added: "Listen, today it's not like it used to be. There are a lot of kids who don't want to join up at all, they pretend to be nuts to get discharged or to get a job close to home, so they can have it easy while others get killed in Lebanon. That's the youth of today for you."

Ezra ordered the materials he needed and when they said good-bye Herzl said: "Hang in there, and let's hope it all ends well."

Further down the street was the fruit and vegetable shop, which had recently been taken over by Arabs, who were busy arranging their wares in front of the shop, and then came the ladies' hairdressers, Yaffit, which at this hour was still closed. Ezra crossed the street and started walking home on the opposite sidewalk. The lottery booth wasn't open yet. Next to the Heritage of Our Fathers synagogue, attached to the old-age home of the same name, stood a group of old men waiting for a tenth man to make up the quorum for the morning prayers. Eyal had read the Torah there on the occasion of his bar mitzvah. Ezra would gladly have gone in to pray with them, so thirsty was his heart for purification, but he had to hurry home with the bread for breakfast and sandwiches for the children, who were already up and whom he would soon drive to school. On this side of the street most of the shops were still shut — Orli, the holocaust survivor Mr. Zaltzman's sportswear and shoe store; the stationery, school supplies, and toy shop owned by Batya Daniel, the widow of Shlomi, who had fallen in the Six Day War and whom Ezra had known well; Levy and his wife's pharmacy. Only Reuven and Haim's bicycle repair and car parts shop was open, and Ezra satisfied himself with a wave and a call of "Good morning!" before quickening his pace and hurrying home.

In the evening Ezra waited impatiently to hear from Menashe, but the call failed to come. After the television news Ezra couldn't control himself any longer and he called his brother.

"I left a message for him and I'm waiting for him to get in touch with me," said Menashe. "He could call at any minute, let's leave the line free."

"Just a minute, Menashe, you left a message for him somewhere, you know where he is? Why don't we go there now?"

"Ezra, you said that from now on you were going to do what he wanted, so let's do what he wants. I'll call you the minute I hear from him."

"I want to see him!" cried Ezra.

But Menashe hung up and probably didn't hear him.

Ezra smoked one cigarette after another, the room filled with smoke, and Ruthie said to him: "Ezra, you should start trying to smoke less now, if you're going to quit like you said you would."

It grew late, Ruthie went to bed, and he switched off the television, put out the light in the room, and tried to sleep in his armchair.

The phone rang after midnight and startled him out of a half-waking, half-sleeping state.

"Ezra, I just spoke to him," said Menashe. "I told him what you said. He said he doesn't need anything and for you not to worry."

"Why did it take him so long to call you?"

"He only just came home and got my message," said Menashe.

"Home? So he's got somewhere to stay?"

"He's staying with some guy who lets him live there."

"Who is this guy?"

"Someone who felt sorry for him and took him in from the street."

"Menashe, I don't understand anything. When can I see him?"

"It's up to him," said Menashe. "It's late, Ezra. I've been waiting up all evening too for him to phone, I'm dead tired and I have to get up early tomorrow to go to work. The main thing is that he's safe and sound and he sounds okay. Don't worry about him. Good night."

Pedro brought a big bag with all his clothes and possessions, and he's going to stay here with us. I knew it would happen, I was expecting it. He isn't working anymore, and apparently he's got nowhere to stay. When he put his things in the living room, she came up and looked me in the eyes with a pleading smile. She said: "Okay?" And of course I nodded my consent. And again she covered my hand with her little palm, which feels so nice. And I said to myself: I only hope he's good to you. Because I was still in some way afraid of him.

When he began coming to take her place on Sundays and sat watching television all the time without paying any attention to me, drinking beer, smoking one cigarette after the other, jigging his knee nervously without stopping, putting his hand inside his pants, rubbing and scratching there enthusiastically — I always had the feeling that this fat little man might suddenly burst out, attack, destroy, do terrible things, who knows what. Even after I became accustomed to him and even grew to like him, I still didn't feel safe with him and was always on the lookout for trouble. But I was glad she had a boyfriend, and it felt nice when the three of us were together, like a family. Now I also thought: I only hope my daughter comes and sees that he's living here, maybe she'll even bring her "social worker" with her. Just let her say a single word of objection and she'll hear me yell. It would be worth it just for that.

At lunchtime she made my food, like my daughter had taught her, attached the board that serves as a table to my wheelchair, and brought the food into the living room. I refused to even taste it. She tried to feed me and I clamped my mouth shut. With my good hand I pointed to the kitchen and then to her, Pedro, and me. She understood what I was getting at but she wouldn't do it, apparently she was afraid to disobey my daughter's instructions. She stood her ground and so did I. I kept my mouth shut and wouldn't let her get the spoon into it. They spoke to each other, and by their movements, expressions, and voices I guessed that Pedro was trying to persuade her to let me have my way, and she was explaining why she couldn't. In the end she gave in.

When their food was ready, she wheeled my chair into the kitchen and I sat at the table with them to eat the food she had prepared. The food tasted foreign, with a spiciness I'm not accustomed to, but I could understand the taste and I wanted to like it. I enjoyed listening to them speaking their language, of which I would never understand a word, and again I thought to myself: Let us be together like this for as long as I have left here. And once I had discovered, on that evening sitting with them in the playground, that for the first time after so many years, when I had already forgotten that such a thing existed, I now felt love, this new desire came to me too, as strong as pain — for them to love me.

In the evening the two of them watched television and I sat with them in the living room. He sat at the end of the sofa, and she lay on it with her head in his lap. There was some love or gangster movie in English on, she was watching it avidly, and he, after giving up the sports programs for her sake, stroked her hair and her face. Against the background of the shouts and explosions in the movie, and the noise of the car chases, there was something gentle and beautiful and quiet about it. Whether because of the usual fatigue of the evening or the pleasant coziness enveloping me, my eyes closed, and in spite of the noise coming from the television, I fell asleep. When I woke up, I felt that my wheelchair was being pushed. I opened my eyes and saw her standing in front of me, smiling at me. And I, with my crooked face, tried to smile back at her, to show her that I was happy. Pedro was lying on the sofa, his head on the armrest, watching some television program. She completed the usual arrangements, put me to bed, and said as usual: "Now sleep. Good night."

She returned to the living room, and through the open door opposite my bed I saw her sitting in the armchair with him on the sofa. After a while they switched off the television, put out the light in the living room, and went into her balcony room. I heard her door shut and after that they talked and laughed in there, there were moments of silence, and then their voices rose again, her angry and him laughing, him angry and her laughing, and they began to argue. Suddenly her door opened and Pedro, in his underpants, came into my room. I closed my eyes and pretended to be sleeping. He returned to her room and they began arguing again. Now she was laughing and he was angry. And then I saw him dragging her into the living room, she struggled but he was stronger. In the weak light coming from the porch they looked like the shadows of two clumsy little bears. He lay her on the sofa, and as he stood next to the arm-chair to take off his underpants, she came running to shut my door. She was naked. The door closed and in the darkness I wasn't sure that I had really seen what I saw, because it was only a shadow. But the door opened again immediately. Pedro opened it. I saw him coming into the room, he too was naked. I closed my eyes. He stood facing me for a minute, I heard his breathing. Then he returned to the living room, leaving the door open, and stood there with his back to me. She said something in an angry voice, and he burst out laughing and went and switched on all the lights in the living room. A scream of fear escaped the girl.

From my bed I could see the end of the sofa and half their bodies. He lay on top of her, hiding her face with his shoulders, until they turned on their sides, facing me, and she seemed to be looking at me. I knew that I was in darkness and she couldn't see me, but I couldn't bear that look, an empty, expressionless look. I closed my eyes and told myself that none of this was really happening, that it was a weird kind of dream I had to get through, fall asleep, and forget. But the pain of it gave me no rest, then or now. All night long and in the days to come those pictures never left me, and I asked myself why the things I had seen affected me so powerfully. What was this pain, like the pain of something precious being broken so that nothing could restore it to its former state again? What had been broken? How much time has to pass until the pain weakens and dies down, leaving only some distant, unexplained memory, waking sometimes and going back to sleep again?

I didn't sleep all night. I was waiting for her to get up and go to the kitchen for a drink of water, as she sometimes does. But she didn't get up. The next morning, when she came into my room, she didn't even say "Good morning," like she always does. She washed me, dressed me, doing everything in silence and with a serious look on her face. Then she seated me in my chair, wheeled me into the living room, and went to the kitchen to make breakfast. He stood next to the door between the passage and the living room, leaning against the wall, looking at me from a distance, with a sidelong look. I beckoned him to come to me. He walked up slowly, with a swagger, to hide his embarrassment, and when he reached me, I took his hand and squeezed it. He burst out laughing, not the cheeky kind of laugh he usually laughs, but a short laugh of surprise. She brought my breakfast from the kitchen. And I pointed to the three of us and to the kitchen again. She wheeled my chair there.

We sat at the kitchen table. It was quiet, they didn't talk. There was some tension between them. And suddenly she said to me: "You want Pedro to go away?" I shook my head, "No, no," Pedro smiled and looked at her curiously. She asked: "You want me to go away?" I shouted and shook my head again. I didn't know if she was content with my answers. I didn't know how else to convey to her my feeling that she wasn't to blame for anything, that I was to blame. That night I had seen something I wasn't supposed to see, and I was drawn to see it. Even though he wanted it. He had dragged her into the living room, he had opened my bedroom door after she closed it, he had switched on the lights. He had done everything so that I would see them. But I shouldn't have looked.

And to this day I don't know why he did it. Perhaps he wanted me to know that she was his and nobody else's? And perhaps he wanted me to see who the real master was in my house? I don't know. He did what he did and I did what I did. He had seen to it that everything happened in the light, in front of my open door, but he hadn't forced me to look. I hadn't closed my eyes from the first moment I saw them naked, I hadn't covered my head with the blanket when they were on the sofa with him on top of her. I wanted to see it, this desire was stronger than any scruple. And only when she turned her face to me, as if she were looking at me, and her expressionless eyes fell on me, did I choke with fear, with insult and pain, and I couldn't bear to see it anymore.

When the three of us sat around the breakfast table in the kitchen, they kept quiet all the while and I was afraid that they were going to leave me. I hoped they would stay with me, that the three of us would always be together. I took her hand and said: "Linda, Linda." She smiled with difficulty.

It was raining hard and the house grew dark. She had to switch on the lights. He was already sitting opposite the television, a can of beer on the table, one hand holding a cigarette and the other hand between his legs, watching the sports programs. She did all kinds of chores in the apartment. Afterward she got ready to go out and do the shopping. I shouted and indicated that I wanted her to take me and for Pedro to come with us, but she took no notice and went alone. Pedro turned his head away from the screen and gave me a long look, I didn't know if he was examining my face or if he was deep in thought. In the end, he said: "Perhaps in the afternoon."

At lunch they were talking to each other a bit and he helped her in the kitchen. There was a break in the rain and the sky cleared, I showed her that I wanted to go out for a walk. She said that Pedro would take me. I insisted that she come too, pointing to all three of us. She agreed, but she had to finish the housework first. Pedro pushed me onto the little balcony and joined her in the kitchen. When he finished washing the dishes, he came out to the balcony and stood next to me. Both of us looked down, I from my chair and he leaning his elbows on the balustrade, smoking a cigarette and dropping the ashes to the ground below. The playground was empty. Perhaps by the time we arrived there would be children there. And perhaps the boy with the dog would come. I hadn't seen him since that evening. Or perhaps he had finally succeeded in reaching Eilat? Suddenly I heard her from the kitchen singing to herself, one of the songs she likes to sing when she's working, with the words that sound so strange you can't tell if they're English or their language. I knew there was going to be a reconciliation. I said: "Linda." Pedro turned around, looked at me, and smiled broadly. I had never seen his teeth so close before, or perhaps I hadn't noticed them: rotten, yellow, with black gaps between them, apparently from too much smoking. He put his hand on my shoulder and left it there a long time. I felt that he wanted to tell me without words that he knew how I felt.

In the playground there were only a few big children, playing with a soccer ball. After us a woman arrived with a little girl and tried to chase them away, showing them the sign at the entrance that said specifically that the playground was intended for small children and ball games were forbidden. But they argued with her and answered her impertinently. She took her little girl and walked away angrily. Pedro and the girl sat on the bench next to my chair and watched the children playing soccer. Suddenly Pedro stood up, threw down his cigarette and trod on it, walked over to the children, and started playing with them. She called him to come back and he paid no attention to her, he was so absorbed in the children's game. She went up and called to him again to stop. But he went on romping with the children and their ball, forgetting where he was. She came back and sat down next to me, looked at me and smiled in despair, as if to say: What can I do with him? Men are like little children.

At those moments, I knew, she loved him.

His white hair, damp with sweat, on the white pillowcase. His closed eyes, his creased forehead, and his aggrieved face. His body responds to her hands, which are turning it from side to side, taking off his wet clothes. The smell of his body — which has become distinct from him and taken on a personality of its own, powerful and mysterious — tempts her to travel with him into the realms of his blindness. Through the towel with which she is blotting up his sweat, her hands are surprised by the softness and limpness of his naked body, his thick chest, the round belly thickening his waist, and before she yields to the impulse to bury her face between his thighs, she feels his hand suddenly stroking her hair. She raises her head to his — his lips are parted in the hint of a smile and his slightly open eyes aren't looking anywhere.

A deafening thunderbolt shakes the house, and then another begins rolling in from the distance. Aviram's dog, whose howls of loneliness have not been heard all afternoon, lets out a yelp of helpless terror and falls silent again. The rain comes down harder, beating against the outside walls with a heavy clatter, as if threatening to break into the circle of lamplight in which she is sitting. She turns on the radio. A female and two male voices, accompanied by antique instruments, are singing the work Oded was playing on his tape when he gave her a lift from Givatayim to Tel Aviv, at any rate she thinks it's the same music that filled the car then with infinite longings for harmony and peace of mind. But if it really is the same work, it's probably a different performance than the one he played, because this time it fails to have the same uplifting effect on her. Perhaps it was the surprise of meeting Oded, the embarrassing intimacy of being alone with him in the car, his attempts to arouse her interest in him, her avoidance of any response that might give him hope — perhaps it was these things that had moved her then to hear what she had heard in the music? Perhaps the change had taken place in her herself, and her mood and expectations now are not what they had been then? We never hear the same music twice. She listens to the work to the end and finds nothing in it but sweet melodies and empty embellishments. To her disappointment, the host of the program announces that it really is the same composition.

She finds herself longing for Ada and calls her.

"Gabi! Where did you disappear to?" cries Ada in a hoarse, sniffling voice.

"What's wrong with you? You sound sick."

"I came down with flu together with the children. But what about you? There's no answer at your house. Aren't you ever home, or have you stopped answering the phone?"

"I'm in that apartment, the one I told you about."

"What, you moved out of your place and went to live there?"

"Yes."

"With the old man?"

"Ada, I told you, he's not old."

"And does he allow you to use the phone there now?"

"Adaleh, I'm going home at the end of the month. It's over."

"So why don't you go home now?"

"We'll talk about it when we meet. I'm sorry you're sick. I'm dying to see you."

"Why don't you come around here this evening? If you don't mind the sickroom atmosphere. I'll ask Gadi to come and fetch you."

"No, I don't like asking him to drive all the way here in this weather, after he comes home from work, and then bring me home again."

"He'll be glad to do it, no problem. But perhaps you can't reveal the address."

"No, I told you, all that's over."

"So why don't you go home?"

"I still have to stay here."

"You haven't given him up yet."

"One feeble little hope against all the odds. Maybe that's my slogan."

"Oded said he saw you in Givatayim and gave you a lift."

"What else did he say about me?"

"He just gave us your regards. If you were at your flat then, in Givatayim, you must have heard all my messages. I was terribly worried about you."

"You know I sometimes disappear."

"So how about this evening, don't you want to come?"

"I'd prefer you to come here. We'll wait till you feel better. Do you want to write down my phone number?"

"Am I allowed to phone you there?"

"Yes, of course, everything's allowed."

And she gives her friend the address and phone number of the apartment.

After hanging up she wonders what Oded said about her. Because her friend, who's incapable of lying, evaded answering her question directly. But why should she care what Oded said about her? The phone rings, she picks it up immediately, and Hezi's voice says grimly: "You were busy. Are you using the phone?"

"What do you want?"

"I want you to leave the apartment right away. Who were you talking to?"

"A girlfriend."

"Didn't we agree that you weren't to use the phone, that I would call you, and you would pick up only at the agreed signal?"

"All those agreements are canceled."

"Then get out of the apartment immediately."

"I'm staying here till the end of the month. Before that you'll have to drag me out by force."

"What are you fighting for?"

"For you."

"For me?"

"Yes. You're the man of my life and I haven't given you up yet."

"But you hate me! You said terrible things about me, you called me a shit."

"I was only quoting what I'd heard from the girls in the office."

"And the way you behaved when I wanted you. And I only came to have a friendly talk with you."

"So that we'd part friends."

"You want to get back at me, you think you can destroy me. You're mistaken. I'm a strong person."

"So am I. Where are you calling from?"

"None of your business. What do you mean that you're fighting for me?"

"I want you, but on my terms."

"What do you want, for me to marry you?"

"At this stage I'm prepared to make do with the role of a mistress, but even a mistress has rights. She's not a toy to play with when you feel like it and throw away when you're sick of her, until you feel like playing again and pick her up from the floor. You can't tell her about your plans to run away to another country and start a new life together, phone her up from abroad and tell her how much you love her and miss her, and then come back and cut off all connections, get her fired from her job, and throw her out of your apartment. It doesn't work that way. As soon as you feel that you've stopped loving her, that she doesn't attract you anymore, tell her so and she'll get out of your life. But not with evasions and double messages."

"I didn't get you fired. I don't interfere in things like that."

"It makes no difference. The mistress doesn't want any apologies from you either, and she's not interested in parting friends, because there never was any friendship between you. But she does want you to treat her with respect. Tell her if you want to go on seeing her, she'll tell you her terms, and you can decide if it suits you or not."

"It sounds to me as if you want to turn me into your mistress."

"Why did you call me when the line was busy?"

"Never mind. But I don't want you to start making trouble there. There are things you don't know and you can't understand. If you're not prepared to abide by the rules we agreed on, then get out of the apartment, and the sooner the better. Why do you insist on staying there?"

"You called before to say that you wanted to come over."

He is silent for a moment, and then he says:

"Yes. That's right. But when I talk to you, you make me mad and I begin to hate you."

"I'm staying here until the end of the month, and you've got until then to decide whether you want to continue the relationship between us on my terms."

"If your terms mean to stop what you call the 'underground,' then you can pack your things and go home now. What do you understand about these things? Have you any idea of what's happening to me?"

"You have time now to examine yourself and decide whether you love me and what you're prepared to sacrifice for that love."

"You're the one to talk about love. You said yourself that you've never loved me and that the thought of sex with me disgusts you. When I came to you, I wanted you terribly, and you behaved like a violated virgin, you wouldn't let me touch you. Maybe I shouldn't tell you this, but when I got back to the office

I had to go and relieve myself in the toilet. Like an adolescent kid, in the stinking toilet."

This intimate confession moves her so much that to her astonishment she hears herself saying something that has never occurred to her until this minute: "I want a child from you."

"Sure, that's all I need now."

"But that's something you really don't owe me."

"Look, I have to hang up now."

"I'll be here till the end of the month. You can call or come and tell me what you've decided."

After she puts down the phone she goes and sits on the bed. Behind the wall she can hear Aviram. "I'm sick and tired, I can't stand this any longer." In the same soft voice in which he often showers the dog with affection he says: "I've had enough, you old slut, why don't you die already." He'd been there all the time she was talking to Hezi, he could have heard every word she said. After a while she hears a yelp of pain, and then more and more yelps at regular intervals, and in the end a long, heart-broken whine dying away in utter exhaustion. By now she knows all the dog's different sounds, the howls of loneliness and longing, the barks of joy, the angry, indignant growls, the battle cries when confronting strangers, and the cries of terror when facing the violence of the elements. But this is something else. Is her neighbor hitting his dog?

She goes out onto the landing and ring's Aviram's doorbell. His steps halt in front of the door and she knows that he's looking through the peephole. He opens the door and smiles through his beard at the unexpected pleasure of seeing her: "I found the note where she wrote her phone number. I was just going to bring it to you."

"Good, thanks. Tell me, what's the matter with the dog?"

"He doesn't feel well. He's terrified of thunder, you saw for yourself when we were outside today. It makes him ill. It takes time before he recovers."

"Before I heard him crying out in pain, as if he was being beaten."

"It's the fear," Aviram explains. "He was probably dreaming of thunder."

"Can't you do anything to help him?"

"I called the vet to ask him what to do, and he told me to take him there so he could see for himself. But it's impossible to get a taxi in this rain. I've been calling all the taxi ranks for an hour already and they all say that all their cabs are busy and they can't promise anything for the next few hours."

"Where is he now?"

"Over there, in his corner," Aviram points to the bedroom. "He refuses to budge. Would you like to come in?"

"If it won't disturb you."

"No, on the contrary, I'm glad you came."

She steps inside and follows him to the bedroom. The window is closed and the blind is down. Aviram switches on a round fluorescent light attached to the ceiling.

A double bed with a frame of pale wood, its mattress covered with a greenish geometric pattern (during the day the bedsheets are apparently stored in the box underneath it), stands against the wall next to her bedroom. Opposite it, taking up the entire wall between his bedroom and his living room, is a closet made of the same pale wood, with a row of tall sliding doors and above them two short, broad sliding doors. At the foot of the bed is a small plastic mat covered with floral-patterned terry cloth, of the kind usually found in bathrooms. And at the head of the bed is a white-painted stool holding a lamp with a blue base and shade and a flexible metal stem, a small book in English turned facedown, with a picture of a smiling, curly-haired young woman, apparently the author, on its back cover, and an alarm clock with phosphorescent hands and numbers on its black face. Everything has an air of imperishable oldness.

And in the corner between the closet and the wall with the window, on a plastic mat matching the one at the foot of the bed, lies the dog. She goes up to him, crouches beside him, and strokes him. His belly trembles as if it is full of suppressed sobs. He raises his head from the mat and turns it in her direction,

looks at her for a moment, and then looks up at Aviram standing next to her, with a despairing question in his eyes. Then he
drops his head again.

She stands up and asks Aviram: "Do dogs suffer from
depression?"

"Yes, they have moods too, just like people, including
depression."

"He looks terribly depressed. Why don't you try to cheer him
up, say something nice to him, that he's a good dog, that you
love him."

"He isn't a good dog and I'm cross with him," Aviram says,
completely seriously.

"What?"

"He has to go out and he doesn't want to go. Okay, he can't.
I carried him downstairs, next to the entrance under the roof,
to let him move about a bit. He just lay there on the ground. I
took him next to the bushes, to do his business there. He didn't
do it. I told him to do it. Do it! Do it! I waited and waited and
nothing. I carried him upstairs, put him down, and suddenly he
can walk, he goes into the living room and does it there on the
floor. I just finished cleaning up when you came."

"You should forgive him," says Gabi, "he's sick."

"That's impossible. He has to be taught a lesson. It's the only
way for him to know what's permitted and what's not permitted."

They leave the bedroom. "I'll give you the note with the
phone number," says Aviram, and he leads her to the living
room. "Would you like to sit down and have a cup of coffee?"

"Thank you, not now," she looks anxiously at her watch.
"Another time, perhaps," she adds and waits in the hall. He
goes into the living room, comes back, and hands her a scrap of
square, yellow paper. She looks at the note. "Where is it?"

"Ramat Hasharon."

"Did she tell you her name?"

"I asked her. She said some name, and then she said another
one. If you ask me, you're wasting your time with her. That survey is already concluded."

Behind his tinted lenses his eyes examine her, waiting for her reaction.

"Look, I know that you can hear everything and you know exactly what's going on here. You don't have to pretend."

"So before you leave I want to tell you something, without pretending: since you came here my life has changed."

"You've already told me that. But in what way?"

"If you like, I'll explain it to you when you've got more time."

"Okay. Just tell me: changed for the better or for the worse?"

"I don't know. It depends on what happens in the end."

"In the end?" she asks in surprise.

Early in the evening an army officer rang their doorbell. Ruthie opened the door and the sight of the officer standing there with a stern, serious expression on his face froze her heart: this was how she had always imagined parents being notified that their son had fallen in battle. After ascertaining that he had come to the right address, the lieutenant said: "I'm here about your son, Eyal. Is the father home?"

"What's happened to him?" cried Ruthie.

"That's what I've come to ask you," replied the lieutenant. "When was the last time you heard from him?"

"I don't know," said Ruthie, "my husband's taking care of it, he'll be out of the shower in a minute."

The lieutenant looked at her in disbelief.

Ruthie showed him into the living room, switched off the television, and sent the children to their room. "Please sit down."

Ezra was in the shower. He had just come home from work. She went to the bathroom door and called to him to hurry up, because a lieutenant was there from the army to talk to them about Eyal. To her relief Ezra soon emerged, his hair wet and his shirt unbuttoned. The officer gave him a searching look. From a big black briefcase he removed a thin brown cardboard file with some sheets of paper in it, took a ballpoint pen out of his pocket, and placed them on the table before him.

"Are you from Eyal's unit?" asked Ezra.

"Unit?" asked the lieutenant. "What unit?"

Ezra understood and kept quiet.

"When was the last time you heard from him?" asked the lieutenant.

"Someone said they saw him next to the central bus station. I reported it to Sergeant Hagai."

"Yes, that's written down here. And afterward?"

"I don't remember," mumbled Ezra, "it was a long time ago."

"Did he get in touch or didn't he?"

"He phoned and said he was okay and we shouldn't worry and that was all. There was nothing to report."

"You have to report immediately on everything, on every contact he makes, on everything you hear about him from any source. You don't know what might help us to trace him. Every detail is important to us. If you don't report, you're an accomplice. Where did he phone from that time?"

"I don't know! He didn't want to tell us anything. The whole call lasted two seconds and then he hung up."

The lieutenant looked through the papers in front of him: "When you reported that he'd been seen next to the central bus station, you mentioned your brother, who went there with you to look for him. Didn't he get in touch with him?"

"Why should he get in touch with him and not with us?"

"Did he get in touch or didn't he?"

"He never said anything about it to me."

"Are there any other uncles?" asked the lieutenant.

"On my side? There's one more uncle, but he's become ultra-Orthodox."

"So what?"

"My son has no contact with him. The others are sisters, and he's not attached to them."

"And on the mother's side?"

"He has no contact with them."

"A girlfriend, close friends?"

"There aren't any."

"If he gets in touch with you or if you hear that he's been in touch with anyone else apart from you, next time you report it immediately."

"Of course," said Ezra.

"I don't have to tell you that your son's life is in danger. When terrorists go looking for soldiers to kidnap and murder, a soldier on the roads, hitching rides, hanging around in all kinds of places, is easy prey."

"Ever since this whole business with my son began," said Ezra, "I've had the feeling that you're not even trying to find him. It's not so important to you. What difference does it make to you what happens to him? Some poor soldier who got into trouble, was thrown into jail, escaped and all the rest, who cares about him? So what's happened all of a sudden? What made you remember him now?"

The lieutenant looked closely at Ezra and at Ruthie, who was sitting off to the side and listening to the conversation in tense silence. "We never stopped looking for him," he announced in a stern, official tone. "We can't inform you of every step we take in this matter. As long as he hasn't been released from military service, after he's finished serving his prison sentence — he's our responsibility."

"Are you telling me that after he goes to jail they're going to throw him out of the army?" demanded Ezra anxiously. "That he won't be able to rejoin his unit and serve like everybody else?"

"I haven't got the authority to tell you anything like that," said the lieutenant. "Such matters are decided by the proper authorities."

After the lieutenant left, Ezra and Ruthie looked at each other in silence, as if waiting until he was out of earshot. And then Ezra said in a whisper, to be on the safe side: "We have to call Menashe immediately, to warn him, so he'll know what to say. Look what I've come to, lying and implicating my brother in my lies. I, who've never lied in my life, not on income tax or VAT forms, not to a single customer of mine, not even to the Arab workers. And who am I lying to? To the army, the thing most sacred to me. What's going to become of us, Ruthie?"

"We'll get through it, Ezra," said Ruthie, but her somber face told a different story. "Anything's worth it if it helps Eyal."

"They won't let him serve, Ruthie. After he goes to jail they'll throw him out of the army, like the criminals and the nutcases. He won't even be able to get a driver's license." Ezra reflected for a moment and a terrible thought crossed his mind: "Ruthie, maybe our Eyal really is mad and a criminal? You heard the way he talked at my mother's house. We think we know our child, but he isn't a child anymore, and we don't really know anything about him. He's a stranger to us. When we think about him, we think of the nice little boy who was supposed to grow up exactly the way we wanted, and that's not what he is today. He's not like us. What do we know about him, about the way his mind works, about what's happening to him? He doesn't talk at all, whatever we ask him he answers: Okay, okay. And who's this man who's hiding him, what kind of a person is he, how did he meet him, why did he take him in? Ruthie, I'm frightened. Before I was afraid for Eyal, now I'm afraid of him."

"And aren't you afraid, Ezra, of what the officer said about the danger of terrorists kidnapping him?"

"He was just trying to frighten us, Ruthie, so that we'd cooperate with them. Eyal's wearing civilian clothes and he's not wandering around the countryside or hitching rides. He's hiding out in this guy's house, most probably in Tel Aviv."

"From the way you're talking about him now, Ezra, it certainly doesn't sound as if you love him," said Ruthie.

"Didn't you see how I lied for him? I feel like a traitor to my country. I'm ashamed of myself, Ruthie, I'm terribly ashamed. And who knows how it's going to end. I'm helping him and I'll go on helping him, in whatever way he wants. But you should know, Ruthie, that I'll never forgive Eyal as long as I live."

Ezra was afraid that before he managed to talk to Menashe and synchronize their stories, the lieutenant would phone him or go to Pardes Katz himself. He called his brother immediately, but he was still at work. His wife answered the phone.

"Has someone from the army been there, or called, to talk to Menashe?"

"Nobody from the army has been here or phoned."

"I have to talk to Menashe urgently!"

"He'll call you the minute he gets home."

"He's a sly one, that lieutenant," said Ezra to Ruthie, "with that Polish fish-face of his, as if he hasn't got a clue. Underneath it all he's got a cold heart and the mind of a lawyer. He wasn't born yesterday, Ruthie, he knows we're not telling the truth. I saw it in his questions. If he finds out that we met Eyal and didn't inform the army immediately that he was at my mother's, that we brought him civilian clothes to help him desert — we're in big trouble."

Ruthie got up and switched on the television. She called the children to come back into the living room and looked at them for a long time, barely suppressing her tears. It was evident from their faces that they had overheard everything, they knew what was going on and understood, in their childlike way, that their big brother was in deep trouble, and so was the entire family. They had already stopped asking their parents about Eyal, because the noncommittal, deceitful replies they received, the impatience, and even anger with which their questions were greeted, had led them to realize that it was a forbidden subject.

Ezra waited in suspense for Menashe to call, smoking one cigarette after another, and when the phone rang he jumped up as if a snake had bitten him. But it was Eyal's voice on the other end of the line, dry, flat, monotonous: "Tell Menashe to get in touch with me."

"Eyal!" cried Ezra. "My Eyal! How are you, what's happening with you?"

"I can't talk now. Tell Menashe. Good-bye."

"Where are you?" shouted Ezra.

The line went dead. Ezra was speechless. From the sofa, opposite the television, the two little ones stared at him, perhaps anticipating that they were going to be sent to their room again. Ruthie extracted the conversation from him with difficulty.

"Why couldn't he talk?" she wondered.

"It's not that he couldn't, Ruthie. He doesn't want to. If you'd answered the phone I'm sure he would have talked to you. He doesn't want to talk to me. He hasn't forgiven me yet."

"You haven't forgiven him either, and you just said that you'd never forgive him. You've forgotten your dream, Ezra."

"I haven't forgotten, Ruthie. How could I forget something like that?"

"Listen to me, Ezra: Eyal will be back with us soon," said Ruthie.

By the time Menashe called, the living room was full of Ezra's cigarette smoke. Ezra told his brother about the lieutenant's visit. Up to that moment, the officer had not shown up at Menashe's house and nobody had called from the army about Eyal.

"What are you so worried about, Ezra?" asked Menashe. "You yourself said that they don't give a damn about what happens to Eyal. Don't you know how those pen-pushers work there in those offices? That lieutenant has to fill in some form about Eyal and hand it in to his superior, so he comes to ask you questions and writes it down and hands it in to his CO and that's the end of the matter, everyone's satisfied, they did their duty. Don't worry, when they come here they won't hear anything different from what you told them. And you know that we can rely on our mother too, she won't say anything she shouldn't. She's stronger than all the rest of us."

"Menashe, from what he said I understand that after Eyal finishes his jail sentence, they're going to kick him out of the army."

"Wait till we get there, Ezra. When the time comes, I'll do what I can with my connections in the army. First let him come back and agree to turn himself in. Then we'll see."

"Do you think he'll come back to us in the end?"

"Of course, he has to. For all his character and stubbornness and willpower, he won't have a choice. Everything's against him, do you understand, Ezra? Everything's against him. He won't be able to carry on like this much longer."

"Ruthie thinks the same. Menashe, he phoned before. All he

said was: 'Tell Menashe to call me.' He didn't want to talk to
me and he hung up."

"Okay, I'll call him."

"Why does he need you to call him, why can't he call you
himself?"

"He called when I wasn't at home."

"He said: 'I can't talk now.' Isn't he allowed to use the phone
over there?"

"What's the problem, Ezra? I'll call him in a minute. What's
eating you?"

"Menashe, I don't know my own child, I don't know what's
in his head, what kind of life he's leading, what kind of people
he's with. Why did that guy take him into his house? Who is he,
what kind of a person is he?"

Menashe burst out laughing. "What's happening to you,
Ezra? What kind of thoughts are running around in your head?
Eyal's fine, he's a grown man and he knows what he's doing.
Stop torturing yourself with all kinds of nonsense."

"Will you phone me as soon as you've talked to him and tell
me what's happening?" asked Ezra.

"We'll see," said Menashe, "if I've got anything to tell you."

"I understand," said Ezra.

"And don't stay up all night waiting for me to phone. I know
you. Maybe he won't be home when I call."

"What, does he walk around outside?" asked Ezra in surprise.

"What do you think, that he stays shut up in the house all the
time and never goes out?"

The doorbell rings and his heart leaps for joy. Ever since she
visited him in his apartment and he dared to tell her that her
presence had changed his life, he has wondered if she would
ever talk to him again, especially since she already received the
phone number she was so keen on getting. And indeed, for
some time he has neither seen her nor heard her speaking on
the phone, with only the music showing that she is still there
behind the wall. Now he hurries to look through the peephole

in the door, and the distorted lens reflects Mrs. Shwartz's haggard face.

"You come now, he say," the old woman announces without delay as soon as he opens the door, and immediately she turns around to go back downstairs to her apartment.

Mr. Shwartz is sitting in an armchair in his blue dressing gown with a woolen blanket covering his legs. His wife, after opening the door for Aviram, sits down on a stool barring the door to the kitchen, her face as stern as a sentry's.

"What's going on there?" the old man asks. "Can you see anything yet?"

"Mr. Shwartz, there's nobody there, nobody would be crazy enough to go there in this rain."

"Do you know what I'm talking about?"

"Of course, about the storeroom," says Aviram.

"Didn't you hear what I told you about the water?"

"Yes, I heard."

"So by my calculations you should be able to see the results by now. Go down and have a look, see what the situation is."

"Now, in this rain?"

"What's the problem? Take an umbrella. Go on, go down and have a look, and come back and tell me what's happening."

"What's the hurry?"

"You ask a man of my age, in my condition, 'what's the hurry?' Don't you understand? You know what kind of medicine I take? You want to see my catheter?"

"No, I've already seen it."

"So is it so difficult for you to do this for me? When I was healthy, didn't I run around for the house, for everybody?"

"Okay, okay, I'll take the dog out at the same time."

"That's right, if it's for the dog you'll do it, but if it's for Shwartz why take the trouble?"

The doorkeeper rises from her stool to open the door for him and immediately locks and bolts it behind him.

The dog has somewhat recovered from his weakness and is able to walk slowly but not to descend the stairs. Aviram carries him downstairs and leaves him to his own devices under the roofed entrance to the building.

Skipping between the rain puddles Aviram makes his way to a spot from which he can see the new neighbors' sunken porch, which is indeed flooded by water, to the height of about one meter. The entire backyard is one muddy puddle. Aviram returns to the entrance, where he finds the dog doing his business in the rain, next to the gas tanks of one of the apartments. He waits for him to finish and urges him to return to the shelter of the roof. His trousers are wet to the knees and a layer of mud is sticking to his shoes. With the sharp edge of a stone he tries to remove the mud from the soles. Then he scrapes them well on the doormat at the foot of the stairs.

After surveying the terrain through the peephole, Mrs. Shwartz opens the door a crack: "Not dog!" she cries. "Not dog!" Aviram carries the dog up to his apartment, puts the dripping umbrella in the bathtub, and goes downstairs to the head of the committee. The old woman follows him on his way to Mr. Shwartz's armchair, pushing a large, damp cloth with her foot to wipe his muddy footprints off the floor.

"More than a meter in the terrace!" Mr. Shwartz exults with a beaming face. "And did you look inside, from the windows?"

"It's impossible to reach the windows, the whole place is flooded, it's like a swamp. And anyway it's dark, you can't see anything."

"The water isn't sinking anymore, eh? You understand, the basement there's like a hole in the ground, and under the floor they made is groundwater. And the more it fills up, the more that water keeps rising. All their concrete and tiles are a joke. The water is already coming up from the floor to the same level as it is in the terrace, even though they made a big step between the terrace and the room."

When he sees Aviram's indifference he examines his face suspiciously: "What's the matter, isn't a man of my age and in my condition entitled to a little satisfaction too? Let me tell you, it gives me health! And believe me, a little health won't hurt me now. Oy! I wish I could be there when they turn up, that woman with her dirty mouth and her husband who makes himself out to be some poor stooge, to see their new apartment. Oy! I only hope I live to see that moment!"

Mr. Shwartz's face takes on an amused expression. He winks at Aviram and calls to his wife: "Hindeleh, will you help me downstairs when they come to see the water in their new apartment?"

"You crazy," answers his wife from her place on the stool barring the door to the kitchen.

Menashe's voice on the telephone: "Eyal's coming home!"

Ezra said nothing.

"Ezra!" Menashe called over the phone: "Did you hear me?"

"When?" asked Ezra.

"This evening."

Ezra looked dumbfounded. He pulled up a chair and sat down.

"What's the matter, Ezra?" asked Ruthie, upset by his appearance. "What did he say?" Her heart told her that the worst had happened.

"Eyal's coming home," said Ezra.

"What's going on there, Ezra, are you in shock?" asked Menashe.

"I didn't believe it would happen," said Ezra.

"I told you it was only a question of time."

"When will we see him?"

"Come to Mother's this evening, he'll wait for you and go home with you."

"And what's going to happen to him?"

"Tomorrow morning you'll take him to the nearest police station and they'll hand him on to the proper authorities. Ezra, listen to me: don't inform the army now and don't tell anyone. If they ask you later on, tell them that he came home late at night and you took him in first thing in the morning. Do you understand what I'm saying to you?"

"Yes, sure."

"Because you sound confused to me."

"I'm fine. It's all clear. I'll do exactly as you say. Why did he go to Mother's and not come straight here?"

"He needs to rest. He hasn't slept for a few nights, he's been wandering around, he didn't have anywhere to go. He didn't want you to see him like that, unshaven and in dirty clothes."

"So he isn't living in that guy's house anymore?"

"No, he left, he didn't want to stay with him anymore."

"Why?"

"Ezra, leave that now, what difference does it make to you? The main thing is that Eyal's coming home. Come at about ten."

"So late?"

"Yes, he's gone to sleep. Listen Ezra, I promised him that you wouldn't ask him where he's been and what he did and why and so on. No cross-examinations and no Zionism. Do you understand? I promised for you. Without that condition he wouldn't have come back. So if there's anything you want to ask, ask me when we're alone, don't ask him. He's turning over a new leaf now, and we have to give him a chance. In any case he's in for a rough time now, with another court martial and another jail sentence, let's not make it any harder for him."

"Absolutely," said Ezra.

"So be patient with him, go gently, and don't overwhelm him and gush over him either."

"Okay, Menashe, don't worry. I've made too many mistakes in this whole business already, and without you and your brains, who knows what would have become of him and of us. Trust me, I'll do exactly as you say."

After he put down the phone, Ezra dropped into his armchair and told Ruthie everything Menashe had said. Then he lit a cigarette and sat there for a long time, tired, silent, and thoughtful. Ruthie examined his face and couldn't understand what the matter was. He sensed her looking at him, met her eyes, and saw the question in them.

"It's strange, Ruthie," he said, "ever since this nightmare began I thought that when he came home, if he ever did, it would be the happiest moment of my life. Like I felt when the nurse lifted him up to show him to me, behind the glass, after he was born, and I saw my son for the first time. You didn't even understand then why I had tears in my eyes."

"Why do you think I didn't understand, Ezra? I certainly did understand, and I remember to this day how it moved me."

"That moment was the happiest moment in my whole life. And I thought that if Eyal came home and went back to the army, it would be the same as then, as if he were being born again for us. And now, when Menashe told me on the phone, I didn't feel any joy. My heart felt empty. Of course it's a good thing that he's coming back, and maybe things will finally start getting back to normal. That terrible worry will leave us, we'll be able to breathe freely again and sleep at night. But Ruthie, I don't know why, there's no joy in my heart."

"Both we and Eyal will have to get used to a new beginning. He'll have to get used to us again and we'll have to get used to him," said Ruthie, "and it will take time."

"That's not it, Ruthie. Look, he's not really coming back to us, and the person who's coming back isn't actually our Eyal. It's somebody else, a stranger. There are things in his life that we don't know and we may never know. And he has conditions: what we can and can't talk to him about. He's coming like a guest. Why did he go to my mother's first instead of coming straight home to us? If he looks dirty and neglected, then my mother can see him and we can't? He has to rest at her house, and bathe and shave and dress in our honor, get himself ready to meet us? What's it all about? It doesn't make sense, Ruthie. You know why he's behaving this way, Ruthie? Because he doesn't have any family feeling for us, and that's all there is to it. He doesn't feel that he really belongs to us."

"He's sure of his grandmother's love, Ezra. He knows that she loves him unconditionally. And with you he has a problem. You see him as a failure, for you he's a traitor, he betrayed the family, the army, the motherland, the values most sacred to you. And you didn't hide it from him, and even if you had, he would have sensed it. The question is whether you'll be able to convey to him that you love him as he is, in spite of everything he did, in spite of everything he might still do. That's the question. Because family feeling isn't a one-way street, it has to be mutual."

Ezra lit another cigarette.

Ruthie said: "In my opinion, Ezra, you should stop smoking now. You took an oath."

"Just a minute, Ruthie. I said: 'If Eyal comes home safe and sound and the whole thing blows over — then I'll stop smoking.' I'm not sure yet that it's all over. I wish! But don't worry, I'll keep my oath."

Ruthie went over to the neighbors to ask their daughter to stay with the children while they went to her mother-in-law's house in Pardes Katz. Ezra went into the side room that served as his office, lit himself a cigarette, studied his work schedule, made a few notes about things he had to do the next day, and called a few people about the job, as he did every day of his life.

SEVEN

"Nice!" Ilan calls and examines Aviram as he enters the office with a smile of demonstrative surprise. "Very nice! Hats off to Mali! This is more like it, I must say — you're a different person!"

"Really?" asks Aviram doubtfully.

Mali says: "That's not all."

"Yes, I know," sighs Aviram, "the beard."

"And the glasses," says Mali.

"The glasses? Are you serious? What's wrong with my glasses?"

"Why not clear lenses, so people can see your eyes?" says Mali enthusiastically, encouraged by her success. "Nobody can see that you've got blue eyes, they're small to begin with and that yellow-gray tint covers them completely."

"But the color of these lenses changes according to the light. In the sun they go dark, like sunglasses, and in the shade or in the evening they're clear."

"They make your eyes look sick," says Mali.

"Listen to her. You can see that she's got taste. Go and choose new glasses with her today," proposes Ilan.

Aviram is older than both of them and they treat him like a child. In order to get the embarrassing ceremony of his first appearance in his new clothes over as quickly as possible, he says nothing, sits down at his desk, and switches on the computer. Outside the sky is clear after days of heavy rain, and the big window reflects the square, bathed in wintry sunshine. Next to the bank entrance the Russian accordionist stands at his post playing his ancient tunes. Aviram can't concentrate on his work. The new jacket sits heavily on his shoulders and neck, hindering his movements, but he can't take it off, because the office is chilly. He misses the cozy, comfortable warmth of his zippered woolen cardigan, his soft, flannel plaid shirt. When he asked Mali to accompany him and help him buy new clothes, she agreed gladly and remarked that it was about time, because his old clothes and beard made him look like a settler, all that was missing was a knitted yarmulke and an Uzi hanging over his shoulder. He is grateful to her for her help. Soon she'll go out on her rounds, and in the meantime she looks at him with a satisfied smile. She's a nice, friendly woman, far from being a fool, and she has already grown accustomed to his attitude toward her and learned how to behave with him. There is immediate understanding between them, a good feeling of closeness, mutual esteem — but no fire. And he, with one foot already reaching for the trap he has set himself, is not prepared to settle for anything less than fire.

"And if you ask me," says Ilan, "at your age you can afford to wear a tie."

Mali gets up to go out on her rounds with the clients. And at the door she asks Aviram: "Are we going to the optician at lunchtime?"

"We'll see."

The telephone rings and Ilan picks it up. Mali leaves. Aviram studies the computer screen and begins the morning's work.

"And did you get what you were entitled to under the contract?" Ilan asks his interlocutor. "There's a clause that covers this kind of contingency. Yes? Okay then, that's all right."

Ilan covers the mouthpiece of the telephone with his hand and calls in a low voice: "Avi." Aviram raises his head. His partner points to the phone, signaling that something of interest to Aviram is going on there.

"Yes, I understand, definitely," Ilan says into the mouthpiece, "we'll do exactly as you wish, absolutely, you can go ahead with your trip and leave it to us."

Ilan sets up a meeting in the office with his interlocutor, says, "Bye, see you later," and hangs up.

"Guess what that was about?" He smiles mysteriously at Aviram.

Aviram thinks he can guess but shrugs his shoulders and shakes his head.

"The 'fucking' apartment! The tenants are leaving before the lease is up. They want to rent it out again, starting next month. It was the son on the phone. Last time the old man came in himself, from some moshav next to Hadera, I think, where they live. You know him from when they lived in your building and you didn't want to deal with it. Now he's sick, so the son's taking care of it. What's going on there? Why are they leaving?"

"I don't know," says Aviram. "I don't think anything much is going on."

"There's no activity lately?"

"Nothing, I think."

"Nothing to see or hear?"

"No."

"Which goes to prove that my thesis was right, that the fucking was only a perk and the real function of the apartment was something else."

Aviram doesn't understand how this proves or disproves Ilan's theory, but he doesn't want to get into a discussion about it.

"He told me that they paid the rent for next month too, on condition that they undertook not to let anybody in until the end of the month. He's coming by in two days' time, because he's going abroad and he won't be here at the end of the month. He'll take the lease to his father to sign and bring it back to us with the key. I promised we'd only start taking clients to view the apartment from the beginning of next month. And until then we'll hide the key. I'll tell Mali too.

"Don't you get it, Avi? The guy realizes he's been burned and he has to find somewhere new. And there are all kinds of things there that have to be finished by the end of the month, people that have to be informed of the change in address, telephone and fax number, and if you ask me, he won't be taking the lady with him to the new place, it isn't healthy to mix business with pleasure."

"I'm sure you're right," says Aviram. And he pictures Mali and their clients entering the apartment on which all his dreams are focused, showing them the kitchen, the bathroom, the living room, the bedroom.

At lunchtime he goes with Mali to the nearby shopping center where he bought his new clothes with her guidance and good advice. At the optician's the sales assistant shows them various frames and tries them on Aviram, while Mali examines his face judiciously. Aviram is invited to go behind the screen to have his eyes examined by the optician, leaving Mali to make up her mind about the frames.

When Aviram emerges from the examination, Mali shows him the frame she has selected, and the sales assistant says: "Your wife's right, that one suits you best." His heart contracts, and he is too embarrassed to look at Mali. Earlier, the salesman at the clothing store referred to him as Mali's "husband." But Mali only smiles and shows no sign of embarrassment. Aviram knows that it isn't only the fact of their being together that is misleading, but something in the way they relate to each other, perhaps even in their body language, their tone of voice, in the unquestioning way they take each other for granted, like a couple who have been living together for years.

"When you see them on you, with these frames and the clear lenses, you won't recognize yourself," Mali promises him as they go down to the car in which she will drive him home, as usual.

She is full of the joy of creation as she sees her work nearing completion, the remodeling of Aviram according to the dictates of her vision. From time to time she steals a gratified glance at the fruit of her labors sitting next to her in the car, inspecting some detail in the whole, considering what more needs to be improved, added, or subtracted.

Familiar voices, which have not been heard there for some time, rise from the backyard of the building. He goes inside immediately and hurries upstairs. The visit to the optician has delayed his homecoming and it's getting late. When he passes Shwartz's apartment the door opens and the old man, who has apparently been lying in wait for him, stands there, leaning on the doorpost with a gloomy expression on his face.

"Please help me downstairs," he pleads, "she refuses to do it. You hear what's going on there?"

Mrs. Shwartz is standing a few steps behind her husband, signaling to Aviram not to do as he asks, emphasizing her message by tapping her finger to her forehead to indicate that the old man has lost his wits.

"For two hours I've been sitting at the window and looking at the street, waiting for you to come home for lunch," the old man complains. "They're carrying on there like nobody's business and I can't see a thing."

Trapped between Mr. Shwartz's complaints and his wife's warnings, and his wish to see how the dog is and take him out, together with the hope of bumping into Gabi, whom he hasn't seen since her visit to his apartment, Aviram is seized by rage, and he doesn't know who to take it out on. And before he can decide what to do, the old man takes the initiative, abandons the support of the doorpost, shuffles up to him, and lays his hand on his shoulder. "Take me there," he says in a weak but commanding voice. Aviram begins walking toward the stairs and the old man scolds him: "Not like that!" and shows him how to put his arm around his back and support him under his armpits. They go down a few steps like this, and the old man whispers: "I can't," and he closes his eyes, his head wobbles, and he appears to be overcome by giddiness. Aviram stops and wonders what to do. He looks up at the landing. The old woman is standing there, leaning on the balustrade, looking at them with a bitter smile on her face. For a long moment she lets them go on standing there locked in an embrace on the stairs, and then she comes down, pushes Aviram aside, and grips her husband under his armpits. Shwartz opens his eyes: "Go and see and come back and tell me," he says to Aviram. His wife lifts him until his feet are barely touching the floor, carries him upstairs, takes him back into their apartment, and slams the door behind them.

The dog no longer greets his master with barks of joy as he climbs the stairs, but Aviram is not surprised. Ever since he was upset by the thunderstorm his behavior has changed, he has grown weaker, and he no longer keeps to his old habits. But Aviram knows that the dog has heard him coming and is waiting for him behind the door. And nevertheless, in the seconds between opening the door and seeing him raise his head and wag his tail, Aviram's heart always pounds in dread. A familiar smell greets him from the doorway. He goes inside, and the dog is there, with a puddle of urine beside him. "You poor thing, you waited so long and you couldn't keep it in anymore," he says and strokes the dog, "it's my fault, for being so late." And before cleaning up he inspects the other rooms to see if everything is in order there. On the other side of the bedroom wall he hears her voice. She's talking on the phone. It's a woman on the other end of the line. Is this the call to Ramat Hasharon? No, she's talking to someone close, and in the end she says to her: "So I'll see you here this evening." Will this help or hinder his own plans for the evening?

The dog proceeds slowly from step to step, and before completing the first flight he stops and looks at Aviram. This is the day for taking old men downstairs, Aviram sighs to himself, and he carries him outside. The dog moves around the garden, finds his favorite spot next to the gas tanks, and does his business there.

The repeated sound of water hitting the ground comes from the backyard. The ginger woman and her husband are drawing pails full of water from the basement and the sunken porch and emptying them out on the ground. They are both wearing rubber boots and their trousers are wet to above the knee. Judging by the level of water remaining on the porch, they still have a lot of work to do. Aviram stands on the concrete pavement where the garbage bins used to stand and keeps an eye on the dog in case he is tempted to approach the big puddle of water. On the balconies and windows overlooking the yard the neighbors are standing and watching the spectacle. The ginger woman stops to rest from her labors, putting her pail down on the concrete wall around the sunken porch and wiping the sweat off her brow with the back of her hand. Her husband too takes a break, and emerges from the water, and when he sees Aviram he comes up to him, as to an old acquaintance, to complain about his troubles.

"You see what happened to us here?" says the man in the red cap with its Olympic hoops and soft drink. "God is punishing us. What did we do wrong?"

Aviram has no answer to his question.

"Why don't you want us here?" the man asks in a dejected voice. "What harm have we done you that you hate us so much?"

His wife turns to the spectators at the windows and on the balconies: "We're not so easy to break. Nothing will help them. They think that if a bit of water comes in we'll get a fright and run away. They don't know us. That dying old man from their committee, he's the one who put a curse on us, damn him to hell. We know a woman who knows how to really curse people, for a few dollars she . . ."

"You're not too bad at cursing either!" someone calls from one of the balconies, and sounds of laughter greet his sally.

"What did we want that's so terrible," says the husband, "all we wanted was somewhere for our daughter to live when she gets out of the army."

"Like hell!" screams the woman. "You think we'll let our daughter live here? Over my dead body! We'll buy her a luxury apartment in Ramat Aviv, next to the university! You think I'll let her live here with this rotten lot who love Arabs and hate Jews? If that's what they want they can have it! We'll bring them Arabs, we'll bring them gangsters, junkies, whores, who'll make their lives hell until they wish they were back in Poland!"

She picks up the pail and starts dipping it again into the water flooding the porch, and her husband hurries to join her, after parting from Aviram with the melancholy conclusion: "God is punishing us, I don't know why."

One of the spectators calls out something that Aviram fails to catch, and again laughter rises from the opposite building. The woman puts her pail down at her feet, in the water. "Don't worry!" she yells at the heckler. "Everybody will pay! First of all that bastard of a contractor, who said that water couldn't get in here, tricked us and took our money, and then the liars who sold us the place and swore that there was no dampness in the winter. There'll be court cases, don't worry, we'll send them people who'll get our money back with interest and damages! We weren't born yesterday!"

Aviram is in a hurry, he has to keep his promise to Mr. Shwartz to go back and report on the situation, and then eat something before returning to work, but the sight of the man and the woman laboriously drawing up the water that has flooded their apartment reminds him of a legend his father read to him as a child, about a bird that avenged itself on the sea for flooding its nest. The memory brings with it from that distant time the obscure fear and unease to which the legend gave rise in him then, and the fear remains as obscure as ever.

Mr. Shwartz is lying in bed. The old woman ushers Aviram into the bedroom, which does not seem to have been aired out for a long time and smells suffocatingly of a mixture of urine, sweat, and medicine. She drags a chair up to the edge of the bed for him and goes to sit on her stool at the kitchen door. Aviram tells the old man about the events downstairs, and he closes his eyes and nods his head, as if his expectations have been confirmed. He points to the little radio on the bedside table at his head.

"Every half hour I turn it on to hear the weather report. They say there'll be more rain tomorrow or the next day, just as much as before. So after they finish taking out the water, the whole place will be flooded again. I only hope I live to see it! But I mustn't be greedy, I can die in peace now too, after seeing that justice and truth exist in the world."

Aviram gets up and says good-bye, and the old man raises his head from the pillow and points to the kitchen entrance, where his wife is sitting on her high stool. "She's a good woman," he says in a low voice. "She always loved me, even when I didn't deserve it. She gave me her life."

And his head falls onto the pillow, exhausted.

"This is Hezi's mistress speaking, from the secret apartment . . ." Perhaps she should open the conversation like this, if a woman answers, and listen to the silence that would fall for a moment on the other end of the line.

"You were looking for us to fill in a questionnaire for your statistical survey. I was very busy then and I couldn't find the time to answer you. Now I have time. What exactly do you want to know? Do you want us to meet or is it enough if I answer your questions over the phone?"

The woman at the end of the line hangs up immediately, or says it's a wrong number — that's one possibility. The other possibility is this: the woman tries to draw Gabi into a conversation and asks her questions. Or she makes an appointment to meet her. This is a less convenient option, one she should try to avoid.

And while she reflects she is suddenly startled by the ringing of the phone. When it rings for the fourth time, she knows it's Ada.

"Am I disturbing you?" her friend asks, hearing a hint of coolness and impatience in Gabi's voice.

"No, of course not! How do you feel?"

"You thought it was him, right? You're expecting him to call. Should I phone another time?"

"No, Adaleh! After all these years, you still astonish me. You make me feel transparent."

"That must be a horrible feeling. I'm sorry you feel that way."

"I'm used to it by now. How about you, are you all right now?"

"Yes, it was over quickly this time. We're all functioning at the top of our form, like Gadi says."

"I want to see you. Will you come and visit me in my 'Backstreet'?"

"Don't remind me. I was so sorry then for telling you about that movie. It was tactless of me. Altogether, that evening was strange and unpleasant."

"If you'd been tactful, you wouldn't have been Ada, and we wouldn't have been friends. So are you coming here?"

"When?"

"This evening."

"Yes, if that's all right with you," says Ada.

"It's fine."

"You're not expecting . . ."

"Of course I am," Gabi interrupts her. "I'm always expecting. Aren't you?"

"No, Gabi, I'm not expecting anyone or anything."

It's been a long time since they met, and after Ada inspects Gabi's face, to see if it's changed, she looks curiously around the apartment, hoping to find some clue that will help her discover the secret. Gabi suggests they sit in the kitchen. It's warmer there, and also — "I have an admirer here," she explains as they sit down at the little table, "behind the bedroom wall, and he can hear everything that goes on here."

She puts coffee and home-baked cookies on the table.

"Why don't you go home right away?" Ada opens without beating about the bush. "If he wants to find you, he can call you there."

"From the minute I go back home, I never want to hear from him again. He has to choose now. If he wants me, let him solve his problems and pay the price. If he doesn't want me, I'm not interested in him anymore and he's lost me forever."

"As simple as that!"

"Yes."

"But you still love him?"

"He's the man of my life. I've never loved anyone like this before. That's why I'm risking everything against all the odds."

Yelps of pain rise suddenly from the direction of the bedroom.

"What on earth was that?" asks Ada in dismay.

"The neighbor's dog. I think he hits him."

"That's terrible," says Ada. They are silent for a moment, listening to the yelps. Ada frowns and looks frightened. "You remember in 'The Outsider' there's an old man, Salamano, who lives in Meursault's building and curses his dog and beats it. You can hear the howls in the stairwell."

"You don't like this place, do you?" says Gabi.

"I like your place. This apartment isn't like a home. It's like a station where you're waiting for something to happen to you."

"This is where I knew the love of my life," says Gabi in an affected, dramatic tone, with a sad, ironic smile.

The yelping begins again.

They look at each other in silence, and Gabi can guess what her friend wanted to say to her but didn't, because there are limits even to Ada's tactlessness: "'That neighbor of yours probably loves his dog too, perhaps it's the love of his life too.' That's what you were thinking now, right?"

Ada blushes, evades the question, and says in a low voice: "I knew you were suffering. You said you felt you were going to war. And war's war, with all the cruelty and suffering and absurdity involved. Now I feel like a tourist paying a visit to your battlefield."

Their conversation goes on for a long time, and it grows late for Ada, whose family life obliges her to get up early in the morning. She gets up to say good-bye.

"I prepared myself to hear from you this evening," says Gabi, "about the quiet, gentle beauty of resignation, of reconciliation with life, of compromise with what it has to offer — to be glad of every moment that passes without calamity, without anything happening, not to expect anything."

"I spared you that lecture this time. You already know it. And I don't like being the one who says: You see, I told you so!"

"Wait, Adaleh, we don't know that yet."

Ada looks at her with an embarrassed smile.

"Do I look all right?" asks Gabi.

"You've matured."

"I'm growing old, you mean."

"You still look younger than your age. But your face shows what you're going through. Oded said that you looked tense and worried."

"The man hasn't yet been born who won't say that a woman who rejected his advances is lonely, miserable, disturbed, and frustrated."

"You really don't know Oded."

"He asked me to come around to his place and listen to music. It revolted me."

Ada shrugs her shoulders uncomprehendingly and refrains from replying, in order not to fan the anger distorting her friend's voice.

Gabi goes out to accompany Ada to her car, which is parked in a nearby street. On the landing she puts a finger to her lips, and they go downstairs in silence. Outside the sky is clear and the air is very cold, and Gabi, who came down without her coat, hugs Ada's coat sleeve with both arms in an attempt to warm herself. In this position they walk slowly down the dark, deserted street, maintaining the silence that began in the stair-well, and Gabi feels that their closeness now is stronger than all the things that were said and not said before, and perhaps Ada feels the same.

"Don't disappear again," Ada says before getting into her car, "let me know what's happening to you. I guess there's no point in inviting you to come around on Friday night."

"I'll still be here, at my post," says Gabi, and she hugs Ada and kisses her on the cheek, which feels cool and dry to her lips after its exposure to the cold night air.

She hurries home to escape from the cold and opens the door of her apartment — which is completely dark. But she'd left the light on in the kitchen. She presses the switch a couple of times in vain. The heater is also off. The lights in the other rooms too refuse to go on. But the fridge is still working. She goes out to the landing and opens the fuse box. The fuses are the old-fashioned porcelain sort and she has no idea what to do with them. Her house in Givatayim is equipped with the new fuse panels, which are easy to handle. Perhaps the heater has caused a short? She gropes in the darkness of the kitchen and pulls the plug out of the socket. For a moment she stands there at a loss and then she goes out to the landing and listens at the neighbor's door. She hears voices from the television and rings the bell.

The door opens and he is revealed to her for the first time in his new incarnation: gray tweed jacket, pale blue shirt, dark blue woolen trousers, gleaming black shoes, and new glasses with clear lenses in narrow metal frames, with his small blue eyes, pink and watery, looking out at her. She apologizes for troubling him so late at night, tells him about her problem, and asks him to help. He goes up to the open fuse box and looks inside. "Oh, the old fuses!" he exclaims in surprise. His voice sounds peculiar, higher than she remembers it from previous occasions, and his gait seems unsteady. Perhaps he had fallen asleep in front of the television and she had woken him up when she rang the doorbell? He pulls out the porcelain fuses one by one, examines them, and finally shows her one whose thin copper wire connecting the two screws is broken in the middle. "Here's your short," he says, a silly smile on his face.

Is she only imagining the smell of alcohol on his breath? She should have gone to bed in the dark and called in an electrician to repair the damage in the morning. "Just a minute," he says, and he goes back inside and returns with a little toolbox, puts it down at the foot of the fuse box, removes a screwdriver, and tries to fit the edge into the groove in the little screw of the fuse. Again and again his hand fumbles until the screwdriver finally goes in and he loosens both screws and removes the torn wire. From one of the compartments in his tidily arranged toolbox he takes a plastic envelope and with a little pincer he exposes the slender copper wires inside it, separates three of them, cuts them to the desired length, and twists them together into one piece of wire. Then he stretches this triple wire between the two screws and again he fumbles with the screwdriver until he gets it into the screws and manages to tighten them. He seems to be well-versed in this kind of job, but this time his performance is somewhat faltering. In the end he returns the fuse to the panel, and the kitchen light goes on.

"It must have happened because of the heater," says Gabi. "But I've already pulled the plug out of the socket."

"Try to connect it again," he suggests and bursts out laughing. His laughter makes his face look ugly behind his beard.

Hesitantly she pushes the plug back into the wall, and the heater goes on again and begins to warm the air.

"With those old fuses the wire sometimes disintegrates after a few years, either from metal fatigue or from corrosion," he supplies the scientific explanation.

She thanks him, but instead of picking up his toolbox and returning to his apartment, he stands there waiting. Something about him and his new clothes arouses her pity. She offers him a hot drink, and instead of declining politely, referring to the late hour, he agrees at once, without hesitation, as if he were expecting her to invite him in as a matter of course.

His eyes seek out her bedroom, and he steps into the living room. She directs him to the kitchen, where it's warmer. She offers him coffee, as the drink appropriate to his situation, but he prefers tea with lemon, since coffee, he says, will prevent him from sleeping. The remaining cookies she baked for Ada are still on the kitchen table, and she offers them to him and makes lemon tea for both of them. After serving the tea she sits down opposite him, and for a moment they drink in silence, and he smiles his silly smile at her.

"You did it," she says to him.

He bursts into the ingratiating laughter of someone caught in a mischievous prank, denying everything and laughing, denying and laughing.

"Aren't you ashamed of yourself, a grown man?"

"What did I do?" He tries to stifle his laughter and fails.

"You waited for me to go out to see my friend off in order to arrange a short in my apartment."

"No! Nonsense!"

"And in order to get the courage to do it, you drank vodka or brandy, I don't know which."

"No, I never drink."

"What do you want from me?"

"I need your advice."

"My advice?"

"It's for a good friend of mine."

What is it that amuses him so much in this childish game? And why is she so happy to join in?

"What's your friend's problem?"

"He fell in love with someone who came to live in his neighborhood. He knows he hasn't got a chance with her: she's beautiful, really nice, and with a dancer's body. And he's not young, not in the least attractive or successful. From the first moment he set eyes on her, when she came to live there, he felt that his whole life as he had lived it up to then was exploding. He realized that he'd never known the real thing, and that apparently he never would. Ever since then he can't think of anything else. Because he, the way he looks, usually goes to prostitutes. But he hates them and afterward he feels disgusted with himself. So he says to me: 'Listen, Avi, I have to, I simply have to do it once with someone like her, just once in my life. Just to know what it's like. But someone like her wouldn't even look at someone like me, who am I to her, what am I to her?'"

"And what did you say to this friend?"

"I said to him: 'Are you crazy? Put her out of your mind, everyone has to know their place. In love it's like it was in the Middle Ages — society's divided into classes and you can't cross the lines. People are born into their class and die in it. It's the same thing with love — there's the aristocracy of love and the serfs of love, at the bottom of the heap. And they have to be content with what's offered them, ugly and pathetic as they are. So put that dream out of your mind and learn to live with what you can get.'"

"Quite right. And he wasn't convinced?"

"He won't give up. He says: 'But I'm not talking about getting married, living together and all that. I know that's not realistic. If I was rich, for example, or famous, or an important person in society, it's not unusual to see beautiful women married to men like that. Either they're attracted to their power or else they want comfort and luxury and they're ready to sell themselves for those things even if the man is old and ugly and dreary and repulsive. But I,' he says, 'have nothing to offer except my ugliness and dreariness, so obviously that's not what I have in mind. But maybe this girl has a kind heart, and she'll agree just so a person like me will get the chance to go to bed once in his life with someone like her.'"

"And what did you say to him?" asks Gabi, who finds herself deriving a curious pleasure from this conversation, and the sillier and more childish it gets, the harder it is for her to stifle her laughter.

"I said to him: 'The world of women is a mystery to us. We should ask a woman with brains and experience to tell us if in her opinion such a thing is conceivable at all.' And I decided to ask you if it would be possible at all to ask such a thing of a woman like that, the kind of woman every successful man dreams of, if she would consider doing someone like him a favor on a one-time basis."

Gabi says nothing and looks at him with a smile.

"So what do you say?" he asks.

"Tell your friend that he's playing with fire."

"That's it exactly! He wants the fire!"

Again she smiles in silence.

The ease and confidence lent him by the alcohol are beginning to fade, and gloom descends. Now he looks more like the neighbor she is used to seeing in his old clothes and worn-out sneakers. He leans his head on his hand and mutters: "What nonsense I'm talking. Oh my God!"

"No!" she cries in pretended innocence and tries to go on with the game. "I think it's very nice of you to want to help your friend, and I can tell you something that might help him. I too have a good friend, and she, when she was a student, many years ago, worked as a proofreader at a newspaper. There was some old proofreader there who made advances toward her and kept pestering her and wouldn't leave her alone. One day she couldn't stand it any longer, and she said to him: 'Leave me alone, I don't want to hear another word! If you don't stop I'll complain about you.' So he said to her: 'Tell me, where's the justice? What am I asking of you after all? For you it's at most ten disagreeable minutes, and for me it's a great boon, heaven on earth!' And she gave him such a slap that he flew off his chair and fell on the floor. After that he never came near her again. Tell that to your friend."

"I don't feel well," says Aviram, his face pale under his beard, his head hanging, and he rises with difficulty from his chair, supporting himself on the table. "I have to go home now."

She goes up to him, takes him by the shoulders, helps him to straighten up, and leads him to his door. His hand trembles and he can't get the key into the lock. She takes the key from him, opens the door, and leads him inside. He leans against the passage wall and whispers in a dreamy voice: "It's a misunderstanding, we're a couple of strangers." The dog comes out of the bedroom, moving heavily, and stops in front of them. He looks at his master with a critical expression, but there seems to be a great deal of compassion in his tired eyes. Aviram suddenly detaches himself from the wall and runs to the bathroom, slamming the door behind him. There is a loud, retching sound of vomiting. The dog follows him, resigns himself to the sentence of the closed door, and lies down in front of it.

She hurries back to her apartment, but on the landing, under the fuse box, she sees his toolbox lying open on the floor. Various tools, wires, nails and screws, a tube of glue, and a paintbrush, appliances whose nature is a mystery to her, arranged in layers and compartments with obsessive order, with an almost fetishistic love, signal to her in an archaic male code she will never be able to decipher. She closes the box and carries it to his apartment. The door is still open and she goes inside. Aviram is standing in the bathroom door, the dog lying at his feet, and applying a damp towel to the stains on his new jacket and shirt. She puts the toolbox down in the hallway.

"Are you feeling better?" she asks.

He raises his head and looks at her. His face is washed, his hair and beard are wet: "Forgive me for everything that happened. We're strangers. I had no right."

When the door opened to let them in, they saw him sitting in the armchair with his back to them, watching television. His grandmother called him from the doorway, and he got up and stood facing them, wearing a uniform that had been washed and ironed, the collar starched, his beret folded under one of the shoulder straps of his khaki sweater, his black army boots shining, his face fresh and his hair cut short. This was how Ezra had imagined his son as a soldier before the lad was drafted and the trouble started. And to Ruthie it seemed that he had grown thinner and taller since she saw him last, that now he was taller than his short, broad-shouldered father.

The grandmother said: "I'm going to make coffee."

Ezra asked: "Where's Menashe?"

"He'll be here soon," said his mother.

"My Eyalie," said Ruthie, and she went up to embrace him, but he evaded her outstretched arms. Taken aback, she murmured: "I'm so glad you've come back. We missed you terribly. Are you well?"

"I'm okay," said Eyal.

"Menashe only told us this afternoon," said Ruthie, "I haven't even had a chance to make something special for you, one of your favorite dishes."

"No need," said Eyal, "Grandma keeps feeding me all the time."

"You must be strong, Eyalie," said Ezra. He chose his words carefully, in accordance with his promise to his brother. "You know that you have a hard time ahead of you."

"I've been through hard things already," said Eyal and suddenly he smiled, a pale smile that froze at the corners of his mouth without affecting the rest of his face, or his tired eyes hiding in the shadow of the thick, black eyebrows he had inherited from his father.

"I know you're a strong person," said Ezra.

Eyal turned his face away.

The grandmother served coffee. Ezra lit a cigarette and he didn't know what else to say to his son.

"Gili and Yaniv don't know that you're coming home yet," he finally said. "We wanted to surprise them. They ask about you all the time, they miss you. Tomorrow morning, when they wake up, they'll find you at home.

"Or maybe you want to leave the house early, before they get up," added Ezra.

"Whatever you want," said Eyal.

A pain pierced Ezra's heart.

"What do you want?" he asked.

"It makes no difference to me," said Eyal.

"Do you want to see Gili and Yaniv?" asked Ruthie.

"Whatever you like."

"You still look a little tired," said Ruthie.

"Maybe we should go home now," said Ezra.

"Menashe will be here in a little while," said the grandmother.

"What were you watching on television when we arrived?" asked Ruthie.

"Nothing special," said Eyal.

After a while Menashe arrived, in high spirits. "I just dropped in for a minute to see how you were getting on. I have guests and I have to get back," he said and went up to Eyal, put his hand on the back of his neck, and pressed so hard with his fingers that the boy bowed his head and his face twisted. "Have you ever given us a lot of trouble!" he said. "Thank God it's over. It's over for us, that is, but for you this is only the beginning of a whole new story. I know that you can get through it and they won't break you. I want you to know, I told your parents all the time, and I'm telling you now, in front of them: You've proved that you're a strong man. You have willpower and endurance and character and you're as stubborn as a mule, and if you put it all to good use you'll go far. Bless you, my boy, and hang in there!"

"Okay," said Eyal.

They drove home, the three of them sat in the cabin of the pickup truck, and Ruthie put her arm around his shoulders. And again he shook her off and said: "No, Mother, I can't stand to be touched."

An oppressive silence fell and it lasted for a long time. Ezra switched on the radio and the eleven o'clock news covered up the silence.

"Eyalie," said Ezra, "tell me how you want to do it tomorrow morning — do you want to go to the police station yourself, or do you want me to take you there?"

"Whatever you want."

"So tell me if this suits you: I'd like us to walk there, the two of us together, down the main street, so that everyone will see that I'm not ashamed of my son, that I'm proud of you. You heard what Menashe said about you, and I think so too. And I want everyone to see how handsome you look in your uniform. It'll make me feel good."

"Okay," said Eyal.

They stopped in front of the house, Eyal remained in the truck, and Ezra and Ruthie went inside to send the baby-sitter home. Then they took Eyal in.

"Do you want anything before you go to bed?" asked Ruthie.

"No, nothing," said Eyal. "I'm tired, I want to sleep."

Ruthie accompanied him to his room, where she had already made the bed. "Tonight at least you'll sleep in a clean, comfortable bed, your own bed, in your own room," she said. "Good night."

He put out his hand and gripped his mother's elbow without saying anything. His hand was so cold that it sent shivers down her spine, and the corners of his mouth stretched again in the strange smile that didn't change the expression on his face. She averted her face and there was a tremor in her voice when she repeated: "Good night, Eyalie."

He shut himself in his room and Ruthie went to her and Ezra's bedroom. Her husband was waiting for her, sitting on the bed in his clothes like a beaten man. "Shut the door," he said.

Ruthie shut the door and looked at her husband. From the way he looked she understood that she would have to be the strong, optimistic partner again.

"What do you say, Ruthie?" he whispered.

"He's terribly tired, Ezra. I hope that after a good sleep in his own bed, at home, he'll get up with renewed strength to help him face what's waiting for him now," she said.

"When we were at my mother's house, I thought that maybe he was putting on an act for us of some nutcase or retard who doesn't know what he wants and doesn't give a damn what happens to him, and all the time he was thinking of all kinds of plans and ideas about how to run away again and make a whole lot of new trouble. But when he wouldn't let you hug him and told you afterward in the truck that he couldn't stand being touched, I began to be afraid that he's really gone crazy."

"Maybe precisely that apathy will help him get through his jail sentence without any trouble, he'll do whatever he's told without any objections, without any arguments, and he'll have a chance to get over this crisis and come out stronger and more mature. Ezra, I believe in his strength."

"I remember what he said the last time, that he can get out of the army by pretending to be crazy. What if he's already beginning to act that part?"

"Ezra, our Eyal isn't an actor and he's never known how to put on an act. He's an honest, straightforward boy. The way he looks is the way he feels."

"If it's not an act, then there's no chance that they'll take him back in the army. Straight after jail they'll discharge him as mentally unfit. Ruthie, it'll haunt him for the rest of his life."

"Is that what you're worrying about now, Ezra?" asked Ruthie. "Wait for him to wake up in the morning, after a good sleep at home and a good breakfast, and then you'll see that he'll be the same Eyalie we've always known."

"They say that with the gentiles it's not like it is with us," said Ezra. "In America, for example, when a boy reaches the age when he's supposed to be independent, he leaves home, goes wherever he can get a job, gets married, and afterward, once a year, at their Christmas, he phones his parents to say hello and how are you, and when he has a child he phones to let them know. That's all the contact they have. And only when one of the parents dies, they let him know and if he can get away he comes to the funeral and sees the family. That's all. They don't have the kind of ties that we have.

"And maybe it's better that way, Ruthie? Eyal's already over eighteen. At his age I'd already been going out to work for a few years and bringing money home. It's a man's age. He's entitled to live his life the way he wants to, and if he wants to go mad, let him go mad. But we live his life all the time, take part in everything that happens to him, worry about his worries, plan his future for him. Maybe it's not healthy. Maybe as someone who understands psychology, you know this. But I have to admit, Ruthie, that even if it's not a good thing, I can't cut that tie. In spite of everything, even though he's like a stranger now, I feel that he's still mine, that he's part of me, like a part of my body. I can't change that, I can't let it go."

"That means you love him, Ezra," said Ruthie, "and I'm sure that he feels it and that it's important to him."

Ruthie got undressed and got into bed, and Ezra went on sitting on the bed for a while and thinking, until he too got undressed, set the alarm clock, and lay down next to her. She was already asleep. Ezra looked at her in admiration: what a strong woman she was — able to fall asleep like that, immediately, after everything they had been through during the day; and in gratitude: how privileged he was to have won a wife like her, to love him and be a faithful friend, a sure support in times of trouble, and when he gave way to dread and despair, to strengthen his spirit with her understanding, with her inner serenity.

EIGHT

"What happened?" cries Ilan in alarm. "Avi, are you with me?"

"I'm telling you that I can't come in today."

"Okay, but tell me what's the matter. Did something happen to your parents? You don't sound right."

"The dog died last night."

"I'm sorry," says Ilan with a sound of relief in his voice, "I know how attached you were to him." After a moment of silence Ilan speaks again: "Mali wants to say something to you."

"Avi," Mali's voice, practical and authoritative, "when did it happen?"

"Last night, while I was sleeping. He died peacefully. When I woke up this morning he wasn't waiting next to my bed, like he always does. He was lying dead on the floor."

"He was old."

"Yes. The vet said it was apparently a heart attack. He's been going downhill lately. On Saturday he was terribly weak. I thought of taking him to the vet today. Now I have to take the body there. He agreed to bury him for me. I can't do it, I don't know how to do it by myself."

"Where's the vet's clinic?"

Aviram guesses why she's asking and tells her where it is.

"Good, that's right near here. I'm coming to take you there. When do you want to leave the house?"

A narrow crack into his private life has opened up to her, and she won't miss the opportunity to widen it, to establish another foothold in his world, to deepen their intimacy. But he's grateful to her for it.

"Listen, that would be really nice of you. In this rain it's impossible to get hold of a taxi, and knowing those guys none of them would agree to take a dead dog anyway."

She says good-bye to him as if she's taking leave of a mourner: "Be strong, Avi, and know that we love you." Just so, in the plural.

He goes out in his old clothes, his scuffed sneakers and the glasses that cast a brownish gray shadow over his eyes, carrying the dead dog in his arms, and descends the stairs hoping that he won't bump into anyone. The rain keeps coming down, and he waits for Mali's car under the portico. The red Fiat Uno stops promptly opposite the building, Mali waves to him and opens the back door wide for him. He runs to get into the car and sits down on the backseat, the dead dog on his lap. Mali says: "You can put him next to you." On the seat at his left she has taken the trouble to spread a towel, but he leaves the body in his lap.

All the windows of the car are closed. The din of the rain and the traffic filter in like a muffled roar in the background, punctuated by the regular clicking of the windshield wipers. They drive in silence, wisely uninterrupted by Mali, who only turns her head from time to time, when they stop at a traffic light, and smiles at him sympathetically.

When they reach the clinic she parks the car and gets out to open the door for Aviram.

Outside, with the dead dog in his arms, he tries to thank her: "You're so good to me, you spoil me."

"I know how you feel," says Mali. "I only wish I knew how to do more."

The rain's been pouring down without stop for a few days now and it's impossible to go out. When she has to do some shopping, she goes out by herself and comes back wet; only rarely does he consent to tear himself away from the television and go in her place, and then only because his supply of beer and cigarettes has run out. He's a lazy fellow. No wonder he lost his job.

Sitting inside all day is having a bad influence on their relationship. It affects me badly too. It gets on my nerves and gives me a feeling of insecurity. They argue a lot and often get into real quarrels. They yell at each other, and even without understanding what they're saying, I know that she's right. She works hard, he's living at her expense, and he doesn't want to give her any help. When she asks him to do things for me — I understand this, because she points to me — he becomes angry, drinks beer, lights another cigarette, and goes on watching television. Once she lost her temper to such an extent that she went over to switch it off. He grabbed hold of her hand and struggled with her until she was forced to yield. The question is, when will the violence in him break out on her, a violence I discerned the first time he came to take her place on her day off?

But when the atmosphere calms, when they make up and she shows him love, I forgive him too, and feel affection for him. Because like her, he too has become a part of me.

On Sunday morning a quarrel broke out between them again. She put on her Sunday clothes that she wears when she goes to pray in their church in Jaffa, and he refused to let her out of the house, he locked the door and hid the key. In the beginning it was in fun, she looked for the key in his clothes, he ran away from her and she ran after him and tried to catch him. They ran about all over the house, fighting and laughing like a pair of children. But it was getting late — she has to take a bus there and walk some distance as well. She began to get angry, and he stubbornly refused to open the door. The argument between them grew heated, she yelled at him and apparently said something that insulted him. His face changed and he attacked her and hit her. She fell down. I couldn't control myself any longer and shouted at the top of my voice. He came and stood in front of me and opened his mouth and shouted back, mimicking me. He bent down and brought his head right up close to mine, until our foreheads were almost touching. He stood like this for a long time, a fat little savage, his hands on his hips, his back bent, his little eyes, like the eyes of a wild beast, trying to swallow my eyes, as if to say: What are you going to do about it?

I turned my head and looked at her. She was lying huddled up on the floor, her face hidden by her arms, crying. I've never heard such crying: short, strangled, shrill shrieks, interrupted by seconds of silence. I thought that something inside me was about to explode in pain and rage. He moved away from my chair and stood in the middle of the room, put his hand into his shirt, took out the key, and threw it contemptuously on the floor. Without revealing her face, which was still hidden by her arm, she stretched out her other hand, snatched the key, got up, and ran quickly to the door, opened it, and ran outside. It was raining and she didn't even take an umbrella.

He went and sat down in the armchair, lit a cigarette, and sat for a long time sunk in gloomy thoughts. Then he stood up, went into the kitchen, and came back with a can of beer and opened it and began to drink. From time to time he glanced at me questioningly, then returned to his thoughts. After a while he went back to the kitchen and fetched a glass, poured some beer from the can into it, and without raising his head put it down on the board attached to my chair. Then he returned to the armchair and looked at me, waiting to see what I would do. When he saw that I didn't touch the glass, he raised his can as if in a toast.

I hated him at that moment as I had hated him when he hit her and knocked her to the floor, and when he stood opposite me to show me who had the power here. Now he was afraid he would be thrown out of the house and his good life would be over. I had no doubt that there would be more outbursts from him, and even worse. Outside it was raining hard, and to increase my pain I imagined her running and running to get to her church in time, wet through and through, in her Sunday best, ruined by the rain. How dare he rob her of her only hours of freedom, one day a week, in all the days and nights that she's shut up here, and on that day too she has another job cleaning somewhere. Why shouldn't she want to get out a bit, meet her girlfriends who come there from all over the town, and pour out her heart to God? I couldn't forgive him. The way he treated her, her pain and humiliation and her strange crying, gave me no rest. But a voice from the depths, what it is I shall never understand, cried out to me to betray her, to take his side, to learn to love even the wild animal in him. I raised the glass and tasted the beer.

In my former life I enjoyed drinking a glass of cold beer, especially in the summer, but this beer tasted different, more sharp and bitter, or perhaps it's my taste that has changed. After a moment I began to feel the influence of the alcohol. My heart started beating fast, and a pleasant tiredness spread through the living parts of my body, enticing me to yield to the power of life, which apparently stems from a strange mixture of love and hate, kindness and cruelty. He was looking at me all the time, now he rose to his feet and came over to me and stood at the side of my chair, holding the beer can in one hand and placing the other on my shoulder. For a long time he stood there like that without saying a word, and the touch of his hand on my shoulder gave me a real family feeling, and I didn't ask myself who was the father here and who was the child.

I woke from a deep sleep. He shook my shoulder until I opened my eyes and saw him standing opposite me. Lunch was ready and he wheeled my chair into the kitchen. I felt muzzy, perhaps because of the beer I'm no longer used to drinking, but with relish I ate the dish she had prepared and he had warmed up. He didn't touch the food on his plate, averting his eyes with a frown. I made a sound, he looked at me, I pointed to his plate, and he shook his head and sunk into thought again. He was sorry for what he had done but he wouldn't learn a lesson; it's impossible to learn a lesson.

When she came home, she ran past us in the living room, went into her balcony room, and shut herself up there. He looked at the door with impatience and concern. After a while she came out dressed in her everyday clothes, having hung the wet ones on a chair in her room to dry. She walked past us carrying the plastic bag in which she puts her work clothes when she goes to her Sunday job. She came up to me and asked: "He give you lunch?" I nodded. Yes. She smiled at me and I put out my hand to her, to feel her soft palm and say to her: Linda, Linda, but she didn't see it, because she ran out of the living room and left the house.

Once more the two of us were left alone. He stood up and

switched on the television, which up to now he had heroically restrained himself from watching — perhaps in order to punish himself — and the sound of sports filled the air again.

There was a pause in the rain and at least I didn't have to worry that she would get wet again. But some unclear fear gripped me, my heart was full of foreboding. He watches the television, devouring the pictures with his eyes. The beer can is in front of him, the cigarette is in his hand, and his other hand is fumbling between his legs. As if nothing has happened. Has he decided to forget what he did and what the consequences might be? Like a blind savage he destroys what has been created here, and who knows if it can still be repaired? Again I felt hatred for him and at the same time the wish to wreak vengeance upon him, to hurt him, to kick him out of the house. But I couldn't think of it seriously: he too is part of what has come into being here, and like her, he too is a part of me.

This house has already seen such things in my former life, and that man was no better than Pedro. In some strange way things have to repeat themselves. I once read an article about reincarnation. I have never believed in such things. But lately I've been thinking about it, especially since the mixed-up boy in the park said about his dog that in a former life she had been a great saint. People like that sometimes know things that they themselves don't understand. I said to myself: According to this belief, the soul is reborn in order to atone for the sins of its former incarnation. So if he was a great saint, why did his soul pass into the body of a miserable stray dog, what was this punishment for? Perhaps the sin was being a great saint? And when I arrive at this hypothesis, my train of thought stops, it's impossible to go on from there to anything, like banging your head against the wall, and all the pain and the fear.

It's already dark. I try to pass the time by napping, but I can't overcome my fear. It's getting late. She should have been home by now. He looks at his watch, offers to go and make my supper. I signal that I don't want to eat. He doesn't want to eat either. He stays where he is and goes back to watching the television. All my thoughts are concentrated on the front door, to hear it opening, to see her coming in. From time to time he looks at his watch, in the end he gets up and looks at me questioningly, with a worried expression, he doesn't know what to do.

It's already late and he offers to make me supper again. I don't want to eat and show him with a gesture that I want a drink. Tea? He asks. He knows that this is my drink. I nod. He goes to make me a cup of tea. After a while he returns and puts the cup on my little table, goes back to the kitchen, and brings himself a cup as well. I've never seen him drink tea before. He usually drinks beer or coffee.

He switches off the television and wheels me into the bathroom to prepare me for bed. I don't want to go to bed, I want to wait for her on my chair, but I don't object, I let him do what's necessary, and he does everything slowly and silently, with a serious expression, without showing his feelings. After all the preparations are complete, he wheels me into the bedroom, picks me up and puts me gently to bed, covers me with a blanket, switches off the light, and leaves the room. From my bed I can see him making up a bed on the sofa, bringing the bedclothes from her balcony, where they usually sleep together. Then he closes the door to the balcony, gets undressed, and shuts off the lights. I hear the rustle of the sheets when he gets into bed, and when my eyes get used to the dark, I see him raising his head from the pillow. He begins to cough, and after the coughing subsides, he sighs and puts his head down on the pillow again. And after that nothing breaks the silence. Everything is over and back to the beginning again.

Rhythmic tunes rise from the apartment. Is he waiting for her there? Did the cleaning woman forget to switch off the radio when she left? Did she come late and is she still there? Gabi rings the doorbell repeatedly without getting a response. The door is locked, the key turns twice in the lock. Inside the lights are on. Before closing the door behind her she calls out: "Hey! Hey!" and the radio goes on playing its tunes. A khaki parka, an umbrella, and a plastic bag are hanging on the rack in the hall. She enters the lit living room. The carpet is rolled up next to the wall, on one of the armchairs are a pair of jeans, a shirt, and a gray sweatshirt. At the foot of the sofa, white sneakers and socks. On the table, a bunch of keys. She turns off the radio and all is silent. Again she calls: "Hey!" and there is no reply. In the bathroom is a pail full of water with a rag inside it, and the mop handle leaning on the wall. There is no one in the kitchen or the toilet either. She goes into the bedroom. At the foot of the bed is the body of a naked girl, with her face on the floor and a big pool of blood around her head.

She escapes from the bedroom, closes the door, returns to the living room, and drops into the empty armchair. When she opens her eyes she has no idea how much time has passed since she closed them. Her glance falls on the other armchair, where the clothes are lying. Nothing has changed there. She realizes that she has to summon help and phones Hezi's office.

"He's left the room," says the secretary. "Who's calling?"

"It's from his home, it's urgent!"

"He's gone upstairs, as soon as he comes back I'll tell him to phone home right away."

"No. Please call him and tell him that it's extremely urgent. I'm waiting on the line."

In the moments of waiting she begins to feel the effects of the fear gnawing at her insides like a hungry animal, it seems to her that she is shrinking rapidly, soon there'll be nothing left of her but a dot. Is it possible that she fears him more than what she saw in the bedroom?

"Who is it?" his voice comes angrily over the line.

"The Filipino maid's been killed," her voice chokes in terror.

"It's you!"

"I just came back to the apartment and I found her lying there on the floor, murdered."

"The Filipino maid?" he says in astonishment, as if this is the only thing that surprises him in what she said.

"Yes."

He is silent for a moment. "Listen! I'll be there in a minute. Don't do anything, don't touch anything, and don't call anyone."

"The police?"

"No! Wait till I come. You must be in shock, I'll take care of everything. Do you understand what I'm saying? Wait for me and don't do anything."

"All right."

She pulls the telephone cord into the kitchen and sits down there. On the marble counter are a couple of rags and cleaning agents in plastic containers, and she doesn't dare approach them. She can't move from her place at the table, not even to boil a kettle of water and make herself a cup of coffee. And every few minutes she looks at her watch.

Twenty-five minutes later, when he still hasn't arrived, she calls his office again, and there's no reply. It occurs to her to call the number in Ramat Hasharon, but to do this she would have to go into the bedroom, where she left the note with the phone number. And perhaps she should run away right now, go back home to Givatayim and leave all this behind her. Let Hezi take care of it when he comes, he was the one who rented the apartment and hired the cleaning woman. But she can't move from her chair, as if the connection between her will and her body has broken.

When he still hasn't come after forty minutes, she calls Ada.

At the sound of her friend's voice her sense of reality begins to return.

"Something terrible's happened, Ada, come quick and help me!"

"What happened?"

"Murder! Someone's murdered the Filipino maid who comes to clean the apartment. I came home and found her dead, I don't know what to do. Come quickly!"

"Have you told the police?"

"No! I don't even know how! Come quickly and help me!"

When the intercom buzzes, she manages to pull herself together sufficiently to get up and answer it. Ada's downstairs.

Once she lets her friend into the apartment and feels her closeness, Gabi breaks down and bursts into tears. Ada embraces her and tries to comfort her, and she turns into the living room, but Gabi protests: "No, not there," and pulls her to the kitchen.

"Where is she?"

"In the bedroom."

"I'm going to see."

"No, don't go in there! It's horrible!"

Ada goes anyway.

"Don't touch anything," says Gabi.

When she returns Ada's face reflects her horror, but she controls herself. "She's naked. They must have raped her."

"I didn't think of that at all," says Gabi and bursts into tears again.

"Okay, we have to call the police," says Ada.

"He told me that he was coming immediately."

"Who?"

"I called him at the office and he told me to wait for him to come, not to call anyone and not to do anything. He would take care of it. That was almost an hour ago."

"And he didn't come," says Ada, as if it is obvious.

"He didn't come. He's left the country. He's run away. He's sitting on a plane at this very moment, he'll disappear and no one will ever find him."

"I'm calling the police," says Ada.

"Just a minute, Ada, I haven't got the strength now for policemen and questions and all the rest, I have to have a cup of coffee first. But I can't go to the kettle, because of the things she left there on the counter, I'm afraid to go near them."

Ada makes the coffee according to her instructions. "An hour is a long time," she says, "they'll tell you you should have called them the minute you saw it. Perhaps she was still alive and they could have saved her?"

"No, she wasn't breathing, I saw she wasn't breathing."

"How did they get in, did they break in?"

"No, the door was locked, I opened it with the key."

"Is there anyone else with a key?"

"Apart from me, the only people who had keys were Hezi and the cleaning woman, and her keys are on the table in the living room."

Ada gives her the coffee.

"I never knew how strong you were," says Gabi.

Ada shrugs. "I wanted Gadi to come with me, but I couldn't find him at his office."

"Did you leave the children at home alone?"

"It's all right, don't worry. So what do you think," asks Ada, "could it be Hezi?"

"Why, what on earth for?" protests Gabi.

"Do you believe he would be capable of something like that?"

"I don't know. I don't know him at all. There are all kinds of things he does with the firm's money, and if I opened my mouth it could ruin him. But he knows that at this hour on Sundays she works here, and I'm never at home."

"I'm calling the police."

On the other side of the wall a different sort of music was playing: pop songs in English. From time to time furniture was moved, something thudded on the wall or floor. He took off his clothes and went to wash. When he emerged from the shower and stood drying himself, the bathroom was full of steam. The mirror was misted over. He opened the bathroom door and wiped the mirror with his hand. From the plastic bag he removed the shaving soap and the razor he had bought earlier in the day, covered his face with lather, and passed the razor over it carefully. Clots of lather, gray with the hair of his beard, were washed off the razor in the stream of water from the tap and dropped into the basin.

After he finished shaving, he washed his face well and patted it dry. A stranger's face glared at him from the mirror: how dare he wreck its hiding place and disturb its rest! Below the shadows under his eyes his jutting cheekbones gleamed, and this gleam lent the stranger's face an uncanny power and masterfulness, without any promise, forgiveness, or surrender, only the demand for obedience.

He went into the bedroom and began to get dressed. On the other side of the wall the radio went on playing the American tunes, accompanied from time to time by singing or humming from the room. In his new clothes and clear glasses he stood in front of the mirror on the closet door and the stranger examined him with commanding, loveless eyes and a certain curl at the corners of the lips, perhaps doubting his ability to pass the test?

The stairwell was cast in gloom and there was nobody on the stairs. He opened the fuse box, pulled out the light fuse, and laid it at the bottom of the box. After closing the fuse box, he took the key out of his pocket, inserted it in the lock, and opened the door of the apartment. A shriek of alarm rose from the little shadow that emerged from the bedroom and froze where it stood. He locked the door from the inside, returned the key to his jacket pocket, and looked at the silhouette at the end of the hall. And when he realized with a shock that she wasn't her, and he wasn't him, and that this delusion was the trap he feared, perhaps he could still have retraced his steps and set the clock back. But a strength not his filled his scrawny body. He had never known such strength, and it pushed him forward. He walked slowly up to her and she cried out in a strangled voice: "What do you want? Who are you?"

And he replied in a whisper, "I love you," and he didn't understand why he said it.

But she understood, and she screamed: "No, no!" and burst into tears.

They struggled silently in the hall, and only when she felt that her strength was running out did she begin to scream. He had no fear that someone would hear her and he made no attempt to silence her. When he dragged her into the bedroom she bit his hand, and the pain shot through his body like a life-giving elixir and sharpened his lust. And then he threw her onto the bed, tore her sweat-soaked shirt off, and pulled down her short trousers. She stopped resisting him and lay with her eyes closed, her naked body trembling and her lips mumbling something.

Only after he got off her and stood next to the bed to fix his clothes did he want to see her face. She remained lying on the bed where he had thrown her, frozen in fear, whispering without a pause: "No, no, please, no." He bent over her and saw her eyes looking straight into his, and even in the darkness of the room he could read in them that she knew what was going to happen to her now.

Before leaving the apartment, he looked through the peephole in the door. The light was on in the stairwell. Someone was hurrying up the stairs. Was it her, returning home? This was the first moment of fear he had known since entering the apartment. He immediately stuck the key in the lock and turned it so that she wouldn't be able to open the door from the outside. With a pounding heart he listened to the footsteps ascending the stairs, until they stopped, and there was the sound of a door closing on a floor below. When the light went off in the stairwell, he left the apartment, locked the door, opened the fuse box, and returned the porcelain fuse to its place. Suddenly the sound of cheerful, rhythmic music burst out of the apartment, and his heart missed a beat — the reconnection of the electricity had turned the radio back on, but in the seconds that passed before he realized this, he felt as if a hand had been laid on his shoulder.

Back at home, under the light, he saw the bite wound on his hand, which was still bleeding and had stained the sleeve of his pale blue shirt. He took off his clothes, went into the bathroom, and held his hand under cold running water until it stopped bleeding. After drying his hand, he dressed the wound with a plaster. He looked into the bathroom mirror, and the stranger's face was very remote and denying, as if it had never seen him before. He went into the bedroom. On the other side of the wall the radio went on playing the pop songs in English. He put on his old clothes and shabby sneakers. He took the key out of his jacket and put it in his trouser pocket. He bundled up his bloody shirt together with his new jacket and new trousers, put them into a plastic bag, tied up the ends, and put it into another plastic bag. Then he glimpsed through the peephole in the door, saw that there was no light on in the stairwell, and hurried out.

Outside, dusk was descending and the rain had stopped. A big American car, old and brown, pulled up in front of the building, and the owners of the basement stepped out of it. They walked past him, the woman gave him a searching look but said nothing. Perhaps they didn't recognize him without his beard, and perhaps their minds were occupied with other matters; presumably they had come to see what the week's rains had done to them. Aviram went into one of the yards in the next street and threw the plastic bag with his new clothes into the trash can.

A fine rain began to fall. He quickened his steps, in a hurry to reach the roofed sidewalk of Ibn Gvirol Street. Before entering the Northern Star building he was suddenly overcome by fear — perhaps they were lying in wait for him there. He crossed the road to the opposite sidewalk and looked up at the second-floor windows. There were no lights visible. Because the blinds were drawn? Or perhaps it was more likely that his pursuers would lie in wait for him in the darkness? He went upstairs and entered the office, switched on the light, and locked the door behind him. There was nobody waiting for him. The office greeted him with its three desks, its iron cabinet, and its wall of shelves, which had been emptied of its files since they had started using computers. Everything was steeped in memory, veiled in a film of longings. Was this how a person felt when he came home from far away after years of absence, or when he was about to set out on a journey from which he would never return?

Ilan's desk, newer and bigger than the other two, was neat and tidy as always. Under the black plastic bowl, full of paper-clips joined together like links in a chain, was a folded sheet of paper. He pulled it out, unfolded it, and lay it on the table. Most of the page was covered with crowded rows of writing, straight as a ruler, small, round letters stuck together, in short and long words — all completely illegible. There was something touching about Ilan's handwriting, something vulnerable, shy, and defensive, in striking contrast to his self-confident appearance. He felt a sudden affection for his partner, and gratitude for the years they had worked together. He folded the page and returned it to its place under the plastic bowl.

On the back of the chair next to Mali's desk hung her sweater, an old white angora cardigan, which she had brought in because of what she considered to be the "freezing cold" in the office on these winter days. He placed his hand on the fluffy wool and it seemed to him that he could feel the warmth of Mali's body stored inside. And he immediately pulled the sweater off the chair and buried his face in it.

Afterward he returned the sweater to its place on the back of the chair, sat down at his desk, and imagined that all three of them were there in the office again. He had never realized how good he felt with them and how much he enjoyed being there. Suddenly the phone rang. Holding his breath and sitting still, he waited for it to stop ringing, and when silence returned, he took a deep breath and stood up. His farewells were over.

He went up to the iron cabinet, opened the lock, took the key of the apartment out of his trouser pocket, and returned it to its hiding place. After locking the cabinet, he went to the door and looked upon the office once more, before turning off the light and leaving.

On the street he hailed a cab and went to his parents' place.

"Who's there?" his father called from behind the door.

"It's me."

"Aviram?"

"Yes."

"Just a minute."

After a rattle of locks and bolts the door opened a crack, held by a safety catch, and the little man's face looked at him through the slit and recoiled for a moment at his appearance. Then the door shut and opened wide again. His father inspected him with a smile.

"You shaved your beard. For a minute I didn't recognize you."

When he passed the mirror in the hall he peeped at his face, and his father, who noticed, said: "It's good, it suits you much better without that beard."

"Where is she?"

"In your room," said his father, "she's busy there with all kinds of old clothes. She has to do something."

Aviram went up to the open door of the room and looked at her. She was sitting on the edge of the bed where he had once slept, in the light of the bedside lamp he had once read by, and talking softly to a pair of black woolen socks that she was turning inside out and examining.

His father went in.

"Look who's come to visit us, our Aviram!"

"Can't you see that I'm busy now?" she replied. "I have a lot of work to do."

Aviram sat down at the table in the living room and his father suggested: "Should we have a cup of coffee?"

"Yes, why not?"

His father went into the kitchen to make the coffee, and Aviram stood up and walked around the room, which like the rest of the apartment had hardly changed at all since his childhood. The same old furniture, the same old volumes on the bookshelves — only the television and the long armchair that went with it stood disdainfully apart in their corner. He went into the kitchen and stood next to his father, who was busying himself with the coffee, and his father looked at him again in astonishment: "I'm still not used to your face without the beard."

"Is all that new, the steel door and all those locks and bolts?" asked Aviram.

"There've been a lot of burglaries around here lately. In the evening and over the weekend the offices that have rented the apartments are closed and we're left almost alone here. If we shout no one will hear us. There are all kinds of criminals, or just crazy people, roaming around the streets here, and they're ruthless: they'll kill old, sick, helpless people to get the money to satisfy their craving for drugs. We put up bars on the windows and the balcony to keep them from breaking in. At night all kinds of dubious characters sometimes sit on the steps, apparently perverts and drug addicts. And once in a while they knock on the door and ask for something. I don't open. We've been warned not to let strangers in. When we wake up at night and hear a noise in the flat we're afraid."

"You should have sold this place long ago and moved into protected housing."

"It's not so simple, as you know yourself. But let's not get into that argument again."

The coffee was ready and they carried their cups into the living room. His father went to call his mother, for whom he had made coffee too. "Can't you see that I have work to do?" she said. "You can take a break from your work for a minute," said his father. "Our Aviram has come to visit us. He wants to see you. Don't you want to see him?" "Not now," said his mother. "Some other time perhaps."

His father returned to the living room and they sat down at the dining table in the middle of the room. Aviram didn't ask about his mother's condition and his father too said nothing about it, in order not to get into that old argument either.

Aviram said: "When I was a child, you once read me a story from *The Book of Legends* about a bird that takes revenge on the sea for flooding its nest. Can you find it for me?"

"No problem," said his father. He stood up and went over to the bookshelves, pulled down *The Book of Legends* by Bialik and Ravnitzky, put it on the table, and immediately found the story. He held the book out to Aviram, but his son asked him to read it aloud to him, as he had in his childhood.

"A bird built its nest on the seashore. The sea rose and flooded its nest. What did it do? It began to take water from the sea with its beak and spit it out on the shore, and to take sand from the shore and drop it into the sea. Its friend came and stood on its back and said to the bird: What are you doing wearing yourself out? The bird replied: I'm not moving from here until I turn the sea to land and the land to sea. The friend said: You fool, how much difference can you make?"

"What a terrible fate," said Aviram.

"It's a parable," said his father.

"And what is this parable saying?"

His father reflected for a moment. "Perhaps it shows us the vanity of revenge. It's never enough, it never gives satisfaction, because what's done can't be undone."

"And perhaps it tells us that right from the outset we're in the position of this bird after the catastrophe, and the whole of life can be compared to the attempt to dry up the ocean drop by drop with sand in a bird's beak."

"What a pessimistic point of view!" his father exclaims in horror. "Life is a wonderful gift, just as it is, in spite of everything that happens to us, with all its troubles and catastrophes. How did you come to such a dreadful conclusion?"

The sound of shuffling footsteps preceded her appearance in the living-room doorway.

"Our Aviram is here! He's come to see you!" his father called out to her.

She responded with a hushing gesture, of the kind usually employed to dampen untoward enthusiasm, and shot a suspicious glance at Aviram. Then she went into the hall, stole a quick look at the mirror, and came back to announce that the woman was standing there again.

"Yesterday," his father said, "she sat down next to the mirror and told that woman how badly I treat her, that I leave her alone in the house all day, that I don't feed her and that she's hungry all the time."

He stood up and went over to her and put his arms around her and stroked her hair. "We love her," he said, "she's ours, right?"

She extricated herself from his embrace. "You're talking nonsense," she scolded him and jerked her head in Aviram's direction, indicating that such behavior was unseemly in the presence of a stranger. Then she turned around, with a resolute expression on her face, and said: "Sir, we don't have time now."

"It's our Aviram!" cried the old man. "Do you want to send him away? We love him!"

"Yes, yes, of course," she said, clearly unconvinced, "but now we have to shut up the house, we have a lot of work to do."

Aviram rose from his chair and his father pleaded with him: "No, don't go. You understand what's happening to her."

"Where is your home, sir? Don't you have a home? Don't you have a mother?" she asked and put her hands on Aviram's shoulders and pushed him toward the hall.

"I have to go," said Aviram.

"I see so little of you," his father sighed.

"I can't take it."

His father accompanied him to the door and his mother followed them. As he left, Aviram turned his face toward them, to see them again for a brief moment, before the door shut and his mother said: "Thank God he's gone!"

There was no light in the stairwell. From the landing above him a faint light filtered down, there was a sound of movement on the stairs, and human shadows flitted past. Aviram made his way carefully down the stairs and emerged into the dark, deserted street.

Like an endless plateau the flat, arid deserts of time stretched out before him, bathed in a pale inner light stemming from some unknown source, until they dissolved into an invisible horizon, and in all these silent expanses there was no sign of life, no object to take hold of, nothing to remember.

Sometimes, when I wake up at night, I don't remember where I am. The room looks like an office, with its white walls and the small, pale light illuminating them from below. Only when I look at the three other beds in the room, which look like cages, and which are occupied by strangers, do I remember that I am one of them, and gradually the place returns to itself.

Pedro stayed with me until they sold the apartment and secured a place for me in this home for invalids. He did his work silently and seriously, without looking me in the eye.

When he had no work to do he sat in the armchair and smoked cigarettes, frowning and staring at an invisible spot on the floor. When he wanted to turn on the television, he asked permission. One morning, when he put me in my chair, I took his hand and gave it a friendly squeeze, but he quickly snatched it away, as if from fire. I began to long for his jokes and wildness; they were a part of our lives, in the days when the three of us were together and I was happy. If I could speak to him, I would tell him that I'm not angry with him, that he's not to blame for anything. Once he was like a father to me, now he's turned into a frightened child. Perhaps he wanted to go on working for me. I thought it would be best too, I'd grown accustomed to him. But my daughter didn't agree. She hated him from the minute she set eyes on him. I let her do what she liked. At first I thought that perhaps he would come and see me at this place, but in fact, why should he come?

In the hall that serves as the dining room we sit around the tables in our wheelchairs, six or seven men and dozens of women, almost all of them without a clue as to what's happening to them. They sit side by side, their eyes closed or rolled up so almost all you can see are the whites, their mouths open, and none of them know that there's somebody else sitting next to them. Each of them is buried alone inside himself. And I too follow their example, accustom myself to not seeing them, to ignoring them completely, to sink into the little that still remains to me of myself, until that little is gone too, and all that's left will be to wait for something that doesn't exist.

But sometimes, when I wake up at night and I don't remember where I am, I call out to her, and she doesn't come. Then I repeat to myself "Lin-da, Lin-da," like music that I want to hear over and over again. Something was born in me when she came into my life and died with her. Perhaps she'll come back to me, and together with her I'll be resurrected? Not that I believe in this hope, but I cling to it with all my strength, like a drowning man, trying to convince myself that one night I'll wake up and call her, and she'll come to my bed in her Mickey

Mouse T-shirt, her smell will fill me again, and she'll say in her English: "Okay, now sleep, good night."

And she'll switch off the light.

All night Ezra couldn't sleep. He couldn't stop thinking about Eyal's situation and wondering whether the boy had really been broken — as Menashe had predicted from the start and he himself, why deny it, had hoped for too — and at the same time had lost his willpower and his zest for life, or whether perhaps he was as determined as ever and was pretending to be crazy in order to get out of the army and avoid going to jail. At moments he tended to believe in one possibility and to foresee its consequences, and at other moments he found grounds for the other possibility, whose consequences were no less harsh.

Whenever he closed his eyes and hoped for the blessing of sleep, he was tortured again by the sound of Eyal's lackluster voice echoing in his ears: I don't mind . . . okay . . . whatever you like. . . . It makes no difference to me. . . . Do what you want. . . . But Ezra himself no longer knew what he wanted: which of the two possibilities should he hope for? The longer the night lasted, with sleep as far away as ever, the more he began to hope that Eyal's spirit was still strong, his will resolute, and his behavior only an act calculated to deceive the military authorities and his parents. More and more he clung to this hope, finding grounds for it in various signs shown by Eyal's behavior that evening and in his words, which were intended to make them feel sorry for him and to remove all suspicion from their hearts.

For hours he lay like this, listening to Ruthie's quiet, steady breathing as she lay sleeping soundly at his side, and regretting that he couldn't share his thoughts and conclusions with her and hear her wise, reasonable reactions. But the hope growing stronger in his heart brought a measure of repose with it, and sleep no longer seemed so far away. If only he could get a little sleep in the time remaining before the alarm clock rang.

Needing to use the toilet, he switched on the bedside lamp and got slowly out of bed. In order not to disturb Ruthie's sleep he went barefoot, on tiptoe, opened the bedroom door quietly, and tiptoed down the hall. When he passed Eyal's room he heard a strange sound coming from behind the closed door. Quietly he approached the door and pressed his ear to it.

At first Ezra refused to admit what he was hearing: perhaps the boy is laughing, he said to himself, perhaps he's coughing or groaning in his sleep. But the truth, like an unbearable weight, sank into his body from his ears and his head to his heart and stomach and legs, and he stretched out his hands to lean against the wall. The terrible weeping dissolved one by one all the thoughts he had been turning over as he lay awake in bed, all the suppositions and possibilities and conclusions and hopes. Little by little he groped his way to the toilet and slammed the door shut behind him. He did this on purpose, to draw Eyal's attention to his presence there, so that he would stop crying. And indeed when he returned, there was silence in the boy's room.

When he entered the bedroom Ruthie's eyes were open and she was waiting for him, but when she saw him her face turned grave and her eyes asked him what was wrong. He closed the door, got into bed, and made up his mind not to tell his wife what he had heard in Eyal's room, in order not to grieve her.

"I didn't sleep all night, Ruthie," he said. "The thoughts and worries wouldn't let me fall asleep."

"In a little while you have to get up."

"Yes. To take our child to prison."

"And we, Ezra, were looking forward to this day," said Ruthie.

"No, Ruthie, you weren't looking forward to it, I was. And now . . ." his voice choked, "I only wish I could go there in his place."

Ezra got up early and went out to the truck, and while the engine was warming up he listened to the news on the radio. He drove to the shopping center, bought a newspaper and fresh bread, and when he came home, he went to wake Eyal. The boy was already waiting in his room, washed and shaved and dressed, ready to do his father's will.

Ruthie woke the little ones and told them that their brother had come home during the night, and soon he would go back to the army. They got out of bed immediately and went to see him. He was sitting at the table in the dining room, opposite his father, who was hiding his face behind the newspaper with cigarette smoke spiraling above his head. Eyal smiled his strange smile at them. They stood next to him and looked at him for a long time, curiously and silently, as if he were a stranger visiting their home for the first time. In the end his sister asked him: "What will they do to you in the army, will they punish you?" And Eyal said: "It will be okay, sweetie, they won't do anything to me, don't worry." "Will they forgive you?" asked Gili. "Sure they'll forgive me," said Eyal. He asked Yaniv: "How's tricks, kid?" The child was embarrassed, and he shrugged his shoulders and ran to his mother in the kitchen.

After breakfast, Ezra took the children to school and Eyal stayed with his mother. She sipped her coffee with her eyes fixed on his sealed face.

"I have the feeling, Eyal," said Ruthie, "that you want to tell us something, but you're not saying it."

"Tell you what?" asked Eyal.

"Should I make you more coffee?" asked Ruthie.

"Okay."

She went to the kitchen and came back with the coffee.

"Are you angry with us, Eyalie?" asked Ruthie.

"No."

"Because you're not talking at all."

"There's nothing . . ."

"When you're there," said Ruthie, "will you be able to write to us? Are you allowed to send letters from there? Just to let us know what's happening to you, how you're feeling. Perhaps there's something we can do to help you. Menashe has connections, you know."

"Okay."

Ruthie, despairing of getting him to talk, cleared the table and went to the kitchen to wash the dishes.

When Ezra came home, Eyal stood up, ready to set out, and his father said to him: "Go and say good-bye to your mother."

The boy went into the kitchen. His mother was standing next to the fridge and wiping her eyes with a paper towel. He went up and touched her elbow. "Good-bye, Mother," he said.

She put out her arms and he allowed her to embrace him.

"Take care of yourself, Eyalie," said Ruthie, "be strong, don't let them break you."

"Mother," said Eyalie softly, and it was evident from his face how hard it was for him to express what was in his heart, "Mother, forgive me."

A soft, winter's morning light filtered through the white film covering the sky, and in the northwest the clouds piled up, dark and heavy.

"That Menashe, what a guy, eh? He's got a head on him!" said Ezra. "If it wasn't for him, I would have done a lot of stupid things, more than I actually managed to do."

Eyal walked beside him in silence.

"Family's the thing," added Ezra, "when things get tough, you can only rely on your family."

At this hour the main road was already full of activity. Among the passersby were acquaintances of Ezra's, who responded to his good mornings and hurried on their way. There were a few people sitting and eating in the Sharoni brothers' restaurant. From the doorway Ezra waved to Menahem, who was busy cutting slices off the meat on the spit and didn't notice him. Shirazi's butcher shop was empty and the butcher was standing with his back against the counter and reading the newspaper. Avram the grocer was serving his customers next to the till. Ezra called to him from the doorway and Avram raised his head. "My Eyal's going back to the army!" said Ezra. Avram smiled, called out a greeting, and returned to his affairs.

The dark clouds that had gathered in the northwest spread and obscured the sky. The two of them approached the building and plumbing supplies store. Ezra thought of going in and talking to Herzl about an order in connection with his work, but he stopped in the doorway. His spirits fell. He looked at his son stepping silently at his side and wondered what he thought he was doing. He felt ashamed of the ridiculous idea of this promenade that he had come up with so naively. People were preoccupied with their own affairs and they weren't interested in Eyal and his fate. Like the stab of a knife the pain of loneliness pierced his heart. He stopped and the boy, like a shadow walking at his side, stopped too. And while he was wondering whether they should walk faster and make straight for the police station next to the junction, a few kilometers away, or go home and drive there in the truck, it started to rain and the decision was taken out of his hands.

"Let's cross the street," said Ezra.

They ran across the road to the opposite sidewalk and stood in the portico at the entrance to the old-age home attached to the synagogue.

"I'm going to get the truck," said Ezra, "don't come with me. Why should we both get wet?"

"Okay."

Ezra gave Eyal a long look, and his eyes cried out to him: "Run as fast as you can! Don't wait for me."

All the way home in the rain he called to his son in his heart: "Do what you want to do, Eyalie, not what you're told to do. You know better than anyone what's best for you. Don't think of us, don't think of anyone, think only of yourself! Be a man again! Like you were before, when you cursed the army and the country, and you weren't afraid of anyone. That's the way I love you. You don't owe anything to me or the family or anyone. Only to yourself. Don't give in, pull yourself together, go back to being what you are!"

When Ezra reached home, his clothes soaked by the rain, but he didn't go inside to change because he didn't want to meet Ruthie and tell her about the tempest raging inside him. He sat down in the truck, started the engine, and drove slowly back. When he turned onto the main road, he prayed to God that Eyal wouldn't be waiting where he had left him, that it would turn out that the boy really had been putting on an act, pretending to be backward or disturbed, that in fact he still had all his wits about him and had only been waiting for the right opportunity to run away again.

But when he approached the synagogue Ezra saw him standing where he had left him, with an old man standing next to him and talking to him, gesturing energetically with his hands. Ezra stopped the truck, got out, and beckoned to Eyal on the opposite sidewalk. The boy saw him, took his leave of the old man, and ran across the road.

"Who's that man, what did he want of you?"

"He's from the old-age home. He told me to repent and return to religion."

"God forbid!" cried Ezra.

"Don't worry. I'm not thinking about it," said Eyal.

"Tell me Eyal, what are you thinking about?"

"Nothing."

Ezra kept quiet. They hadn't had such a long conversation for ages, and it too led nowhere. The rain beat down furiously on the roof of the cab and the wipers weren't working fast enough to clear the windshield. Vision was poor. They left the neighborhood and turned onto the expressway, which was jammed with traffic. The column of vehicles advanced slowly, they reached the junction, turned off onto a side street, and after a while they stopped not far from the police station.

"Eyalie, are you sure that you want to go there?" asked Ezra. His son looked at him questioningly.

"I'm letting you off here and leaving," said Ezra. "You do what you want to."

"Okay," said Eyal, and he got ready to get out of the truck.

"Be strong, Eyalie," said Ezra with a tremor in his voice, "just do what's right for you. Whatever you do, you'll always be ours, we'll always love you and stand by you! My Eyalie, do you understand what I'm saying to you?"

"Okay," said Eyal, and he got out of the truck.

Ezra turned the truck around but instead of driving back to

the junction he stopped, raised his head, and looked in the rearview mirror. He saw the boy running through the pouring rain to the police station, going up the steps, and vanishing inside the building.

Ezra drove to the junction, stopped at the red light, and felt the need for a cigarette. He took the pack, opened it, hesitated for a minute, and gave the cigarettes one last look. Then he closed it, crushed it in his hand, opened the window at his left, flung the pack into the field next to the road, and took the lighter and threw that out too. Someone behind him honked impatiently; the traffic lights had changed.